*T*was sure more than a minute had gone by, but I could easily have lost track of all time. I opened my eyes. His were the lightest shade of gray I'd seen yet. "You can kiss me, Jude."

I expected just about anything else than his forehead lining as his eyes darkened. "I know I can," he said, his voice tight. "I'm just not sure if I should."

The ache that originated at the very core of me began to spread. There was only one way to alleviate it. "You *should* kiss me, Jude."

His eyes went another shade darker, but they never left mine. "I shouldn't," he said, sliding a hand behind my neck, skimming a finger beneath the collar of my tank top. "But right now, I don't give a damn."

Also by
NICOLE WILLIAMS

CLASH

CRUSH

NICOLE WILLIAMS
CRASH

Simon & Schuster

First published in Great Britain in 2012 as eBook original by Simon & Schuster UK Ltd
This paperback edition published in 2013 by Simon & Schuster UK Ltd
A CBS COMPANY

1 3 5 7 9 10 8 6 4 2

Simon & Schuster UK Ltd
1st Floor, 222 Gray's Inn Road
London
WC1X 8HB

Simon & Schuster Australia, Sydney
Simon & Schuster India, New Delhi

A CIP catalogue record for this book is available from the British Library.

eBook ISBN: 978-1-47111-760-2
PB ISBN: 978-1-47111-761-9

Printed and bound by CPI Group (UK) Ltd, Croydon, CR0 4YY

www.simonandschuster.co.uk

www.simonandschuster.com.au

For the fine and fabulous girls of the FP. Not a day passes where I don't find myself thankful to have each and every one of you. You inspire me to become a better writer, as well as a better person. You encourage me, let me vent, and aren't afraid to tell me to suck it up. Write until there's nothing left to be said. Then write some more.

Love and glitter cannons to you all!

ONE

*S*ummers turn me into a sucker. That's why I was glad this one was almost over.

Every year since puberty, from mid-June to early September, I'd been sure I was going to meet the real-world equivalent to Prince Charming. Call me old-fashioned, call me hopelessly romantic, you could even call me a fool, but whatever I was, I knew the end result—I was a sucker. To date, I'd never found a guy who was worthy to stand in Prince C's shadow; no real surprise there, as I'd discovered more and more that guys were something of a pain in the ass. But here, working on my tan at Sapphire Lake's public beach just a couple of weeks before I was all set to start my senior year at a new school, I'd just found me a Prince Hot Damn.

He arrived with a whole mess of guys, tossing a football

back and forth, and specimens like this confirmed there had been some kind of divine rule in the universe, because no natural selection process was up to the task of creating something like him. This was some god's handiwork somewhere.

He was tall, his shoulders were wide, and he had those dark ringed eyes with black lashes that had the power to undo a girl's best intentions. So, in nonsucker terms, he was just my type. Along with every other woman in the northern hemisphere.

My blue raspberry Slurpee couldn't even compete for my attention. I didn't know his name, didn't know if he had a girlfriend, didn't know if he wanted one, but I knew I was in trouble.

However, it was when his dodging and tackling and sprinting ceased when he glanced my way that I knew I was in big trouble.

The glance was immeasurably longer than every other glance shared with a stranger, but what was conveyed in that shortest of connections cut through me, letting some piece of this stranger work his way inside. I'd experienced this before a few times in my life, nothing but an eye connection with a passing stranger begging me to take notice and follow.

To date, I never had, but the last time I'd let one of these moments pass was at a restaurant my family went to. This boy dropped a pizza on the table, told us to enjoy, and then, right as he was leaving, he winked at me. My heart went boom-boom, my head got all foggy, and I felt this ache inside when he turned and walked away, like we were tied together by a fixed rope. I'd let exactly four of these soul typhoons pass unexplored, but I'd made a pact of the utmost sacredness with myself that I wouldn't let a fifth go by in the same kind of way.

I was never sure if the person on the other end of that look felt the same kind of intensity I did, so when Prince Hot Damn spun away, tackling someone into the sand, I knew I ran the risk of him thinking I was one of those girls who made an art form of preying on beautiful boys minding their own business. I didn't care—I wouldn't let another one of these moments go. Life was short, and I'd been a firm believer in seizing the moment for the majority of my life.

Then he came to another standstill, like my stare was freezing him in place. This time it wasn't a glance. It was a good five-second stare, where his eyes did that dumbfounded thing mine were doing to me. His smile had just begun its upward journey into position when a football whizzed right into the side of his face. It was one of those moments you saw played out in movies: wide-eyed boy staring at girl, oblivious to the world around him until the laces of a football indented his forehead.

"Stop staring, Jude!" the young boy who had thrown the ball called out. "She's too hot, even for you. And since she's got a book, she probably knows how to read, so she's smart enough to know to avoid guys like you."

I slid my glasses into place as serendipity boy chased after the pint-size teaser, and turned my attention to the book sprawled out beneath me.

I saw the attraction in his eyes, that and more. It was only a matter of how much time he wanted to play it cool until he came over. I had all day.

That's how I reassured myself as he threw the boy over his shoulder and sprinted into the lake, dunking up and down until the boy was squealing with laughter. I reassured myself again when he and the boy trudged from the water and returned to the cluster of boys playing football and picked up right where he left off, oblivious.

I tried to distract myself with my book, but when I found myself reading the same paragraph for the sixth time, I gave up. Still not another look my way, like I was invisible.

When a second hour passed in the same way, I decided it was time to take matters into my own hands. If he wasn't going to come to me and I wasn't quite ready to go to him, I'd just have to make him. I'd found boys were fairly simple creatures to figure out, at least on a primal level—on a mind, heart, and soul matter they were about as confounding to me as thermal dynamics—and since primal was just a nice term for raging hormones, I decided to use their overabundance of teenage boy ones to my advantage.

Grabbing a liter of water from my beach bag, I rose to a stand, making every movement slow and deliberate. At least without looking ridiculous. His eyes weren't on me as I adjusted my bikini just so, but a few male sets were. Good sign I was doing the right thing, but bad sign he wasn't noticing, since this whole stunt was set into motion for him.

I pulled the clip from my mass of hair so it fell down my back, and I shook it into position for good measure. I practically cursed under my breath when I chanced another peek. Nada. What's a girl got to do to get a boy's attention these days?

I walked back toward the picnic table, where the newest addition to our family, the furry kind, was still smiling through his panting. So new, in fact, I had yet to name him. "There's a good boy," I said, kneeling beside him, where he was using the shade of the table to his advantage. "Since you're of the same gender, although I find your species to be more appealing on so many fronts, do you have any suggestions for how to make that boy mine?" I asked, pouring some more water into his bowl as I watched Jude pry a football from the air. The boy played the best game of beach football I'd ever had the pleasure of watching.

My furry friend offered a few licks over my arm before his wet nose nudged at my leg. I could have been reading into the nudge of encouragement a bit, but when his doggy eyes tracked over to Jude and his doggy smile stretched further, I laughed. "Yeah, yeah. I know it's a woman's world and all, but there are still some things where I'm old-fashioned," I said, scratching behind his matted ears. "Like the guy approaching the girl. Don't call the feminist movement and rat me out, or else no steak for you tonight."

I patted his head as he yapped his vow of silence. Then I headed back to my blanket, watching Jude surreptitiously as he sailed the football to another little boy. If standing, stretching, and swimsuit adjustment weren't working, with dinner not even an hour away, I'd have to resort to drastic, more desperate, measures. I was stubborn and I was a sucker, and since I'd waited this long for him to come over, I wasn't going to give up now. Giving up was not in my blood.

I stretched on my blanket, stomach down, twisting my arms behind me to pull the string free of its tension. In my experience as a seventeen-year-old girl, seven of those years having boobs that required a bra, undoing that one little knot at the center of your back had about a 95 percent accuracy rate of attracting any male within a five-beach-towel radius. Jude might have been right on the five/six cusp, but it was all I had left. The last trick in my bag.

I made a pillow of my sundress and pretended to be concerned with nothing more than minimizing my tan lines, but as I took a quick survey of the area, every male eye within five beach towels was staring. Except for him.

A few whistles even sounded from his fellow football players' lips, of which I played ignorant, but still, nothing from him. One of my friends at my old school had once told me that if ever a day came where our intended male targets didn't flock our way after this last-ditch effort, it would be time to send word to the Vatican—that it was time for a miracle.

Get Rome on the phone, because a miracle was playing out in front of me as the only boy I wanted to notice was the only one who didn't. Darn you, providence and soul typhoons.

I'd give him five more minutes before I'd force myself to swallow my pride and make a move. I knew if I had to approach him, I'd likely get denied, but I wasn't going to let another one of these pass me by. Carpe diem, baby.

I noticed something whizzing above me from the corner of my eye, but it didn't seem of much importance until a certain body I'd been lusting over snagged it right before falling back to the earth from his impressive suspension in the air. Or at least falling right over the top of me.

He didn't crash into me all that hard, leading me to

believe it was intentional, but I still managed to shriek like a little girl. I knotted my top back into place while he struggled to reposition himself.

"The name's Jude Ryder, since I know you're all but salivating like a rabid dog to know, and I don't do girlfriends, relationships, flowers, or regular phone calls. If you're down with that, I think we could work out something special."

So that serendipitous moment I'd been angsting over the better part of a glorious summer afternoon? What a waste. There had been nothing on the other side of that loaded look than an opportunistic summer . . . ahem, *fling*. Lord help me, I was going to become a nun if my male radar didn't realign toward guys who were not walking penises.

"And I'd give you my name if I actually wanted to pursue anything more with you than telling you to get the hell off me," I said, twisting onto my back once I was confident everything up front was covered. However, whether it was my twisting motion or his twisted sense of self, his leg caught my hip as it rotated and followed it all the way around. Super, the boy was all but straddling me now, and despite being angry beyond appeasing, I felt my heart pounding through my chest like it never had.

He smiled down at me. Actually, it was more of a grin. A grin full of attitude and ego. It was a tad sexy too, and it could have been hella sexy if I hadn't already decided to not fall into this boy's traps. "I was wondering how long it would take to get you horizontal," he said, eyes sweeping down to my belly button. "Although I'm not really your missionary-style kind of guy."

Whatever was left of my romantic notions of male chivalry and love at first sight had just been obliterated. I'd never verbally admit I was a romantic; that was one of the many secrets I kept to myself, but it was a special ideal, and one guy took the last bit I'd clung to.

Pushing his chest was like trying to move a tank. I removed my sunglasses so he could see my glare. "Is that because it would require a real, living, breathing female—not one of the imaginary or blow-up kind—to have sex with you?"

He laughed at that, like I'd just said something as cute as a kitten. "No, a supply of girls is never a problem. But if they're the ones who come a-knockin' at my door, why should I be the one to do all the work?"

That nasty taste in my mouth might have just been a bit of vomit. "You're a pig," I said, shoving him again. Harder, so my hands slapped his chest, but it was like nothing more than a gust of wind had come at him.

"Never claimed to be anything but," he answered, raising his hands in surrender when I came at him again with my palms. "I also knew you wouldn't stop your staring until you learned the cold, hard truth. So, consider yourself warned. I might not be the kind of guy who reads textbooks at the beach," he said, glancing back at my open book, "but I'm smart enough to know girls like you should stay away from guys like me. So stay away."

My glare was now officially a glower. "That won't be a problem once you stop all but holding me down," I said, waiting for him to move. He did, but it was still with that cocky grin. I hated that kind of grin. "And you can consider yourself warned that you are trespassing on my personal property"—I grabbed my pink beach blanket in explanation as an eruption of barking sounded behind me; I knew that dog was a kindred spirit—"and beware of dog." I sneered up at him as he sat himself beside me, still in a straddling position. "You can go now."

That wiped the smile from his face. "What?" he asked, the lines of his forehead pulling his gunmetal-gray beanie lower. And what kind of a person wore a cotton hat to the beach on a scorching-hot day? The mentally deranged ones I needed to stay away from, that was who.

"Scrambo," I said, waving him off. "I'm done wasting my last few precious minutes of a perfect summer afternoon on you. Thank you for the eye-candy distraction, but I can see it's nothing more than that. Oh, and by the way, your butt is not nearly as impressive up close as it is at a distance."

I didn't have time to curse myself for my latest bout of verbal vomit, because his mouth fell open for a second. It was exactly the reaction I'd been hoping for. "You girls speak a language I'll never understand, but are you saying what I think you are?"

"If it involves you getting up and walking out of my sunshine and my life from here until the end of time, then we're on the same wavelength," I answered, sliding farther down on my towel to realign my face with the sun, trying to pretend his face wasn't the thing dirty thoughts are made of. Save for a long scar that ran the diagonal of his left cheekbone, it could have been classified as mind-dumbingly perfect.

Perfectly not my type. I had to remind myself of that. And convince myself, too.

His eyebrows were still squished together, like he was trying to figure out the most riddling of riddles.

"What's that dumbfounded look for?" I asked.

"Because I have yet to come across a girl who sends me packing," he said, watching me with something new in his eyes.

"So sorry to upend your world of nonrespect for women, but it seems my work here is done." I sat up, shuffling my textbook into my bag.

"What kind of dog is that?" he asked abruptly. The low notes were gone from his voice.

I peered over at him as I continued tossing my beach day must-haves into the bag, gauging to see if he was serious. He'd just gone from all but riding me on the beach to casual conversation. "He's got a bunch of breeds in him," I began slowly, watching him from the corner of my eye to see if this was some new trap.

"So he's a mutt," he said.

"No," I said, admiring the shaggy bundle still baring his teeth in Jude's direction. "He's well-rounded," I added.

"Well that's the best attempt I've heard yet at making a piece of shit seem less shitty," he said, spinning the football on his finger.

"No, that's my way of seeing something for what it actually is," I said, sure I sounded more defensive than I'd intended. "That 'piece of shit,' I'll have you know, was hit, kicked, underfed, and lit on fire by his previous owners, who dropped him off at the shelter when he had the nerve to devour an unattended tuna fish sandwich. That 'piece of shit' was scheduled to be put down today for no other reason than drawing the short straw in life."

Jude's eyes returned to the dog. "You just got this guy today?" he asked, making a face. "Out of all the dogs you had to choose from, you picked the one that was the sorriest excuse for a dog I've yet to see."

"I couldn't let him be killed because some slime of the

earth ruined him, could I?" I asked, wincing as I wondered what my parents would say. "I mean, look at him. He's been brutalized by humans, and the only thing he's concerned about right now is protecting me. How could I not save him?"

"Because he's the ugliest dog I've ever seen," Jude said. "He's all but hairless—and I don't want to get any closer because I fear he might rip my balls off—but I'm pretty sure that putrid smell is coming from him. Unless . . ." He leaned into me, moving my hair behind my shoulder as his nose all but connected with my neck. My instant reaction was to shudder. This boy knew what he was doing and how the lightest graze of fingers over just the right patches of skin or a warm breath fogged over the right spot of the neck could all but crush a girl's most virtuous of intentions, but I fought the shudder down. I wasn't going to be one of the girls who shuddered in his presence. He didn't need another boost to that bloated ego. "Nope, I only smell sweet and innocent coming from over here," he whispered against my neck. He smirked at me, knowing exactly what he was doing and knowing exactly what I was trying not to do. "I'd suggest taking that fleabag through a doggie car wash a few times." He laughed as the dog began barking again at Jude's proximity to me, but he leaned away from me again. "What did your parents think when you brought Cujo home?"

This time I grimaced.

"Ahh, let me fill in the blanks. They don't know their precious daughter snuck behind their backs and brought this animal with a questionable past into her life."

My grimace deepened as he verbalized what I was planning to sugarcoat.

"And since I'm on a roll here, let me fill in the blanks as to what their reaction will be." He tapped his chin, staring at the sky. "They're going to tell you to drop that thing like a bad habit and send him back where you found him."

I blew out a rush of air. "Probably," I said, attempting to form a rebuttal that would be convincing to my parents. I already knew Dad would be on board by default, but Mom was another story, and my dad had learned years ago that life wasn't pleasant if he wasn't on the same parenting ship as Mom.

"So why did you do it?" he asked, still staring at the dog like he was a puzzle. "Because you don't strike me as the kind of girl who rebels against whatever her parents say."

"I don't," I answered. "But we made kind of a big life change recently, and I wasn't able to give this up." I'd been adopting and rehabbing dogs for the past three years. Every employee and volunteer at the nearby shelters knew me by first and last name. This might have been the "do-gooder" deed that was closest to my heart, but it certainly wasn't the only one I'd been involved in.

At my last school, I'd been the president of the Green Group, overseen the Toys for Tots drive three years running, volunteered weekly for after-school tutoring at the nearby elementary school, and spearheaded a quarterly bake sale where the proceeds went to the local military families who had loved ones overseas. I was about to start a new school my senior year, and I didn't know what to expect, if I could expect anything. Would my new school have the clubs I was used to, and if so, would they welcome a newcomer from a private school?

"Life change? Give this up?" he repeated. "Okay, my interest was piqued when you shot me down. Now I'm absolutely smitten since you made dog adoption out to be a vice." He smiled at me, and I swore I could feel my stomach bottoming out. "So what's this big life change you're up to those gorgeous blue eyes in?"

I slid my sunglasses back into position out of principle. If he was going to find a way to be condescending about my eyes, he didn't get to look into them. "We sold the house I grew up in and moved to our lake house," I began, trying to sound as carefree as I could about it, "and this place we live in has the most ridiculous, restrictive rules, so it would only make sense those idiots won't allow a dog off leash, right?" I was getting worked up just thinking about it, and my hands were flying all over the place. "We don't have a kennel, I can't keep him inside the house because my dad's allergic, and you try putting a leash on this guy and he all but transforms into the Tasmanian Devil." The dog was still eyeing Jude warily. "It's like the idea of being tied to something sends him over the edge."

"I know the feeling," he said, admiring the dog with something new in his eyes. Camaraderie, was it?

"Yeah, yeah," I said, reaching for my melted Slurpee. "Already got the spiel about you not one to be tied down to things like girlfriends. No need for the instant replay."

As I took a long and final sip of blue raspberry syrup, Jude leveled me with a gaze that was too deep for a guy of shallow character. "There are others ways to be tied to something than through a girl. In fact, I'd say I'm tied to just about everything else but a woman."

Okay, I so wasn't expecting this moment of vulnerability to slip from a guy who probably thought a nice first date included a visit to the backseat of his car. "Care to elaborate?" I asked, setting the empty cup into the sand.

"Nope," he replied, staring out into the water. "But thanks for asking."

"Jude!" someone yelled down the beach.

Glancing over at the shouter, a middle-aged man who

was rotund at best and grossly obese truthfully, Jude waved his hand. "Coming, Uncle Joe."

"That's your uncle?" My eyes flicked back and forth between Jude and Uncle Joe, finding no resemblance other than gender.

Jude nodded. "Uncle Joe."

"And those are your cousins?" Again, I surveyed the handful of boys ranging in age from probably kindergarten to high school, finding no definitive feature that would tie them to each other.

Another nod from Jude as he popped up.

"Do they all have different moms?" I asked, teasing only partly.

I felt his laugh all the way down to my toes. "I think you might be onto something."

Accepting the end was near, I decided to cut the tie early. "Well, it was"—I searched for the right word, coming up empty—"*something* meeting you, Jude," I said, as that smile of his angled at my word choice. "Have a nice life."

"You too . . . ," he said, his brows coming together as he searched me for something.

"Lucy," I offered, not sure why. I'd said my name a million different times and ways, but telling it to him seemed oddly intimate.

"Lucy," he repeated, tasting the word in his mouth.

Shooting me another tilted smile, he headed toward the trail of boys leaving the beach.

"Oh God, Lucy," I said to myself, flopping down on my beach towel. "What were you thinking? That was a serious heartbreak averted."

Even as I said the words, with as much conviction as I could muster, my eyes weren't able to peel themselves away from him as he ambled down the beach, spinning the football between his fingers.

Stopping suddenly, he spun around, that smile reappearing when he caught me staring at him. "So, Lucy," he hollered, tucking the ball under his arm, "how much farther are you going to let me get before you give me your phone number?"

Whatever premonitions I'd had about Jude and heartbreak going hand in hand flew out the window. I wanted to get up and bust a move, I was so stoked.

However, I still had some dignity in the name of all women and couldn't make this easy on him. "How far do you think the edge of the world is?" I called back, rolling onto my side.

Jude shook his head, chuckling silently. "You playing hard to get, Lucy?"

"No, Jude," I replied, sliding my glasses on top of my head. "I'm impossible to get."

Outright lie, but he didn't need to know that.

"Jude!" Uncle Joe shouted again, this time sounding a special shade of pissed. "Right now!"

Jude tensed, the smile faltering. "Coming!" he shouted over his shoulder before loping toward me. Kneeling beside me, his eyes locked on mine. "Number?"

"No." I was so close to breaking that if he asked again, I knew I'd cave.

"Why?"

"Because you have to work harder than some lame attempt to get it," I answered, hearing my conscience asking what the hell I was doing. This type of guy was every type of wrong on the surface, but there was something more going on, something I'd seen in that flash of vulnerability that sucked me in.

Leaning in so close his nose was almost brushing mine, he asked, "How much harder?"

I sucked in a slow breath, hoping my answer wouldn't make it seem like I was hyperventilating. "Use your brain, since you've made it clear you don't use it for academics."

He waited a few seconds, maybe waiting for me to retract my "hard to get" routine. I sealed my lips tighter.

"I'm going to come up with something good," he said finally, sliding my glasses back into position. "Really good."

"You come up with something that good," I said, glad my eyes were covered so he couldn't see the party in my pupils, "I'll not only give you my number, I'll let you take me out on a date." I felt the uninhibited part of me I did my best to repress surfacing. The part of me I tried to convince myself was bad, evil, wrong, so on and so forth, but the part of me that felt most like I wasn't fighting a current when I went against it.

"What makes you think I want to go on a date with you?" His face was more serious than anything I'd ever seen on a teen boy.

I cursed to myself, wanting to spurt out a string of them as Jude's expression stayed frozen. I was just about to reply, "Nothing," or grab my beach blanket and bag and scramble out of here with my tail between my legs as a smile split Jude's face in half.

"You're kind of beautiful when you're tortured, you know that?" He laughed, giving the football another spin. "Hell yeah, I want to take you out. Even though dates aren't really my thing, I think I can make an exception for a girl who rescues varmints"—right on cue, a snarl sounded beneath the picnic bench—"one who reads quantum physics at the beach"—I could have corrected him that I was brushing up on biology, not quantum physics, since I was in serious need of improving my GPA this upcoming year, but I don't think he would have cared, or known the difference—"and one who adheres to the European way, not to mention my favorite way, of suntanning by going topless."

Jude's smile pulled higher, and he gave me a knowing raise of his chin.

"For someone who prefers the sans top thing, you must not follow that policy personally," I replied, skimming my eyes down the long-sleeve thermal clinging to his chest from sweat or water or some combination of both. Apparently full sun and ninety-five-degree heat didn't warrant shedding the layers in Jude's book.

He shrugged. "There's a work of art, a true masterpiece, hiding beneath this shirt." His muscles rolled and stretched to bring the point home. Not that I needed to be convinced. "I can't let all this be displayed for free to the public."

If there weren't already about three dozen red flags up as to why I should steer clear of the grinning, flexing, wrapped-head-to-toe-in-caution-tape boy in front of me, here was three dozen and one. So what did I do?

Exactly what I knew I shouldn't.

"So what's the price of admission to the Museum of Jude?"

His smile faded into nothing, his eyes doing the same. "For girls like you, with the world-is-yours futures," he said, toeing at the sand, "it's expensive. Too expensive."

Another flash of vulnerability. I didn't know if he had a bad case of mood swings or deep down he was a sensitive guy banging against the walls to be set free. But I wanted to find out. "Was that you just inadvertently telling me to stay away from you?"

"No," he answered, meeting my eyes. "That was me telling you directly to listen to your gut and what it's screaming at you right now."

"What makes you think you know what my gut is saying to me?"

"Screaming," he corrected. "And experience."

If Jude thought experience had given him the instruction manual to Lucy Larson, he'd never been so wrong. "So I'll see you around then?"

He shook his head, and his smile broke through again. "I'll see you around then."

TWO

fter begging the Darcys, who I used to babysit for across the lake, to take the pup for one night while I figured out what I was going to do with him, my sensible left brain had finally asserted itself over my free-spirited right brain.

Jude Ryder wasn't only trouble, he was trouble with a side of danger and a dessert of heartache. I didn't talk the lingo of stereotypes, but I knew the path Jude was on and the one I was on would never intersect unless one of us surrendered to the other.

I'd worked too hard for too long to allow mine to dead-end.

Even as I veered off Sunrise Drive to bounce down the pitted dirt road to our once secondary home and current primary and sole home, the reasons I should delete Jude from my mind continued to pile up. I knew why I shouldn't have anything to do with him, and that all made sense, but there was another thing deep inside of me that just didn't give a hoot about what I knew.

Something was fighting back, telling my gut to take a hike. Something wanted Jude Ryder in my life, no matter the consequences or the outcome.

And whatever that something was, I craved it.

I cut my little Mazda's engine outside the garage, since it was filled to the rafters with boxes and pieces of furniture from our old house, which was about four times as large. At one time, we never worried about money, but after Dad's business empire came crashing to the ground, savings dried up and things like second homes and European vacations became luxuries of the past. Mom's job as an architect paid just enough to keep a family of three alive but not thriving. Even if we still had all the money we'd once had, alive but not thriving would still describe the Larson family unit. We'd just been going through the motions for five years now.

Sliding my cover-up over my swimsuit so I wouldn't have to hear the always-to-be-expected and ever-so-creative lectures of disapproval from my mom about giving the milk away before someone bought the cow, I jogged up the rickety steps of our front porch.

"Hey, Dad," I said as I pulled the screen door open. After five years, I no longer looked for Dad sitting on the worn blue armchair. He was always there if it was any time before seven p.m., entranced by the television or a crossword puzzle. After seven, he transformed into a gourmet chef, whipping up Italian cuisine with such flair you never would have guessed he was Norwegian.

"Hello, my Lucy in the sky," was his expected response, as it had been for years. My dad was nothing if not a Beatles fan, and I, his second-born, had been named for his all-time favorite song, to my mother's mortification. She was, if there was such a thing, the anti-Beatle. I don't know how my dad managed to get not one, but two children named after the band that created a generation, in my dad's words, but there were plenty of things that didn't make sense when it came to my parents' relationship.

"How was your day?" I asked, only by habit. My dad's days were all the same now. The only variation was what color shirt he sported and what kind of sauce he whisked up for dinner.

He was just opening his mouth when the first few notes of the *Jeopardy!* jingle sounded, and like clockwork, he was out of his seat and striding into the kitchen like he'd just declared war on it. "Dinner will be ready in thirty," he announced, cinching his apron ceremoniously.

"All right," I said, wondering why, after all this time, I still mourned what my dad and I had been. "I'm going to take a shower, and I'll be down to set the table." I lunged at the stairway the moment I heard the *click-clack* of heels pounding gravel, but I was too late.

"Lucille." The screen door screeched open, letting in an inescapable cold front also known as my mother. "Where are you running off to?"

"The circus," was my response.

The ice queen went subpolar. "Judging by the way you're dressed, or barely, and given your plummeting GPA the past few years, I would say a career as a trapeze artist isn't that far-fetched."

Her words didn't even hurt anymore, no more than a superficial wound. "Good to know I'm living up to your expectations," I fired back. "I'll be sure to send a postcard when I hit the big time with Cirque du Soleil."

Always a proponent of getting the last word, I whipped around and flew up the stairs before we really got wound up. However, I was only delaying the inevitable. We'd pick up right where we left off in thirty minutes, when Dad chimed the cowbell. Fireworks could be expected at dinner.

Slamming my door shut, I leaned against it, forcing myself to take deep breaths. It never really calmed me like those exercises were supposed to, but it backed me down from the ledge enough so I could get on with the next thing in life, hopefully something that didn't involve Mom.

I'm well aware most teenage girls believe their moms hate them and are out to ruin their lives. The thing about my mom is that she really does. Hate me, that is, and wish my life will one day be ruined the way I ruined hers.

She wasn't always this way, the definition of a dried-up, ball-busting, daughter-loathing career woman. In fact, the day my father became a borderline shut-in with some serious issues, I lost the woman who used to leave napkin notes in my lunch box that were signed ♥ Mom.

That person was never coming back, but I still found myself wishing she would whenever I slid my tray through the lunch line and grabbed a handful of napkins.

THREE

S ome people had roosters. Others had alarm clocks.

I had the Beatles.

My dad was as prompt as he was predictable, and this morning "Come Together" was playing at three-quarters volume, which meant it was seven a.m. For a teenager on summer vacation, the Beatles were as welcome as a fire alarm blasting into my ear at the crack of dawn.

Groaning my way out of bed, I slid into the first pair of matching sandals I could locate. A smear of ChapStick and a quick tear through my hair with my fingers and I was ready for the morning. The invention of the yoga pant and the pairing with a tank top ranked on my list of top ten most life-changing inventions. The stretchy duo served as sleepwear, exercise attire, everyday duds, and the perfect outfit for a morning in the dance studio.

There were a lot of things I could go without—shampoo, licorice, red toenail polish, sleep . . . hell, boys—before I could go without dance. Ballet to be specific, but not exclusive. Any and every opportunity I got, I was dancing. I'd been breaking, hip-hopping, waltzing, tangoing, and pirouetting my way through life since age three.

When it was announced we'd be simplifying—aka downsizing because we were running out of money—our lives, I had one request.

Actually, it was more like a demand.

That dance lessons at Madame Fontaine's Dance Academy go on uninterrupted. And not canceled due to insufficient funds. That's the main reason I chose to work summers at one of the cafés around the lake. I wasn't going to let money, or the lack thereof, get in the way of my dreams. Since our lake house was only a forty-five-minute drive from our old house, I'd been able to continue my dance lessons through the summer. One of the few lucky things to have sprung up in my life.

I didn't care if I no longer got to wear the name-brand clothes and had to shop on half-price day at the local thrift store, or if my car was replaced by public transportation, or even if we had a roof over our heads. I had to keep dancing.

It was the only thing that kept my head above water

when I felt I was drowning. The only thing that got me through the dark days. The only thing that seemed to still welcome me with warm arms and a mutual love. The only thing that hadn't changed in my life.

Throwing my pointe shoes over one shoulder and my purse over the other, I opened my bedroom door a crack. The cabin was a rickety old place, with lots of character, as my parents put it when they bought the place a decade ago, which had just been a nice way of saying it was a hunk of junk that was lucky to still be standing. But I'd learned two summers ago how to oil the hinges and apply just the right amount of upward pressure on the door handle to get the half-century-old door to open noiselessly.

After the "Come Together" chorus, I waited, listening for the *click-clack*s of Mom's heels or her trio of sighs. Then I gave myself the green light.

Mom was either on her way or already at work, so the coast was clear. After last night's dinner, actually, after the last five years of dinners, avoiding my mom was a top priority, right below dancing.

As I leaped down the stairs, an image surged to mind. An image I'd tried to erase from it. An image my best intentions had been useless against.

Jude Ryder, crouching in the sand a breath away from me, appraising me like he knew every last dark secret of mine and it didn't faze him one bit. Jude Ryder, golden from a summer in the sand, liquid silver eyes, stacked muscles pulling through his shirt . . .

My toe caught on the second-to-last step, and had it not been for all those years of dancing, I'm certain I would have face-planted into the ancient plank floor.

Righting myself, ensuring shoes, purse, and pride were still intact, I forced myself to make a sacred vow that I would never allow myself to daydream, think of, ponder, wonder, or lust after Jude Ryder again.

I didn't need a signed petition from the countless girls he'd probably seduced and left high and dry to know he was a one-way ticket to an unwanted pregnancy at worst or a broken heart at best.

"See ya, Dad," I called out, snatching an apple from the fruit bowl. "I'm off to dance practice, and I'll be home sometime before dinner." Grabbing a bottle of water from the fridge, I was out the door two heartbeats later.

It didn't matter how long I hung around—there would be no response from my dad. Not even a nod of acknowledgment. He could have been a mannequin in his chair, staring absently out the window at nothing.

I could have been screwing half the world's population on the kitchen counter and he wouldn't have cared. Or even noticed.

Reminding myself that dwelling on the screwed-upness that was my family wouldn't fix a thing, I adjusted my thoughts to something else, anything else that wasn't family related.

And where did my mind lead my thoughts to?

Jude Ryder.

I was on some sort of sick, self-destructive thought stream.

As I headed toward the Mazda, something caught my eye. Something that stood out because of the way it caught the early morning sun. Something that had not been there yesterday.

It was cyclone fencing, a rectangle of it, containing a miniature house, two plastic bowls, and a knotted rope inside of it. A dog kennel.

A solution to one of the endless problems that riddled my life.

An answer to a silent prayer.

I strode down the beach from the cabin, biting my lip to keep the phantom tears from forming. I noticed a red bow tied across the padlock door, a folded note hanging beneath it.

I suppose to 99.9 percent of teenage girls, a dog kennel as a present ranked just above a bad hair day on prom night, but to me—a girl who couldn't have fit the mold of normal if she tried every day of forever—it was like finding the latest Hollywood heartthrob wrapped beneath the Christmas tree with a tag that read, *Bon appétit*.

Beaming like the schoolgirls I rolled my eyes at, I ripped the note from the bow, not even caring who had built the kennel. This meant mini Cujo could stay with me until I'd rehabbed him so he could be adopted into another family.

My smile that felt like it wouldn't end vanished as soon as I read the words.

So. How about that date?

It was signed with nothing other than a *J*, but I didn't need the perfect punctuation or the following three letters to know who'd left it. Just the man I needed to, yet couldn't, stop thinking about.

Just the man I never needed to see again. Just the man I wanted to see right now.

If my history of failed relationships didn't already prove it, this did. I was going to end up an old, malevolent shrew.

Taking a quick scan of the area, I saw no sign of a man whose face, body, and smirk shunned the gods. I was irritated at myself for being disappointed.

Certain a guy like Jude knew exactly what he was doing and what his next play was going to be, I shot one more smile at the kennel before jogging to the Mazda. Mirror walls and wood floors were beckoning to me, and I was resolved: Dance came before boys.

With perhaps the exception of one.

Shaking my head and putting a heavy lid on my irresponsible, internal evil twin, I turned the key over in the ignition and blasted music until the speakers sounded like they were about to explode.

I still couldn't erase Jude Ryder from my mind.

I wiped out. Fell so hard on my ass it knocked the wind right out of me. The last time I'd taken a fall of any kind was when I was twelve and on the second day on my pointes.

I was mad the fall had cut my practice short. I was madder that Becky Sanderson, who'd been bragging she was a shoo-in for Juilliard since we were in grade school, had had a front row seat to it. I was maddest I'd have a bruise the size of Cape Cod on my derriere until winter break because I'd been thinking of a certain someone I most certainly shouldn't have been.

Whatever and whyever it was, Jude had set off a grenade in my life that was decimating everything I held sacred in less than twenty-four hours.

I wanted to curse the maker for not completing the female mold with a delete-slash-purge button when it came to men, but I was too superstitious. I was convinced swearing at the divine was followed by a one-way ticket to hell.

And not the otherworld, Satan-and-demon-dwelling hell. Hell on earth.

Let's face it, I was already so close I needed to be on my best behavior every second of the day.

Pulling into the driveway, I slammed my head down on the steering wheel, trying to conceive of a viable equation for time travel so I could fast-forward my life one year.

Because dogs were the most sensitive creatures on this earth, a hot, wet tongue slid up my cheek.

"Why can't you be a teenage boy, Rambo?" I asked, scratching him behind his ears.

He gave me a yap and a doggy smile as his answer. My newest pet project, pun intended, had earned himself a name last night at the Darcys'. Apparently a *Rambo* marathon played all night long, and whenever Mr. Darcy had attempted to switch off the TV, the pup had gone all nutso on him, so he left it on, and by dawn, the "neutered male mixed breed" scheduled for euthanasia the same day I adopted him had a new name.

"All right, boy," I said, frowning at the beach house. "Let's get this over with." Scooping up all of Rambo's twenty pounds, I beelined for the kennel like it was safe territory. Like if I proved I could contain him, I could keep him.

"Here's your new house, Rambo," I whispered as I

shooed him inside. "Be a good boy and don't dig, bark, or tear your doggy house to shreds, okay?"

He began inspecting the kennel right away, growling in the corners where I guessed a certain set of hands had spent a lot of time fastening nuts and bolts together.

"You're not a big fan of Jude's, are you?" I said, kneeling outside the kennel door. "Why is that?"

"Probably because dogs have great intuition."

I was so startled by the voice behind me and its proximity to my neck that I stumbled back, falling on my butt. For a grand total of two times that day. At this rate, I was going to become the first prima klutz ever.

"Dammit, Jude," I said as Rambo began howling up a storm. "There were these great one-syllable words referred to as greetings that were invented so one person"—I motioned at him—"could alert another person before they—"

"Fell smack on their ass?" he finished, offering me that same grin that had been my undoing yesterday and, as my twisting gut was proving, today as well.

"Startled them," I finished, about to push myself off the ground when he reached for my hands and pulled me up. I told myself the warmth, the heat, that trickled into my veins at his touch had everything to do with the hot-as-Hades summer day.

Even in my most authoritative voice, I wasn't very convincing.

His smile ticked higher. His eyes flickered. He knew exactly what his touch was doing to me. And I hated that he knew.

"Sorry I startled you," he said, letting go of my hands.

"Sorry you knocked me on my ass, you mean?" I smirked at him, wishing he wouldn't look at me like he could see everything that was happening in unmentionable places.

His eyes rolled to the sky. "I'm sorry for all prior, current, and future offenses I make in your presence."

From behind, I heard Rambo lapping up water from his bowl. "All jokes and banter aside," I said, "thank you. This is quite possibly the nicest thing anyone's done for me."

Shoving his hands in his pockets, he stared at me. "It was no big deal."

"Yeah, it is," I said, not about to let him wave it off. "Although I'm curious as to how you got this thing built without anyone hearing or noticing."

"It helps that I'm a fence-making ninja," he said, giving me a twisted smile, "and it also helps that I live next door." Pointing his chin at the next cabin over, he arched a brow at me and waited.

"It was your family who bought the place from the Chadwicks last fall?" I asked, gazing at the A-frame cabin next door. I'd been under the impression it was still vacant.

"Yes, indeedy."

"You're my neighbor?" It was every teenage girl's

American dream to have a neighbor like Jude, so why did my stomach feel like I'd just swallowed a brick?

"No," he said, rubbing his hand over his mouth, trying to mask his smile. "You're my neighbor."

"Well," I sighed. "There goes the neighborhood."

He nodded once, those gray eyes of his so light today they were the color of nickels. "There it goes."

Three words. Three words accompanied by that look, performed by those eyes, emitted from that man.

I was lucky my knees weren't buckling beneath the weight of that swoon.

"So"— Jude scanned me—"neighbor, how does Friday night sound?"

"It sounds like Friday night," I smarted back, thankful the strong, very unswoony pieces of me were coming back together. No man, one rung short of divinity or not, would render me a sighing, batting-eyelashes, lovesick maniac.

"Weak, Luce," he said, clucking his tongue. "We're going to have to work on the speed and sharpness of your comebacks if you're going to spend much time with me. I'm hard to keep up with."

"Easy solution to that, then," I said, crossing my arms and leaning into the kennel. "I won't spend much time around you."

"So you've decided to wise up and keep your distance?" he said, his voice quieter.

"Lucy, wise up?" A voice that could line that much ice around words in this kind of heat demanded a particular level of skill and discipline. "That's as likely as me getting to take a three-day vacation any time in the next decade."

I swear if I was a dog, my hackles would have been on end or my tail would have been between my legs. With my mom, I didn't know whether to fight back or cower and expose my jugular.

"I don't know about that, ma'am," Jude said, stepping around me to where my mom hovered over me. "Luce seems like one of the smart ones. One of the ones who has her head on straight."

Mom clucked her tongue three times. "Flattery is not considered a virtue, young man. Especially when, at this stage of life's game, it is utilized by young men hoping to work their way into a young woman's pants."

"Mom," I hissed, spinning around.

"Who's your new friend, Lucy?" she asked, surveying him head to toe like he was as everyday as, and far less useful than, stretch denim.

"Jude." When she was acting like this, I kept my answers to one word.

"And I'd assume Jude," she said, just like she was sinking

her teeth into a lemon wedge, "has a last name."

"Ryder," he offered, extending his hand, which she frowned at like it was a misplaced load-bearing beam on one of her projects.

"Ryder," she repeated, although she enunciated it so it sounded more like *Ride her*. "Of course it is."

Unbelievable. My mom had to be the first woman who had gazed on Jude's face and not felt something thump-thump somewhere inside. Even a guy, a straight guy, would have been more impressed by Jude than Mom was.

"Another dog." Mom sighed. "What number is this? I lost count at five." She scrutinized the kennel and everything in and around it as if it should be shipped away on the next train out of town. "So much for wising up. When are you going to learn that you can't save the world one lost soul at a time?" she said, the hardness draining from her voice, leaving behind nothing but the sadness that really was my mom.

She was halfway to the cabin door and out of hearing range when I offered a response. "Until there are no more lost souls left to save."

"Seems like a great lady," Jude said from behind. I could feel the smile on his face, it was that strong.

"You have no idea." I turned toward him, wishing every time I looked at him it didn't feel like I was falling down an abyss. "So you think I'm smart, huh?"

"Only because you decided to keep your distance from me."

Glancing at the kennel, imagining the time, money, and stealthy planning it must have taken to build it without being noticed, I didn't need to know the finer details that made up Jude Ryder. I mean, who builds a kennel overnight? In a handful of hours? Someone who had a good heart somewhere beneath the layers of muscle and attitude. "Who says I decided to keep my distance?"

"You did," he said, shoving his hands in the pockets of his worn pewter jeans.

"No, I didn't," I said. "And if I did, I reserve the right to change my mind at any given time."

"If that's the case, then I reserve the right to retract my previous comment."

"You make so many of them, exactly which comment are you talking about?" I asked.

Reaching out, he ran his fingers down the laces of my pointe shoes strung over my shoulder, like he was capable of breaking them if he wasn't careful. "The one about you being smart."

He could have been about to say something else, he could have been about to do something else, but it would have to remain a mystery, because at that moment, the Beatles' "Eight Days a Week" blared through the windows. Dinner was in thirty.

"Are you hungry?"

Stroking the pink ribbons one last time, more carefully than hands like his seemed capable of, he glanced back at the cabin. "Maybe."

"Maybe?" I repeated. "You're a teenage boy, a superhuman-sized one at that. You should always be hungry."

He paused, the inner conflict so strong it was lining his face.

"Come on," I insisted, grabbing his hand and giving it a tug. "My dad's the best cook ever, and you just met my mom. Don't make me go in there alone."

Exhaling, he shifted his eyes to mine. "Are you sure?"

"Absolutely, positively, impossibly, certainly"—I peaked a brow at him—"dare me to continue?"

"Make it stop," he said, clamping his hands over his ears.

"Come on, Drama-saurus Rex," I said, waving good-bye to Rambo, who was happy as a clam gnawing his bone, and led Jude up the stone walkway.

"Another weak, weak attempt at humor, Luce," he said, winding his fingers through mine. "So weak."

"Forgive me, O hallowed god of comedy."

Nudging me as we walked up the steps, he smiled that impish one that made me feel my heartbeat in my mouth. "Good to see you're ready to admit I am a god."

"Oh God," I sighed, shaking my head.

"Exactly," he said, all matter-of-fact. "Just the way you should refer to me."

Shooting him the most unamused expression I could manage, I shoved the screen open. The inevitable would only wait so long.

Dinnertime at the Larson home was low on my list of priorities, especially considering dinners as of late had been punctuated by silence and even more silence. Unless you count the frowns Mom fired like ping-pong balls between Dad and me. But sitting down to a family dinner with Jude, a guy I knew very little about other than I was dangerously captivated by him and that, at least on the surface, he was a guy no right-minded parent would want their teenage daughter spending their time with . . . This dinner, I was quite certain, had the potential to be epic.

An epic disaster.

"Something smells damn good," Jude said to me, sniffing the air, which was thick with the scents of wine and mushroom.

His words weren't heard only by me, as attested by both my parents snapping their heads back to stare at him.

Throwing a double punch, my mom's brows peaked at the same time her lips pursed. My dad smiled. You see, where Mom saw the bad in everything, the damn in life, Dad saw the good. Or at least he used to and still did from seven to nine p.m.

Jude chose to address Mom first. "Sorry for the language, ma'am." He stuffed his hands in his pockets. "I was brought up in a house where cursing was like a second language. It comes so naturally I don't even realize it. But I promise to attempt to filter myself when I'm in your house."

Leaning back in her chair, she crossed her arms. "I've always found profanity to be a poor substitute for intelligence."

My mouth fell open. Even for my mom, this was crossing into a new level of cruel.

Jude's expression didn't change. "In my case, I'd have to agree with you. My report cards have been the things of parents' nightmares."

"And from the smirk on your face, I deduce you're proud of that?"

And now, to join my mouth falling to the ground, I wanted to crawl into a hole and hide. Whatever was hidden between the layers that made up a person like Jude, no secret, crime, or offense deserved this degree of nastiness.

Glancing over at Jude, I found his face just as calm as if he was om'ing his way through yoga.

"No, ma'am," he replied, shrugging.

"'No' as in you are proud or you aren't proud?"

Sliding his hand from mine, Jude looked her straight on and answered, "'No' as in I'm proud of very little in my life."

Mom didn't have an immediate response to this. Even in her paint-it-black world, honesty of this sort gave her pause. "Sounds like precisely the kind of overachiever I want spending time with my daughter."

"Mom," I hissed in my warning voice. Not that it affected her in any way.

"That's what I told her," Jude said, "but the thing I've learned about Lucy in the few hours we've spent together is that she's the kind of person who doesn't let anyone make up her mind for her."

The cell phone mom kept within an arm's length at all times buzzed to attention. For the first time in who knows how long, she clicked ignore. "And what else have you learned about Lucy? Since you're the expert."

Taking my hand back in his, he slid me a smile. "She's smart, except when she isn't."

Buzzing again. This time Mom lifted the phone to her ear. "What a revelation," she said to Jude before rising and marching out of the kitchen, offering the party on the other end a clipped greeting, followed by a three-second-long sigh.

"Sorry," I mouthed to him.

"For what?" he said in a low voice. "You can't control your mom's actions any more than she can yours."

"My," I said, tugging him forward. One parent down, one more to go. "Aren't we insightful today?"

"That's a term that no one's ever used to describe me before," he said, tugging at his beanie so it sat just above his eyebrows. With all the long sleeves and beanies he wore, I was beginning to wonder if he had the circulation of an eighty-year-old woman.

"Dad," I called, tapping his shoulder. No response. "Earth to Monsieur Larson," I tried again.

His attention didn't deviate from the pots and pans sizzling and boiling on the gas range. "Hello, my Lucy in the sky—"

"This is Jude," I interrupted, not wanting Jude to see me even more as the little girl I already felt in his presence.

Raising a finger, Dad turned off all the burners. I wasn't sure how he was able to time an entire meal to the same second, but I was sure this was a phenomenon that skipped a generation when it came to me.

Spinning around, he wiped his hands off on his apron . . .

Oh God, how had I forgotten the apron? Jude's eyes bulged, but he recovered so quickly I was certain Dad hadn't even noticed. Not that he would have cared if he did. The apron had been a present from Italy, Rome to be exact, and depicted the sculpture of David in his glory, in *all* his glory, hanging down in anatomically correct places.

"Hey, Jude," Dad greeted, looking quite pleased with the whole transaction.

"Mr. Larson," Jude said, extending his hand. "Nice apron."

Shuffling the spatula into his other hand, Dad shook Jude's hand. "I like you already," he said, wiping a streak of flour from his cheek. "Great name, exquisite taste in culinary attire," he continued, before inspecting where Jude's hand still enveloped mine. "And you like my daughter. You're a smart man, Jude." Winking, Dad spun back toward the stove, unleashing a whisking, flipping, and stirring frenzy.

"It's not hard to recognize something special when life's thrown a lotta shit your way," Jude said.

"I'll raise my hands to the sky at that," Dad said while I worked on confirming my feet were planted to the ground. Something about the way Jude's eyes went all soft when he stared at me and said "special" was doing a job on me. "Lucy in the sky," Dad said. "Why don't you forward the disc a few tracks and we'll play Jude here his Beatles theme song?"

"No," Jude said abruptly. Dad and I both paused, studying him. "My mom worshipped the Beatles, hence the name," he said, the tension gone from his voice. "I've heard that song enough times to last three lifetimes."

Dad studied Jude awhile longer before shrugging. "Well, I won't torture you with it any more, then," he said. "But it's a great song to be named after. Possibly the second best"—looking over at me, he smiled—"right after 'Lucy in the Sky with Diamonds.'"

"It's a song about letting drugs mask the pain of life," Jude said. "I think Mom was still loopy from delivering me when she named me."

Dad stared at Jude again, like he was trying to put his finger on something he couldn't quite pinpoint. "It's also a song about love," he said, "and letting that love in when we need it most."

Jude paused, something so strong going through his mind it was visible on the planes of his face. Finally, he shrugged. "Well, whatever it is, it's just a name."

"A good one," Dad said, waving a spatula at him. "What's your last name, Jude?" Dad glanced up as he plated the chicken.

"Ryder, sir."

"Hmm." Dad's forehead wrinkled. "Name isn't familiar, but you have a face that I feel certain I've seen before."

Jude's hand tensed around mine. "I get that a lot."

"Did you grow up around here?"

"I grew up everywhere," Jude answered.

"Jude's family bought the Chadwicks' place," I interjected, not sure if it was more for Jude's or my hand's benefit. "Maybe that's why you recognize him."

Dad mulled this over as he spooned sauce onto the plates.

"Maybe," he said to himself. "Maybe not."

"Can I help you, Dad?" I asked, pulling Jude with me. I was sure if I let his hand go, it might be the last time I'd have it in mine again.

"These two are ready," he said as he finished saucing the other two. "One thing is for sure, son," Dad said, patting Jude's face. "Whether I've seen it or not, that is one good-looking mug."

I was used to being embarrassed by my parents, kind of came standard when your father was on the bad side of crazy and your mom was the poster woman for the ice queen, but this was hitting an all-time high. Dad, all but stroking Jude's cheek, dancing around the kitchen wearing the naked bust of an ancient statue, beaming like he was mad as a hatter.

If Jude still wanted to see me tomorrow after tonight's ordeal, he could handle just about anything else I threw at him. I hoped.

Glancing up at Jude, I found him staring at me like he couldn't help it. Maybe that's because I could have updated my heritage from Caucasian to Tomato Red.

I glanced at the door, then looked back to him. I wouldn't have blamed him either. As a blood relative of this family, I wanted to escape through that door more than a dozen times a day.

Shaking his head once, he leaned his head down until I

could feel his breath hot against my neck. "You can't get rid of me that easy."

I was fighting off a bad case of full-body chills, but I managed a quick, "Darn."

"Mags!" Dad yelled up the stairs, managing to jolt the hell out of me and rattle the china cabinet at the same time. "Dinner's on!" He paused at the bottom of the stairs, expecting an answer that I'd known for a long time he'd never receive. The only human being on earth Mom neglected more than me was my dad. Another second passed before he turned away and headed toward the table, where Jude and I were taking our seats.

"I hope you like it," Dad said as he placed the chicken plate in front of Jude.

Inspecting me with a laserlike focus, Jude replied, "I already do."

FOUR

'd always loved a campfire. But a campfire at night, sharing a blanket with Jude squished up beside me, with a parent about to retreat to bed, went beyond love.

This was the campfire to top all campfires.

"Night, kids," Dad said, stretching as he stood. We'd made it through dinner, thanks to my mom staying locked in her office, giving someone a tongue-lashing through her cell. Dad, odd as he was, was easy enough to be around if you could get past the fact that reality escaped him. I'd managed to accept this as a fact of life, and Jude didn't seem to have a problem with it either.

"Night, Dad." My heart was already racing. I knew once we were alone something was going to happen. The tension had been that thick between us the past hour, as expectant exchanges, hands playing finger hockey, legs brushing legs, and the unsaid words between us grew louder than had we spoken them.

"Good night, Mr. Larson. Thanks again for dinner," Jude called after my dad, his hand hovering above my knee.

"I like your dad," he said as his thumb circled the inside of my leg.

It was impossible to offer any other response than a smile and a nod.

"The verdict's still out on your mom," he said, chuckling.

Another nod and smile.

"And I like you," he said, his voice low. "In fact, I really like you." Taking his hand from my leg, he lifted it to my face. And then the other hand. He held me so firmly I couldn't look anywhere but at him, but gently enough that, had I tried, he would have released me.

"I like you, too."

Cocking an eyebrow, he waited.

"I really like you," I added, feeling so many damn sparks I could have ignited any moment. "I don't give my number out to just any guy, you know?"

Smiling, he moved his thumb to my mouth. Brushing the line of my lower lip, he studied me like I was something he could consume.

I was all for woman empowerment and all that jazz, but

standing in the heat of that touch, I wanted to be possessed in every way another person could possess you.

I was sure more than a minute had gone by, but I could easily have lost track of all time. I opened my eyes. His were the lightest shade of gray I'd seen yet. "You can kiss me, Jude."

I expected just about anything else than his forehead lining as his eyes darkened. "I know I can," he said, his voice tight. "I'm just not sure if I should."

The ache that originated at the very core of me began to spread. There was only one way to alleviate it. "You *should* kiss me, Jude."

His eyes went another shade darker, but they never left mine. "I shouldn't," he said, sliding a hand behind my neck, skimming a finger beneath the collar of my tank top. "But right now, I don't give a damn."

His words hadn't settled on me before his lips did. They were as powerful as his hands, but as gentle at the same time. He parted his lips, and his groan rumbled against my chest, and before I had time to process if I should or shouldn't, I swung my leg over his lap because, beyond every rational reason, I couldn't be close enough to him.

His tongue against mine, his chest pressed to mine, his hands holding me like they were as hungry as mine were, I wondered if this was one of those moments people remembered on their darkest days and smiled on. I wouldn't only be smiling, I'd be cartwheeling from this memory until the day I died.

My hands slipped beneath his shirt, scrolling up his stomach until there was nowhere left to go but down.

"Luce," he breathed, when my fingers settled on his belt. "Stop." His hands gripped my hips firmly, but his mouth kept pace with mine again.

"I'll stop when you stop," I whispered against his mouth.

"Dammit," he sighed, pushing against me with his hands, but continuing to welcome me with his lips.

"If you're done with her, can I have a turn?" a voice suddenly shouted at us from down the beach.

"Shit," he hissed, lifting me to a stand in one seamless movement.

"What?" I whispered, running my fingers through my make-out hair.

"Go inside, Luce," he said, situating himself in front of me. "Right now."

"Why?" I wasn't going anywhere. Not with a man who could do that to me out here. "Who are they?" I asked as a few dark figures walked up the beach toward us.

He spun on me, and his eyes were so disturbed I couldn't determine if they were more frantic or manic. "Don't why me, Lucy Larson. Get your ass inside that house right now." Grabbing my shoulders, he spun me around, then shoved me in the direction of the cabin. "Right the hell now."

He had a temper, not a good thing. Because I had one too.

Spinning back around, I glowered up at him. "Don't you ever push me again!" I shouted. "And don't you ever tell me what to do."

Jude's expression flattened before turning into desperation. "Please, Luce. Just go inside."

His plea was so raw, his eyes so helpless, I almost did. But then the three figures were upon us.

"You been holding out on us, Jude?" one said, stepping into the firelight. He wasn't as tall as Jude, but he was stockier. Running his eyes down me like he was peeling off my clothes in the same motion, he said, "You unearth some fresh piece of ass and don't have the decency to share with your brothers?"

"Brothers?" I whispered this time, letting Jude step in front of me and stay there.

"Metaphorically, baby," the stocky boy answered. "And brothers who share everything." Jude's broad back was the only thing saving me from another eye raping by Stocky Boy. "Everything," he repeated, telling a crass story with one word.

"Vince," Jude said, his voice murder. "Get the hell out of here before I make you."

Vince laughed. "I know you like yourself a little piece

of ass, whether you're kicking it or screwing it, but I doubt you'd be able to take all three of us down before we took you down." The two other boys, who must have been twins and hygiene-impaired, stepped into the circle. "Right before we took your girl down. Each took your girl down."

I should have been terrified. Every survival instinct inside me should have been firing at top speed. Teenage girls had nightmares about situations like these.

But I wasn't. Whether it was Jude's balled fists, or the fury rolling off him, or the fact that my survival instincts took a hiatus, I felt as calm as calm could be.

"Let's find out how that goes for you," Jude said, his jaw set. "Come on, you dipshits. Which one's going to be the first one to come at me?" Curling his finger at each of them, he waited.

We waited for a while. No one, least of all the stinky twins, looked like they could come away alive, let alone walking, if they came at Jude. From the cautious expressions on their faces, you would have thought he was walking death, with a pair of fists that packed a powerful punch.

"We'll leave you alone," Vince said at last. "Let you finish up what you came here for. One last summer screw."

Jude made a noise that sounded more animal than man. "That's a smart move, but it isn't going to save you from catching an ass-whupping the next time I catch up with you."

"As always, Jude, such a pleasure," Vince said, following after the twins, who were already halfway down the beach. "And a word of advice for you, girlie," he said, stepping to the side so he could see me. When he did, a smile that was nasty by every definition of the word curled his mouth. "Make sure he uses a condom. You don't want to catch what that man whore's got growing down there."

Jude's entire body jolted forward; he wanted to chase after those guys and do who knows what to them, but he stopped. Glancing back at me, his shoulders dropped and then his arms relaxed back at his sides.

The man had been insulted in as many ways as a man could be, threatened, taunted, and teased, and here he stayed. A foot in front of me. A man who I didn't doubt could end all three of them in ten seconds' time, judging from the rage and confidence I'd witnessed in his eyes.

And he stayed behind with me. Whether to protect me in case the three stooges made a return trip or to pick up right where we'd left off, I wasn't sure. And I didn't care.

"Hey, dickweed!" I yelled at the trio ambling down the beach. I made sure to step into the firelight so they could get my full message. Raising my middle finger, I yelled, "There's plenty of this to share!"

"What the hell are you doing, Luce?" Jude hissed, pulling me behind him again. I didn't take Jude for the chivalrous type, but I liked it, more than any woman of the twenty-first century should.

"Not even a fraction of what I'd like to," I said, as the only reply the three gave me was a chorus of laughter.

"Listen, I dig your spunk and your take-no-prisoners attitude, I do," Jude said, turning to face me, "but you don't mess with people like this."

"People like this or brothers like this?" I said, so much nervous energy bouncing out of me from the highs and lows of the past ten minutes I didn't know what to do with it.

Jude sighed.

"Those are your brothers?" I actually said a quick prayer it wasn't true.

"In a way," he replied, closing his eyes.

"In what way?"

Opening his eyes, he reached for my hand. "In the way that doesn't matter."

"Then screw them," I said, letting him take my hand when I knew I shouldn't have before I had some clarification as to who or what he was. "I should have flipped them off again. They're all bark."

"No," he said firmly. "Please, Luce. These are the kind of bastards that have no bark. They sink their teeth into you without any damn warning." Grabbing my arms, he pulled me close, trying to make his words sink in through osmosis.

"Don't mess with them. If you see them coming down the sidewalk, cross the street."

This earned an eye roll from me. Surely he was exaggerating. I didn't doubt the doofus triplets had done their fair share of pot and defacing public property, but they weren't ballsy enough to do the stuff that would earn them hard time if they were caught. Coward was stamped across every one of their foreheads.

"Shit, Luce," Jude said, crossing his arms behind his neck and turning toward the beach. "This is exactly the reason I told you to stay away. So you didn't find yourself eyeballs deep in my shitty life."

Now his words of caution were starting to make sense. Why he'd said I should stay away from him if I was smart.

The thing was, if staying away from him made me smart, I never wanted to be smart again.

"Jude," I said, looping my fingers through his belt.

Turning around, he leveled me with weary eyes. "Yeah?"

"Kiss me."

He paused. Then, he did.

I didn't have a clue what time it was by the time Jude and I were finally able to pry ourselves away from one another, but as I tucked myself into bed that night, I knew the sun would be making its debut in a few hours max. That meant

I'd have to get through a killer three-hour ballet practice on two hours of sleep.

I didn't care. Every minute of sleep lost was spent losing myself in Jude's arms.

I forced myself to close my eyes and shut down my overheated mind. I opened them a heartbeat later. Rambo went off like a hurricane warning.

I jolted out of bed and ran to the window. Rambo wasn't a barker; he growled, smiled, and gave an occasional yap, but I'd never heard him go off like this. It was like either him, or someone close by, was about to have the life strangled from them.

I couldn't make out much other than the gleam of his kennel and what could be shadows winding in the wind or people moving around the perimeter. Lifting the window to get a better look, I saw a wall of flames explode up and around Rambo's kennel.

It wasn't something I thought about. It was purely a gut decision. Crawling out of the window, I scooted down the roof. The only thing on my mind was saving Rambo from another fire. One I could actually save him from.

How or who had started the fire wasn't even an afterthought; I just had to get to him. To save him.

I swung my legs over the edge of the roof. My feet landed on the porch rail, and then it was a mere jump to the ground.

I'd done it a dozen different times, but I didn't think this instance qualified as sneaking out of the house.

Rambo's barks had stopped at the inception of the flames, and I wasn't sure whether that was because he was scared barkless or dead. It seemed wrong to hope for the former.

Grabbing the hose around the side of the house, I cranked it on and sprinted down the yard. The hundred yards to the beach where the kennel was took an eternity to cross. Thrusting my thumb over the end of the hose, I sprayed the kennel door first, killing the flames there so I could open it and free Rambo. Once the flames were extinguished, I slid the padlock open, ignoring the blistering heat still smoldering over the metal. Swinging the door open, I stepped inside.

"Rambo!" I called out, frantic. "Come on, boy." The smoke was burning my eyes and throat, but I took another step inside. Tears were close to spilling. I was sure I'd find Rambo's scruffy little body lifeless on the ground, when that little fur-ball leaped into my arms with a yap. I cried out with relief, letting him lick my face until every square inch had been covered.

"You gave me a scare, boy," I sobbed, ducking out of the kennel. Rambo's crazed licking came to a sudden halt. A low growl rumbled through his body.

I couldn't tell if the laughter behind me had just started or had been going on for a while, but when clapping accompanied it, I finally took notice.

Setting Rambo down on the ground, I glanced over my shoulder. Vince and the twins came at me. Without Jude's formidable frame blocking me, their faces screamed menace. They terrified me.

"So we meet again," Vince said, separating himself from the other two.

I felt like vomiting, but I didn't let that keep me from replying. "I was hoping we would, since I wasn't sure if you got a good look at my parting message." Lifting my hand in the air, I performed a repeat flip-off.

I knew it was childish, I knew it was out of place, and I knew it was useless against three men and whatever they were going to throw my way, but it felt so damn good at the time.

Vince's face dropped, like he couldn't believe I was giving them the bird when my dog had nearly gone up in flames and three boys who personified disturbed were sneering at me like I was next up on their climb toward crime escalation.

"I'm going to enjoy watching you burn, bitch," he said, spitting to the side. "Grab that whore so we can teach her some manners."

I should have yelled, I should have run, I should have at least tried to find a rock or stick I could use as a weapon, but I'd never been the girl who did what she should have.

I glanced over at Jude's house, waiting for him to come barreling out the front door any moment to save me, when two sets of arms grabbed ahold of me, twisting me with such force I yelped.

"You better let me go right now!" I shouted at the two of them, struggling against their grips. "Unless you want a fist dent to your foreheads." Another look over my shoulder revealed no sign of Jude, not even a hint of light in his house.

"He's not coming to your rescue, honey," Vince said, stepping forward. "Jude's not the kind of guy who likes to play hero. He's more the antihero type, if you catch my drift."

This earned a couple of snickers from either side of me.

"Ha," I snorted. "This coming from the person who tried to light some helpless dog on fire to lure a girl out of bed so he could attempt to intimidate her. That sound like someone who would recognize a hero when he saw one?" My mom had told me from the time I was three that my mouth was going to be the death of me, and gauging by the flash of murder across Vince's face, she was right.

"So what exactly are you calling me?"

Narrowing my eyes, I sank my heels in the sand. "A coward."

It didn't seem physically possible that a guy that heavy could move as fast as he did.

"I was going to let you live," he hissed outside my ear,

as his fingers encircled my neck, "but that was before that comment." His fingers left my neck and went to my head. I already knew what he was prepping to do, so I braced myself for it, but expecting it didn't dim the pain when he yanked my hair so hard I was certain he'd uprooted half of it.

I closed my eyes and whispered a prayer I'd said every night as a child before I got into bed, and then, when I expected to hear the scream of another hair pull crawling up my body, I heard another kind of scream. One that was so desperate and enraged at the same time, it sounded like the devil himself had decided to pay Sapphire Lake a visit.

Opening my eyes, the first thing I saw was Vince's face eclipsing from domination to dread, right before something small nailed him straight between the eyes. He staggered back, grabbing at his head, right before he fell backward.

And then Jude was on top of him, seemingly coming out of nowhere, landing fist after fist into any part of Vince he could get to. "You're going to have to tie me up better than that next time, you sick son of a bitch!" Each word followed by a punch, each punch landing like a clap of thunder.

I stood there, still in shock from the fire and the malice behind the fire, and now, also in shock watching Jude beat another man with such hate he didn't seem to care if he killed him or not.

I wasn't sure whether to be relieved he was on my side or

terrified that a person like this existed.

Stalling suddenly, Jude glanced back at me. "Luce," he said, his voice even, not showing any of the signs of being winded that you'd expect him to, "go inside and call 911."

When I stayed frozen in place, he added, "I've got this. I won't let them hurt you." Just then, the cowering-in-the-corner twins decided to unite forces and come at Jude. Or at me, I wasn't sure. "Go, Luce," he begged, motioning back at the cabin. "I'll protect you."

This time, when I tried to put one foot in front of the other, I was able to do it. Rambo, who hadn't left my side, followed on my heels. Striding up the beach felt like I was trying to run a marathon in under an hour, but I pressed on, glancing back every other step to make sure Jude was holding his own against the threesome.

Holding his own would have been the modest term for saying he wasn't taking any prisoners. How and wherever that man had learned to fight like that, I didn't want to know, but I couldn't help but be thankful for it tonight.

I was just staggering around the corner of the cabin when I noticed the red and blue lights, followed by a cop shining a flashlight into my face.

"We're responding to a report that someone across the lake noticed a large fire burning in this general area," he said, walking toward me as his partner came up behind him.

"You see anything, miss?"

"Here," I said, breathing heavily from my jaunt up the beach. "The fire's here." As I pointed down the beach, the officer studied me again, this time really seeing me. His eyes widened.

"Miss, are you in need of medical care?" he asked, continuing to walk toward me like I was mentally unstable, which, at this point, wasn't that far off the mark.

"Maybe?" I answered, not sure. Adrenaline was still firing through me so intensely I couldn't feel any of my injuries, or ascertain if I had any.

"Hal, call for a paramedic."

His partner nodded and jogged back to the cruiser.

"Okay, miss," he said, stopping in front of me. "I'm Officer Murphy. What's your name?"

"Lucy," I said, clearing my throat. "Lucy Larson."

"Good, Miss Larson," Officer Murphy said, his eyes darting over me, trying without success to look at me like something wasn't very wrong. "Is anyone else down there?"

"Yes," I said, grabbing his forearm and pulling him toward the beach. "There are four others."

"What are their names?" Murphy asked, striding ahead of me in a hurry.

"I only know two names. Some guy named Vince."

"And the other?" Murphy stopped, glancing back at me.

I swallowed. "Jude," I said. "Jude Ryder."

"Wait," Murphy said, his face changing. "Jude Ryder's down there?"

I nodded, my brow furrowing.

"Shit," he said under his breath before tearing his walkie-talkie from his pocket. "Hal," he sighed into it, "call for backup. Jude Ryder's here."

Hal muttered another curse back before answering, "Copy that. I'm calling for backup now."

FIVE

*O*ne of my favorite places in the cabin was the screened-in porch. I loved taking in the view, curled into old wicker chair with a blanket twisted around me.

That had changed tonight.

Something about watching the guy you hoped would kiss the wits out of you every night until forever shoved away in cuffs, followed by three more guys who were more stumbling than walking, thanks to Jude's handiwork, all while what was left of the kennel smoldered, had a way of knocking your whole worldview on its ass.

The paramedics had left, because other than a smattering of bruises, I had actually emerged unscathed. My parents finally woke up once three more squad cars arrived with sirens blaring. Mom was still hungover from her double dose of sleeping pills, and Dad had been such a wreck when he found out what happened, he had to be given a tranquilizer. So now, both parents sat as far apart as they could on the wicker love seat, eyes glazed over, glancing between the beach and me and the police cars as if trying to decide if this was all real.

"Mr. and Mrs. Larson?" Officer Murphy tapped once on the screen door before stepping onto the porch. "We're all finished up here. Here's my card, if you have any questions." He slid it into my mom's hand, gazing between the three of us like we were the saddest thing he'd seen tonight. He might have been right. "Otherwise, I'll keep you updated. Now, Lucy," he said, facing me, "I'll need you to come down to the station and give your report first thing in the morning. Will you need a squad car to pick you up or can you get there on your own?"

"I can drive," I answered, giving him a small smile as I continued to stroke Rambo, who had curled up in my lap and didn't have plans of leaving it anytime soon.

Mirroring my smile, he crouched beside me. "Are you all right, Lucy?" he asked, resting his hand on my arm. "Can I get you anything?" He squeezed my arm, examining my parents like he couldn't reconcile why they were over there while I was over here.

"Yeah," I said, trying not to look back at the third squad car from the front, where a bowed head wearing a beanie cap was visible. "I'm good."

"Okay," he said, rising. "I'll see you in the morning."

"Officer?" Mom cleared her throat, sounding half-pleasant. Must have been the sleeping pills. "Just to be clear, Mr. Ryder doesn't live in the house next door?"

"No, Mrs. Larson," he said. "Unless you count squatting in the boathouse uninvited for a few nights."

"Squatting?" she repeated, like she'd never heard the word.

"Also known as breaking and entering in my line of work," he explained. "Also known as a regular occurrence if you're Jude Ryder."

"This isn't his first time being arrested?" Mom asked, staring at me as she spoke.

Officer Murphy chuckled. "Nowhere near it," he said. "We've known Jude and those other three delinquents since they were grade schoolers. Bad eggs, every last one of them," he went on, trying to drive the message home. "These boys are the sort fathers pray their daughters never have the misfortune of meeting. These are the kind of boys who grow into men who spend their lives in prison."

Mom sighed, shaking her head while Dad enjoyed the benefits of la-la land.

"But Jude saved me from those other three," I said, not sure why I was speaking up. As I'd expected, I knew nothing about Jude. I felt betrayed and lied to and duped. But somehow, even with all that stacked against him, I still felt the need to stand up for him. "They would have done something terrible if he hadn't stepped in." I made sure to make eye contact with my mom, driving home that Jude had been the only one capable of saving me, since my parents had been snoring drug-induced low Cs for hours.

"Not to dispute what you're saying, Lucy, but in all my years of dealing with Jude Ryder, I've never once known him to care about anyone but himself," Officer Murphy said to me, his smile sympathetic. "Boys like that are incapable of caring about anyone but themselves."

"I don't believe that," I said.

"I know, Lucy. I know you don't," Murphy replied, opening the screen door. "Jude wouldn't be such a capable and successful repeat offender if he wasn't charming and manipulative, but tell you what. When he gets released in the next hopefully three weeks, but more likely few days, let me know if you hear from him, will you? If he calls you to apologize and beg your forgiveness, or heck, even if he calls just to say hi, you let me know, and I will retract my statement about him not caring for anyone but himself. But if he doesn't, will you do me a favor and forget you ever met Jude Ryder?"

I wasn't sure whether I shook or nodded my head, but Officer Murphy was right about one thing.

I never did get that call a few days or a few weeks later.

SIX

irst day at my brand-new school. Senior year. Those people who say hell doesn't exist are so wrong.

Southpointe High was everything I believed happened only on reality television. The girls were twice as pretty as the average teenage girl, the boys could pass for college students, so-called geeks got tossed into garbage cans, several female teachers made glaringly obvious passes at male students, and I witnessed at least a dozen different drug deals taking place in between periods.

And it wasn't even lunchtime yet.

The teacher was just going over the semester syllabus, which included reading and reviewing books I'd read in seventh grade, when the bell went off like it was a bomb-raid alert. Being the new girl, when everyone had ushered me to the seat closest to the door, I assumed they were being polite. Little did I realize my seat was closest to the bell, which sounded like a sonic boom.

Just like the three periods before, fourth period English earned me more eye rolls and snickers as everyone watched me all but jump from my skin. I was going to need to buy stock in ibuprofen, because I'd be taking it every four hours from now until graduation day on June 3. And yes, I already had a countdown going.

"So you're the new girl the guys are already placing bets on." This from a girl who was so put together, so gorgeous, she epitomized what people meant when they used the word "veneer" to describe a person. "I believe Luke Morrison is in the running for the 'most likely to nail you first' honor."

"Excuse me?" I was all for being friendly, especially when I didn't have a single friend here, but I wasn't one to roll over and expose my throat.

Veneer girl caught on quick that I wouldn't be the personal doormat she could wipe the mud off her stilettos on, because she smiled, waving at the air. "Don't let anything the male species says or does around these parts upset you. I know the general consensus is they've supposedly evolved from apes, but that's just an insult to apes, in my opinion."

"Oh-kay," I muttered, slipping my book bag over my shoulder.

"I'm Taylor," she said, flipping her hair as a guy nudged past her, giving her a look that should strictly be reserved for the bedroom.

"I'm Lucy," I said, not sure if this could be the makings of my first friend at Hell High or someone who subscribed to the keep-your-friends-close-and-your-enemies-closer motto.

"What are you doing for lunch, Lucy?" Taylor asked, weaving her arm through mine and tugging me through the door.

I didn't have a chance to reply.

"You have to sit with me and my girls. I'm not taking no for an answer," she said, leading me down the hall, making that hall her bitch. I swear every head turned as she sashayed down that runway. Guys winked, whistled, and stared. Lots of staring. The girls pretended to ignore her but shot glares or stink eyes from the side.

"Thanks?" I said, uncertain whether I should be thankful. My thoughts turned to my brother, like they did at some point every day. He was a natural when it came to these kinds of situations, making friends in new settings. Making friends had never come easily to me, and it appeared Southpointe High wasn't going to be an exception.

"First impressions are everything, and second impressions are nothing," she said as we walked into the cafeteria.

Same reaction as it had been in the hall. Whatever Taylor had going, it was powerful stuff. "It's all about damage control, but I think we'll be all right if we play it right."

My head was spinning. "By damage control, you mean because the guys are already spreading rumors about who's going to bang me first, or soonest, or hardest, or whatever?" So much for school being a place of higher learning.

"The guys? Of course not," Taylor said, waving at a table in the far corner. "That's the highest form of compliment in their books. It's the girls, more specifically the girlfriends of the guys taking bets on the new girl. Plus, your wardrobe isn't exactly contradicting the slut image."

My nose wrinkled. This girl spoke a language I wasn't familiar with, and she was taking a jab at my wardrobe. My skirt was a teensy bit short, yes, but I had on a cardigan and flats to tame it down, for God's sake.

"They're striking an offensive, a potent one."

"And that would be?" I asked, wondering if at least some of the glares and stink eyes were aimed at me. In fact, that dark-haired girl who didn't know the meaning of less is more when it came to mascara was definitely aiming that stink eye my way as she draped her arm over the guy beside her.

"They've labeled you a slut," Taylor said with a shrug. "I've already seen it scrawled across two bathroom mirrors in last season's lipstick and heard it whispered at least fifty times in the hallways."

Was it possible to hate high school more? Yes, the answer is always yes.

"Fan-flipping-tastic," I replied, holding my shoulders high. "And what did I do or not do to deserve the dumbasses of Southpointe High taking bets on bagging me and the girls who date them labeling me a slut?"

Of course I knew the world wasn't fair. Not everything made sense or followed a logical, harmonious path, but I at least wanted a reason why the world sucked if there was one.

"That . . ." Taylor stopped me, spinning me around so we were staring at the lunch line. My breath hitched in my lungs, and a bad case of vertigo followed. " . . . is the reason why."

His tray slid to a stop as his shoulders tensed. He turned, and Jude zeroed in on me like he knew exactly where I was. I saw a hint of a smile, and I felt my world beginning to spiral out of control.

"I take it from that stupid grin on your face the rumors are true," Taylor said, trying to steer me along, but I wasn't moving. More truthfully, I couldn't move when Jude scrutinized me the way he was now. "But here's rule number one at Southpointe High—if you want to keep even a moderately clean reputation, you don't look at, talk to, or God forbid, date guys like Jude Ryder."

Leaving his tray, he headed my way, carving a path through the packed cafeteria. Anyone who saw him coming moved, and those who didn't were tugged away by nearby friends or shouldered out of the way by Jude.

"He's coming over?" Taylor said, sounding like the world was ending.

"Yeah?" Didn't seem that earth-shattering to me.

Taylor shook her head like I was hopeless. "Jude never ever, in a hundred million years, pursues a woman. He's the pursued, not the pursuer."

This time it was my turn to shrug. "He's just coming over to say hi."

"Exactly. Jude doesn't come over and say hi to anyone," she said impatiently. "I'll repeat, he's the pursued."

It felt like every eye in the cafeteria was pinging from Jude to me. This was high-school hot-off-the-presses drama unfolding right here. "I thought you just said if a girl cared about her reputation, she wouldn't hang out with the likes of Jude. Isn't that why I'm a bona fide slut, according to Southpointe High's unbiased, give-a-person-the-benefit-of-the-doubt population?"

"Yeah, I said that," Taylor said, checking Jude out in a way that made me feel all territorial. "But haven't you noticed that with guys like Jude, a girl just doesn't care about her reputation?"

There didn't seem to be an appropriate answer to that, so

I weaved out of her hold and headed for him.

"What are you doing?" Taylor said behind me.

"Going to say hi."

"You can't do that," she hissed, rushing forward and grabbing my arm.

I wasn't sure if this girl was doing drugs or had forgotten to take them, but she was starting to piss me off. "Listen, Taylor," I said, spinning on her. "If my reputation can manage to get even sluttier by saying hi to someone, so be it." Tugging my arm free, I caught the wounded expression she cast my way.

So much for making friends.

"Hey, Luce."

I felt the hair on the back of my neck rise.

"Hey, Jude." I composed myself as best I could. He was still grinning like this had been the best thing to happen to him all week, and other than the fresh scar crisscrossing his eyebrow, he looked exactly the same: dark clothes, dark hat, dark secrets.

"I didn't expect to see you here," he said, stuffing his hands in his pockets.

"Really?" I said, trying to act like we weren't on a stage for everyone to witness. "I didn't expect to see you here either, especially when the last time I saw you, you were being hauled away in a police car."

His expression twisted as he rubbed the back of his neck. "Yeah, about that. I suppose I've got some explaining to do."

"Some?" I said. "I'd say you've got yourself a whole heap of explaining to do."

"I know," he said, his face shadowing. "I know."

"So when did you get out?" I asked quietly, taking a quick survey of the cafeteria

"It's all right. Everyone already knows," Jude shouted, "what a good-for-nothing SON OF A BITCH I AM!" His voice thundered against the cafeteria walls, followed by a chorus of spoons clattering onto trays. "I got out a couple weeks ago," he said in a normal voice, lifting a shoulder.

I tried not to act thrown. "And you couldn't call?"

"Of course I could have called, Luce," Jude said, his voice tight.

"So you didn't call."

"Do you need an answer to that, or are you just looking for a way to make me feel shittier than I already do?"

"You feel shitty?" I said, stepping forward. "You feel shitty?" I repeated just because it felt good. "My hair was almost ripped out by the roots by a couple of your acquaintances I never would have had the honor of meeting had it not been for you. My dog was almost barbecued. I'm officially an honorary Southpointe High slut because somehow, everyone knows I know you, so that must mean I've slept with you six ways to Sunday." I was giving the audience exactly what they wanted, a damn show, and they weren't missing a hot minute of it.

"That's your answer," Jude replied, his jaw popping. "That's why I didn't call. That's why I didn't show up on your doorstep the second I was released from juvie like I wanted to. I'm cancer, Luce. And not the kind that you can kill off with radiation. The kind that kills you in the end." That vulnerability I'd caught glimpses of before was there again, drowning in his eyes.

I was too pissed, or too hurt, to let those eyes affect me. "Well, thanks for nothing. Have a nice life."

Quite possibly the hardest thing I'd done to date was turn my back on him in front of a wide-eyed cafeteria and walk away.

I didn't know where to go, but I couldn't march angry circles around the cafeteria unless I wanted to add "mentally unstable" to my laundry list of titles. So, swallowing my pride and my opinion that Taylor might be the most manipulative female to have ever walked the earth, I marched my butt right back to her table.

"I didn't expect to see you again," Taylor said, crunching into a carrot stick and giving me a scowl that would have flattened a lesser woman.

"Why's that?" I said as nonchalantly as I could. "I told

you I just wanted to say hey to an old friend."

"That was one hell of a hey," Taylor said, all snarky-like, before taking a sip of diet soda. The group of girls sitting around her, not nearly as genetically blessed, but still pretty enough to lift their surgically molded noses up at me, snickered into their own cans of diet soda.

"What that was, Taylor," I said, pulling a chair out and sitting down. I didn't need an invitation if they weren't going to issue one. "Was one hell of a good-bye."

"Doesn't look that way," she said, staring over my shoulder.

Turning in my seat, I found Jude standing in the exact place I'd left him, watching me with an intensity I'd never experienced before, staring at me like he didn't give a damn what anyone thought of him doing so.

Flipping back around, I tried on my glare for size. "Ah, Taylor. I'm sure you of all people know that looks are deceiving." Pulling an apple from my bag, I sank my teeth into it and gave her a challenging smile.

"Meaning?" she said, leaning forward.

I was pissing off the wrong person, I knew that, but I'd been through enough in life to recognize petty bullshit when I saw it, and this chick was the queen of petty. "Let's take you, for example. Someone like you, pretty in a conventional, surgical"—a combined inhalation spread around the table—"put-together way"—I was doing cartwheels inside, letting this girl have it—"well, someone like that you wouldn't expect to be such an insufferable, nasty, b—"

"Hello, ladies," a newcomer interrupted, nudging a couple of the openmouthed girls before stopping behind the chair next to me. "This seat taken?"

I shook my head, giving him a once-over before pulling a bottle of water from my bag. Smile too bright, streaks too blond, tan too fake, shirt too ironed. Handsome in a very vanilla way and definitely not in a handsome-to-me way.

"So you must be the girl everyone's talking about," he said, taking a seat.

Snickering circled around the table.

His face flashed red as he realized his mistake. "I mean, everyone's talking about in the sense that you're the new girl," he clarified, which did nothing more than earn another round of laughter from the table.

"Of course that's what you meant," Taylor said under her breath.

He shot her a give-me-a-break expression before turning in his seat toward me. "I'm Sawyer," he said, smiling that artificially white smile. "Sawyer Diamond."

Oh, man. Even his name was too . . . annoying. If Dad found out I went to school with a guy whose last name was Diamond, he'd try to shove an arranged marriage down my throat. His Lucy in the sky . . . a Diamond.

"Lucy," I said, taking a sip of my water, reminding myself that making snap judgments in the heat of anger was always a bad idea. Next time I found myself marching away from someone, I'd march a million circles before sitting down at this table again.

"Lucy," he said, pulling a sandwich from his lunch bag. "A pretty name for a pretty girl."

I was mid eye roll when I felt someone hovering over me.

"You're in my seat, Diamond."

I didn't glance back. I didn't need to. I'd recognize that voice if I heard it in my next life, too.

"I didn't realize this seat was taken." Sawyer squirmed in his seat, hunching his shoulders.

"Your mistake," Jude said, gripping the back of Sawyer's chair. "You make a lot of those, don't you?"

Sawyer rose to a stand, turning on Jude. He wasn't quite as tall as him, but close enough, and he was nowhere near as built as Jude.

"Shove off, Ryder," he said, crossing his arms.

"Why don't you leave her alone?" Jude said, staring down at Sawyer purposefully.

I had a premonition I was about to add an all-out cafeteria brawl to my things-that-should-only-happen-on-reality-TV list, but whether or not I was pissed beyond repair at

Jude, I couldn't stand watching him dragged away in cuffs again.

Popping up, I slid in between the two of them. "I'm leaving. You can have my seat if you want." I didn't look him in the eyes. I didn't want a reminder of what I was turning my back on.

Without another word, I stepped away and raced out of the cafeteria.

I wasn't sure what was required for homeschooling, but I'd take ten hours a day, seven days a week, with no bathroom or lunch breaks, if it meant never returning to this cesspool of suck again.

Dodging around students, I didn't stop until I found an empty hall. Ducking into the closest locker alcove, I slid into a corner, curling my head into my legs. I wanted to cry so badly right then. I wanted to let every tear I'd held back for years have their moment, but something wouldn't let them form. Some mental block inside me would not allow the release I needed so badly.

"Dammit," I muttered, slamming my fist into a locker.

"Luce?"

So not what I needed right now. So just what I needed right now.

"How did you find me?" I said, keeping my head ducked.

"It was easy," he said, taking a seat beside me. "All I did was follow the cursing."

I laughed. Hard. I was always emotionally unstable in these kinds of moments, when I needed to cry and couldn't. In fact, emotionally unstable was a fair assessment of who I'd become. Most days I was able to bury my insecurities and my horrible past with my attitude and temper. Days like this reminded me just how fragile I was. Just how easily my supposedly thick skin could be pierced by the wrong person wielding the right words.

So here I was, sitting next to a man who defined "wreck" and who, if I let him into my life, would turn me into an emotional wreck. He scooted close against me, hitching his arm around my neck, and pulled me into him. I should have resisted, at least put up some fight, given I still knew nothing of Jude's past, present, and future. Of course I didn't.

"So?" he said, his voice muffled in my hair.

"So," I said, as a herd of boys shuffled by us. They didn't say anything while they were in view of Jude, but they were elbowing each other so hard down the hall I could hear it. Sitting here alone, snuggled up to Jude, was likely to do wonders for my already shot reputation.

"Explanation time," he said, like there wasn't a choice.

"Explanation time." Now was better than later, although sooner would have been better than now. I knew I'd take what I could get when it came to Jude.

"Ready when you are," he said.

My mind went blank. Like no question or answer would

change anything I felt for him. This was an insane thing for a girl to conclude when it came to someone like Jude.

If it wasn't already confirmed, I had a screw loose.

"Come on." He nudged me. "You can ask me anything, and either I'll answer it or I won't."

"How very forthcoming of you," I said, smiling into his shirt.

"We've only got a few minutes before the bell rings, so you better get started. I don't care about being late, but I'm guessing you're the kind that does."

In fact, I'd had my fair share of tardies. At my straitlaced, blue-blooded private school, I'd been something of a rebel because I wasn't afraid to wear a miniskirt, or slick on an extra layer of lipstick, or skip class every now and again. However, here, at Heathen High, my once rebel ways were going to qualify me for sainthood.

Oh wait, I forgot I'd already been labeled a slut by the student population.

Jude nudged me again, so I tore into it, not easing into the questioning.

"You've been to jail before." It wasn't a question. I already knew, but I guess I needed him to confirm it.

"Yep," was his clipped response.

"How many times?"

"Eleven or twelve. I lost count."

I knew Jude and cops went together, but I'd underestimated just how well.

"What for?" I asked, working to keep my voice even.

My head lifted as Jude shrugged. "Mostly for getting into fights, and one time for having drugs on me."

Holy crap. "What kind of drugs?"

He didn't pause giving his answer. "Meth."

Holy shit. "Were you using it?" Was it wrong to pray he was giving it to someone else?

"Nah," he said. "I was trying to sell it. I was a dumb and greedy son of a bitch at thirteen. Didn't work out well for me, so I quit. I haven't sold drugs in four years."

"And you know those three boys because you all live at the same home?" Other than that first morning after that night of chaos, I hadn't spoken of them. I'd tried not to even think of them, but I was willing to bust open that locked door to unveil who the real Jude was.

For the first time during our question-and-answer session, he stiffened. "Yep," he said, shifting his beanie down lower.

"And Uncle Joe? He runs the place?"

Jude laughed one low note. "If you call lounging his fat ass on a couch while a few dozen kids go ape shit, then yeah, that's his job."

"How long have you lived there?" Sitting upright, I

peeked over at him, and he was someplace else. Somewhere dark.

Like a switch had been flicked on, he flinched. Giving his head a swift shake, he cleared his throat. "The cops didn't tell you?" he said, working his jaw. "They're usually champing at the bit to label me a screwup."

This was land-mine territory I was tiptoeing through, and I wasn't sure how much farther I'd get before it would all blow up. "I kept hoping I'd hear it from you. But someone seemed to have forgotten my phone number. And my address." I smiled over at him, and finally, he softened.

"Five years," he said.

"Do you like it?" I asked.

"It's all right." Another clipped, nothing-to-write-home-about answer.

"Why did you wind up there?" For as desperate as I'd been to ask him all these questions if I ever got the chance, each one was making me squirm in my seat.

"My mom left. My dad went to jail."

"I'm sorry," I whispered. God, I felt like the worst kind of person for thinking bad things about him. "Is your dad getting out anytime soon?"

"Nope." I was waiting for the wall across from us to burst into flames from the way he was focused on it.

"What did he go to jail for?"

"For the kind of crime that jails were invented for."

A cold chill tickled up my spine. "And your mom? Why did she leave?"

"Because she hated being a wife and hated being a mom even worse," he said, the corners of his eyes creasing. "Because she was selfish and wanted her freedom and didn't have any sense of loyalty."

I lifted my hand and weaved my fingers through his. "Do you think she'll ever come back?"

Jude snorted. "Nope. Mom's long gone," he said. "Although I've got this lovely parting gift she left for me I carry around in my pocket," he said, sliding a piece of wrinkled old paper from his back pocket. "Well, this, and the ratty old hat on my head she knit or crocheted or some shit that was three sizes too big for me at the time."

I wasn't sure I wanted to read the note. In fact, I was sure I didn't, but I couldn't say no when Jude handed it to me. I couldn't say no when a person was handing me the only thing they had left from someone they'd loved. I took in a breath and unfolded it. "These are the lyrics to 'Hey, Jude,'" I said, puzzled.

"Right you are," he said, his voice tight.

"This is what your mom gave you before she left?"

"Well, she didn't give it to me, she left it on my night-stand before bolting off in the middle of the night, but yeah, she was thoughtful enough to write down the lyrics to some crummy song. Not even an 'I love you' or a 'yours truly, Mom.' Nice, right?"

Folding it back up, I handed it to him. "Why do you carry it around with you?"

"I don't normally. I keep it in a frame next to my nightstand but pulled it out this morning in a moment of weakness."

"You keep this on your nightstand?" I repeated, feeling like a tiny piece of my heart was breaking away.

"So I can see it every night." The muscles running along his jaw flexed.

"To remember your mom by," I guessed.

The tension in his jaw went up a notch. "To remind myself what can happen when you let yourself love someone." Stuffing the paper back in his pocket, he slammed the back of his head into the locker behind us.

To date, that was probably the saddest thing I'd ever heard.

"And the hat?" I understood why it was so threadbare and worn—he'd worn it every day for the past five years.

"Same reason," he answered, sliding it over his eyebrows.

"Well that's just all kinds of depressing," I said, trying to think of some way to steer the conversation in another direction. "Do you have any brothers or sisters?"

Jude shook his head. "Just me. Thank God dear old Mom and Dad stopped at one," he said. "What about you?"

I froze. That wasn't the dark alley I wanted the conversation to go down. I wasn't ready for Jude to know my past, even though he'd so willingly shared his. I liked to think I was an open book. That was the impression I wanted others to arrive at, but I was anything but an open book. I was the kind of book that had been shut for so long a cloud of dust would have erupted if someone had been able to pry me open.

"I had an older brother."

"Had?"

I closed my eyes, trying to discuss this as neutrally as I could. "He died a few years back."

Jude paused. "What happened?"

I bit my lip. "I'm not ready to dive into that one yet," I said, trying not to sound as sad as I felt. "Especially given the whole your-mom-left-you-and-your-dad's-in-prison thing. My depression tolerance has officially been reached." I tried on a smile, but it didn't fit.

"Sorry, Luce. Life is shit sometimes," he said, giving me a squeeze. "I'm sure he was a great guy."

"The best," I said, studying him. "You know? Sometimes you remind me of him."

He smiled. "He must have been a phenomenal guy then."

I tried another smile, and this one worked. "He was."

"Now we've got our shitty pasts out of the way, do you have anything else you're dying to ask me?" There was a tinge of hope in his voice, hope I was done with the inquisition, most likely.

No such luck.

"Tell me the real reason you didn't call," I said, playing with the hem of my skirt. "Do you have a girlfriend?" I didn't know who she was or could be, but I already hated her.

Jude's relief at the change in questioning was plainly visible. "Hell, no."

"You don't want one," I stated, remembering our very first conversation.

"That used to be my MO," he began, studying my lips for so long I felt them start to quiver, "but now I'm not so sure."

"Okay, so you didn't call me, not because you have a girlfriend," I said, checking off probable explanation number one, moving on to number two. "So you decided you're not all that into me?" I swallowed, bracing myself for whatever answer came out of his mouth.

"Luce, for such an intelligent species, you women can be really dumb sometimes." He laughed, lifting his index finger to my chin and turning it to him. "I didn't call because

I told you, there's nothing good that will come out of you being with me. I might not mean it to happen, but things have a way of going all to shit around me."

"Because you're a cancer," I said, repeating his words, but not believing them.

"Exactly."

I blew out a sigh of pure frustration. "Who told you that?"

Another far-off look. "Someone who used to be important."

It seemed like all these answers should be ticking off the questions in my mind; instead they were only adding more. "Here's the thing, Jude. Everyone already thinks I'm a slut because of you, so how much worse can it get if we keep hanging out?"

"Much worse," he muttered before his head snapped back toward me. I saw the unbridled anger in his eyes. "Wait. You're telling me they're calling you a slut?"

"Um," I stalled, familiar with Jude's short-fuse temper. "Apparently."

Jude punched the closest locker so hard the metal caved beneath his fist. "Judgmental bastards," he hissed, jumping up. "I'll catch up with you soon, Luce." He glanced back at me. "I need to do something."

"Jude," I warned. "It's not worth it." Because it really

wasn't. I had never let what others thought of me dictate what I was, and I certainly wasn't going to start now.

"Like hell it isn't," he answered, already striding down the hall.

A couple of guys greeted him in passing. His reply was another fist slammed into a locker.

I had fifth-period PE and was next to ecstatic when Coach Ramstein told us we didn't need to suit up because there was some sort of first-day-of-school assembly going on.

My elevated mood took a nosedive as soon as I stepped onto the shiny gym floor. I knew everyone wasn't staring at me, but it felt like that. Row after packed row, I was met with knowing eyes and smiles. A few were brazen enough to whisper the *S* word just loud enough so I could hear it.

Dammit, now I was getting pissed. I didn't want to make enemies of everyone here at Southpointe, but I wasn't ruling it out if they didn't start shutting their traps. It didn't seem fair a title had been forced on me without even partaking in the fun to earn such a name.

I walked to the end of the gym and sat in the bottom row of the last section of bleachers. I had the entire bench to myself.

Straightening my back, I looked up, making a point to meet every single stare pointed my way.

"Attention, please!" a tired voice spoke through a microphone. Judging from the decade-old suit and shadows under his eyes, he must have been the principal. The roar in the gym didn't lower a decibel. "Attention, please!" he repeated in an even more tired voice. This poor guy was going to have a rough year if he was already this exhausted on the first day.

I appeared to be the only student paying attention, so that was why, when someone suddenly appeared behind the principal and snatched the microphone out of his hand, I had time to mutter a select curse word under my breath before everyone else realized what was going on.

"Shut up, you sons of bitches!" Jude's voice vibrated the room, and everyone did just as requested.

The principal attempted to retrieve the microphone, but Jude lifted it over his head, a good three feet above the poor, red-faced man. Jude shook his head once and lifted a brow. Our principal got the message and backed away.

Lowering the microphone, Jude looked over at me, again knowing exactly where I was in this crowd of a couple thousand. His gaze lingered on me for another second before he turned his attention elsewhere.

"I put up with you bunch of bastards because I don't give a damn what you all think of me," he began, walking around the podium. "But I won't for one second put up with you trying to ruin the reputation of an innocent girl."

I wanted to gaze around the room, to experience the wide-eyed faces and jaws-to-the-bleachers mouths, but I couldn't take my eyes off Jude. He was defending my honor, and whether he was going about it the right or wrong way, it was the damn sexiest, most romantic thing I'd ever had happen to me.

"Lucy Larson is a friend. A friend whose back I have, and I think everyone knows if she were some random girl I screwed, I wouldn't be up here now." He paused, waiting or threatening anyone to stand up and say otherwise.

I'll be honest, gauging the fury on Jude's face, I feared whoever might have stood up to object would be leaving today's assembly in a body bag.

"If I so much as hear a quiet thought about her being a slut"—Jude's fist clenched, as he seemed to make eye contact with every Southpointe High student—"you better hope you don't like your legs, because I'm going to break both of them."

Now, to match everyone else's, my mouth fell open.

"If anyone needs any further clarification on the matter, you can take it up with me in the parking lot." He let that not-so-subtle warning hang in the air another minute before handing the microphone back to the principal.

The principal motioned to another administrator to take

over before motioning to Jude. Chuckling, Jude followed him out of the gym.

"It wouldn't be a first day of school if I didn't see you in my office before the end of fifth period, Mr. Ryder," the principal sighed.

"Yeah, but this was a worthy cause, Principal Rudolph," Jude answered, winking over at me before exiting the still-silent gym.

SEVEN

om's car was here. That was the first thing I noticed as I pulled up to the cabin after school. She was never home this early; it was like some mortal sin for her to leave the office before five.

So, of course, she'd choose the worst day I'd had in years to break this rule. I would have put the Mazda in reverse if she hadn't been watching me from the kitchen window. She was waiting for me.

Just when you think there's nowhere to go but up.

Unbuckling, I grabbed my backpack and set out to meet the inevitable. Opening the screen door, I inhaled and stepped inside. All I wanted to do was grab an apple, rush upstairs, and snuggle Rambo, because tonight was the last night I'd have him. The Darcys had wound up falling in love with the little fur-ball back when they'd watched him for me, and their kids hadn't let up on them until they'd agreed to adopt him. It was going to hurt like hell when I came home tomorrow night to find my beanbag chair empty. Rambo was the first dog my parents had allowed inside the house—probably because they were feeling guilty for that night they'd snoozed and snored through a kennel fire. But I knew it would take a miracle of the Annie Sullivan variety to sneak another dog by them.

Mom was sitting at the table, two glasses of tea steaming in front of her. The biggest smile my mom was capable of forming slid into position. "How was your first day?"

Epically awful. Worst first day of school in the history of the world. Humiliating. "Pretty good," I answered, reaching for the cup of tea she extended.

"Anything special happen?" she asked, sounding interested.

I was nominated the school slut by the end of first period. "Not really," I said with a shrug.

"Did you make any friends?" She took a sip of tea, still considering me with that ghost of a smile.

I made a lot of enemies. "A few." Lying shouldn't come this easy.

"Did you see any familiar faces?"

My parents were pretty much the anti-fans of Jude. If

they knew, they'd seriously consider pulling me out of Southpointe and busing me to another school district or selling their internal organs on the black market to send me back to private school just to ensure I didn't have to pass him in a hallway. While everything else about Southpointe blew, one very big part didn't. Sure, I didn't have, nor would I likely have, any friends there; the curriculum was coursework I'd started in elementary school; and it was so old every hall, room, and wall smelled like an old gym bag.

But Jude was there. And somehow, nothing else mattered but that.

"Nope." My voice broke, instantly alerting my mom. Okay, so lying wasn't this easy. It wasn't like I enjoyed lying to my parents. It was more of a survival instinct. I told them what they wanted to hear, and in return, they mostly stayed out of my life. "I mean, it's a big school. I'm sure there'll be a few people I recognize eventually."

"Hmm," she murmured into her tea. She was up to something. I didn't know what, but when any parent was "up to something," it was never something good. "I could have sworn I saw a Southpointe bus stop at Last Chance Boys' Home on my way to work."

I wasn't going to let her ruin my only bit of sunshine in that hell. "Is this the part where you're waiting for me to reassure you that I really don't mind—in fact, it's probably for the best—that I was pulled out of a private school my senior year because we're broke, and I was tossed into some mega school that has metal detectors at every entrance?" I said. "Because maybe we can skip the BS and, for once, be honest with each other."

She set her tea down, reaching for her temples. This was the first time Mom had lowered her walls in ages; I didn't know how to handle it.

"Have you heard from the dance schools you applied to?" she asked, sounding weary.

I sighed, wishing I'd never applied in the first place. My self-confidence really didn't need any more rejection. "Nope," I said, trying to make it sound like I didn't care, but darn it, I did.

I'd wanted to attend a top-notch dance program before I could spell. I was a dancer; it had defined my life since I could slip into my own tutu. I couldn't imagine a better life than dancing across a stage in front of an audience until old age or weary legs stopped me, and getting into one of the premier schools in the country would give me that opportunity.

"It's still early, Lucy," she reassured me, seeing right through my blasé act.

I lifted a shoulder. "We'll see."

Having had enough heart-to-heart for one day, I headed toward the stairs.

"Lucy?" I paused on the first stair. Mom was gazing at me like I was the most fragile creature in the world. She wasn't that far off. "How are you? Really?"

After five years, she had to work harder than a cup of over-brewed tea and a few marginally concerned questions to earn the honest answer to that one. "Good," I said, meeting her eyes.

"Really?"

Of course not really. I'd lost my entire family in the span of a day and had never gotten them back. And that was just for starters. "Really." I moved up the stairs faster, but not quite fast enough.

"You know, Lucy, if you ever needed someone to talk to," Mom's voice trailed up the stairs, "I know I'd likely be dead last on that list, but I am here if you need me."

I couldn't have been more shocked if I'd found my legs had transformed into a mermaid tail.

"Uh," I sputtered, searching for the right words. "Thanks, Mom."

Before any other transaction of the otherworldly could take place, I sprinted up the rest of the stairs into my room and slid under my covers all set to dream about a boy with beautiful eyes and an ugly past.

Walking through the metal detectors on the second day seemed less traumatic: The stares that fell on me turned to smiles; a few kids even waved. After my second class, I was wondering if I was in the same school. Everyone greeted me in the halls, five people offered to let me borrow a pen in trig when I asked, and one of Taylor's apostles complimented me on my outfit choice.

It was such a one-eighty from yesterday that either the entire student body had been lobotomized or Jude was a powerful player at Southpointe. Very powerful.

I had my answer at the end of third period, when I caught a glimpse of Jude walking down the hall a ways in front of me. The hall was packed, shoulder to shoulder, but wherever he walked, the crowd parted.

I was so hypnotized watching him part the seas, I didn't notice when a certain someone I'd been trying to avoid all morning nudged up against me.

"Hey, beautiful," Sawyer said, tossing me a wink.

Oh, man. Did guys still get laid with this tired old line? If so, I'd bitch-slap every last girl who fell for this one until I knocked some sense into them.

"Sawyer?" I said, glancing over. His high-beam smile peaked higher. "Retire that line, will ya? It sucks."

His face fell, but all too soon it was back to all its Sawyer glory. "That was some assembly yesterday. Bound to go down in Southpointe history for sure," he said, keeping pace with me as I sped up.

I knew guys like Sawyer—they'd been a dime a dozen at my old school—and what didn't work for me was that they were more boys than men, more talk than action. I was a man-of-action kind of girl.

"Yep, the trombone solo really kicked ass," I said, playing dumb because I didn't care and it was more fun.

Sawyer paused. I could see him scratching his internal head. "So you and Ryder, huh?"

Sawyer had bigger balls than I'd given him credit for. He was the first one to suggest Jude and I were an item in my presence. Gutsy, given yesterday's death threats. "We're friends," I said, trying to put some air between us so his shoulder wasn't stroking mine every step.

"Friends?" he said. "Looked like more than that. It looked like something."

I bit my lip before saying the first thing that came to mind. Just because I had a tendency toward anger didn't mean I had to let my temper rule my life, although now was one of those moments I wished I'd let it off its leash.

"It's nothing," I said, ducking between a few students to get to my locker.

Sawyer glided up beside me. "Good," he said, leaning

into the next locker over. "That will make things easier when I take you to Homecoming."

I don't know how many revolutions I spun the combo on my locker, but it was more than ten and less than a hundred. The only thing worse than not having a date for Homecoming would be having Sawyer as a date. He was the kind of guy who rented a hotel room before picking out a corsage and equated a lobster dinner with an all-night sexathon.

"Let's say I pick you up at eight next Saturday?"

Giving up on my combo, I inhaled. "Sawyer," I began. His face was so damn confident I was tempted to go with my "tell him off" version.

"Luce already has a date for Homecoming."

Jude sauntered up to us and squared himself in front of Sawyer. "Go find yourself another girl, Diamond. This one's off the market and is smart enough to see through your shit even if she weren't."

Sawyer's one-hundred-watt smile was long gone. Pushing himself off the locker, he stood toe to toe with Jude. "I thought you were just friends."

"Well, you were wrong."

"I figured as much," Sawyer said, not turning and running as most people did when they found themselves up against Jude. "You're not the kind of guy who keeps girls as friends. Pardon me for mistaking Lucy as available. I didn't realize you two had a friends-with-benefits thing going on."

Without warning, Jude shoved Sawyer so hard he fell into the herd of students making their way to class.

"Jude." I threw down my bag and grabbed his arm, trying to pull him away, which would have worked if I could bench-press a semi truck.

"Luce," he breathed, glancing at where my fingers circled his arm. "Let me go. I'm good."

Only because I would have been useless had he wanted to make Sawyer's face a punching bag, I did as he asked.

Striding after Sawyer, who was struggling to right himself, Jude stood over him, his veins bulging in his forehead. "Listen to me, you pompous jerk-off, and listen good. You ever," he spat, "EVER! so much as disrespect Luce in that way again, that will be the second-to-last breath you take, because so help me God, I will be so hot on your heels, you won't know what's coming for you until the devil's checking your name off on that roll-call sheet." Everyone had stopped to stare at the three of us, but the only thing I was focused on was Jude. His anger was so intense, it was shaking every last part of him, but he managed to contain it.

"Now, let me clear this up for you, since you're the dumbest piece of shit I've yet to encounter. Luce and I are friends. And I'm taking her to Homecoming. And you will not insinuate, verbalize, or even think anything about her that is less than honorable. You got me?" Jude's face was red, an inch above Sawyer's, and his veins now bulged to the point of bursting. Sawyer was being a dick, yes, but you would have thought he'd just committed first-degree murder from Jude's reaction. I had to admit, as much as I trusted Jude, it scared me.

Shoving up off the ground, Sawyer met Jude's scowl. "I got you."

"There's a little bitch," Jude said, patting Sawyer's cheek. "Now get the hell out of here. Isn't it about ass-slapping o'clock in the locker room for you and your boyfriends?"

The two glowered at one another before Sawyer's eyes latched onto me, where I was still glued to my locker. "See you later, Lucy?"

"Not if I *see* you first," Jude muttered after him, watching Sawyer until he disappeared around a corner.

The looky-loos were dispersing, although a few hung around, hoping for some postgame action.

"Scram," Jude ordered, waving his hands at the stragglers. I hadn't seen Olympians move that fast.

"So you're taking me to Homecoming?" I said, managing to get my locker open in world-record slowest time.

"That's right," he said, rocking back on his heels. His eyes were gleaming, and his face oozed confidence. It was damn sexy, but he couldn't know I thought that.

"Don't you think you need to ask me first?" I focused on exchanging third period's books for fourth's, although the corners of my eyes were burning from watching him.

He sidled up to me, getting so close I felt the heat pulsing from him. "Luce, will you go to Homecoming with me?" His voice was soft, low. And that made me feel things I didn't need to if I was going to make it to fourth period unflustered.

"I thought you wanted to keep up this whole friendship facade." I wasn't playing hard to get; I was making sure he really knew what he wanted. This was a guy who kept a framed note from his mom on his nightstand to remind him what happened when you let yourself love someone. The note didn't scare me, knowing that I would have done the same thing as a reminder of what happened when you opened yourself up to love. Two people with such skewed viewpoints on love should not, in this life or the next, wind up together.

"I don't give a damn about facades. I give a damn about people showing you some respect," he said, heat burning in his words. "Come on, go with me."

"I thought you didn't do the whole flowers, date, girl-friend thing." Zipping my backpack up, I slammed my locker.

"I didn't," he said, giving me that grin that could only mean he saw through me. "But I think you might have changed my mind on all that."

My heart stopped and was doing a handspring the next beat. "Is that a compliment?"

His gaze shifted to the ceiling. "You can take it however you want if you go with me."

"Jude." I rolled my eyes. "You could go with any girl, woman, or supermodel you wanted to. Why me?" It was a question I'd been asking myself a lot lately.

He made a face. "I don't want a girl, or a woman, or a supermodel. I want you." Damn, this whole conversation was not healthy for my heart. "You don't look at me like the rest of the girls do. Like you either want to stay as far away from me as the hallways will allow, or you want to get me into bed so you can brag to your Ivy League sorority sisters about the time you banged the infamous bad boy. You look at me and see me," he admitted, the corners of his mouth creeping up. "I don't remember the last time someone's looked at me like that."

He knew he was wearing me down, and at this stage, I was another cockeyed smile away from caving. He used this knowledge to his advantage.

Pressing himself against me, his hand found my hip. Backing me up against the wall of lockers, his other hand wandered up my arm until it molded around my neck. I went from being a young, marginally innocent girl who liked to dance to a woman with a one-track mind. My whole body ached, and when his lips just brushed over mine, it felt like the ache was about to explode.

"Go with me," he whispered, sucking at my lower lip.

He could have been asking me for my spleen and I would have agreed just as fast. "Okay." I nodded, sounding as shaky as I felt.

He leaned back, his face victorious. "So that's a yes?"

"Jude," I said in between trying to catch my breath, "that was a hell yes."

Brushing a quick kiss on my cheek, he headed out into the hall. "It will be one hell of a night, Luce. I'm glad I'll get to spend it with you."

Homecoming with Jude Ryder.

There was so much wrong with that, it had to be right.

EIGHT

The next couple of weeks went surprisingly smoothly, and a daily pattern emerged. I got to school, Jude was waiting for me. I walked through the metal detectors, Jude walked me to class. I tried to make elementary coursework somewhat stimulating during class, and Jude made the five minutes walking between classes overstimulating. I ate lunch with Taylor and her friends after she'd showered me with a hundred and one apologies and excuses, but my attention was focused on Jude, who sometimes spoke more in his silence than through his words.

He hadn't tried to kiss me again, but I could feel when he wanted to, and I pretty much always wanted to, but he seemed insistent about keeping some distance between us. I wasn't sure if this was just a show for Southpointe or if he'd decided I was more friend than girlfriend material. I would take Jude whatever way I could have him, but I'd prefer the option where I could kiss him whenever I wanted to.

Rambo had moved on to his new forever home, and Mrs. Darcy had already called twice to tell me how wonderfully he was settling in. I was thrilled for both dog and family, but I'd be lying if I said I didn't drench my pillow in tears that first night he was gone. It was an occupational hazard that came with rehabilitating dogs. One that was worth it, though.

"Can you believe this weather?" Jude greeted me, after nudging the student next to me off the bleachers. Surveying me, his eyes widened before he suddenly glanced away.

"No," I chattered. "Could someone please tell the weather it's still summer?" The rain had started first, then the wind, and then the forty-degree temperatures. In the Pacific Northwest, forty was like below zero.

The crowd roared in anger abruptly, throwing popcorn and empty drink containers at the football field. It was Southpointe's Friday night Homecoming game, to be followed up by the dance the next night, and to say we were losing would be an insult to losers everywhere. We weren't even on the scoreboard yet, and the opposing team's side of the reader board read forty-two points. And it was only the beginning of the second quarter.

"This sprinkle?" Jude said, wrapping an arm around me and pulling me against him. Warmth tingled down my spine. "This is fine weather."

I shot him a quick glare. "Says the man who doesn't own a garment unless it's gray."

"Are you implying something, Luce?" he asked, rubbing my arm hard.

"Who, me?" I fluttered my eyelashes. "Why gray? Why not black? Isn't that more your scene—more I-could-kick-your-ass-into-next-week?"

He bit his lip, trying not to laugh. "Black absorbs all colors, accepts them, and lets them define it. Gray isn't anything but itself. It absorbs nothing but itself."

This was clearly something he'd thought about. He didn't wear gray because it was his favorite color; he wore it for a deep-seated philosophical reason. As I'd discovered over the weeks, Jude was every kind of mystery that appealed to a woman and every kind she could never unravel. He was an enigma to which I wanted the answer.

A nasty gust of wind made me bury my head into Jude's chest.

"Didn't you check the weather report?" Jude said over the wind.

I laughed. "Does it look like I did?" I was wearing cutoffs, flats, and a shelf-bra cami. A white shelf-bra cami . . .

"Good thing I did," Jude said next to me as an old blanket parachuted around me.

I sighed with relief and embarrassment at the same time. I'd been so freaking cold I hadn't had enough brain cells working to remember I was wearing white in a torrential downpour. Now all the wide grins of my male classmates around me made sense.

"Thank you," I sighed, snuggling under his arm again as he turned me into a blanketed mummy.

"I could say the same," he replied, giving me an ear-to-ear grin.

I elbowed him, weaving out of his embrace. However, the weaving didn't work; he only held me tighter.

"I'm kidding, Luce," he said, through his laughter. "But come on, you're surrounded by a bunch of jerk-offs who have one thing on their minds at all times. Having an eyeful of you like that"—he eyed below my neck—"is not good for our hearts or hormones."

I don't know if I'd ever turned so red. "And by jerk-offs, are you including or excluding yourself in that category?"

"After seeing you like that," he said, droplets of water running down his face from his saturated beanie, "definitely including myself in the jerk-off category."

I tried elbowing him through the blanket, but he'd bound

me up so tight I couldn't move. I was powerless beside him.

"Isn't royalty supposed to sit in front?"

I scowled down to where eight guys and seven girls sat in saggy crepe-paper-decorated chairs, wearing crowns and holding wands or batons. When Taylor had come bouncing up to me, announcing I'd been voted one of the two senior class Homecoming princesses, I wasn't sure whether I should be shocked or mortified. I was certain Jude had threatened loss of limb to anyone who didn't vote for me, and also, I was anti all forms of voting the popular kids more popular. Homecoming royalty, prom king and queen, student government, best-looking, most likely to succeed . . . cue the finger in the mouth now. Those types of titles never went to anyone other than the top-tier populars, whose parents and grandparents and their ancestors had worn the same titles before them.

That was, up until today. I wasn't a popular, and given my whole opinion on the matter, putting that ridiculous crown on my head felt wrong. I drew the line with the sparkly wand thingy, stuffing it into my back pocket.

"I know you had something to do with this, Jude Ryder." I turned my most powerful glower on him. "And don't expect this to be something I forgive and forget."

He was fighting a losing battle to hide his smile. "I don't know what you're talking about. I can't help it if Southpointe

High has elected you their newest 'it' girl."

I was tempted to tear the crown off and break it in two in front of him when Taylor waved back at me, her own crown proudly sparkling on top of her wet-poodle hairdo. I kept the crown where it was, but as soon as halftime was over, the crown was going in the nearest garbage can.

"Hey, Pinocchio," I said, inspecting his face. "Your nose just grew, like, five inches."

"Whatever, princess."

The crowd showered another string of curses and tossed more garbage down on the field. Then someone behind us threw a half-empty bottle of orange soda, and it cartwheeled right into my temple.

It surprised me more than anything, but Jude's face did the Mr. Hyde thing. He spun around on the bleacher, latching onto the culprit.

"Hey, asshole!" he yelled, shoving through the row behind us. "Where do you think you're going?"

Shaking my head, I turned my attention back to the game, trying to drown out Jude's curses as he shouldered through the crowd. At that instant, the quarterback was sacked so hard the ball went flying into the opposing team's hands.

Another touchdown, and our quarterback wasn't getting up. The crowd went quiet as a couple of khaki-slack-wearing guys ran out onto the field. They crouched down beside him, moving and rotating a few limbs until they sat him up. The injured player pulled off his helmet.

It was Sawyer. More like, of course it was Sawyer.

He was such the stereotypical quarterback. I almost wanted to cheer for the other team until he started limping across the field, using the guys beside him as crutches. I told myself to be nice; he couldn't help it if he was a jackass. That degree of it was born into a man.

"OMG, Lucy," Taylor squealed, appearing from out of nowhere beside me. Her red-and-gold cheerleading outfit and shimmery pom-poms, topped off with the tiara and wand thingamajig, was an embodiment of everything that was wrong with high school popularity contests.

"Please, Taylor, for the love of functional acronyms everywhere"—I smiled angelically over at her—"don't ever say OMG again."

Steamrolling right past my request, she repeated, "OMG, Sawyer is out. Like, possibly out for the season, from what Coach Arcadia just said to Jason, who told Jackson, who told me."

"Wait," I said, grabbing her arms. "Coach Arcadia? As in Bill Arcadia?" From the back, I couldn't tell if that was Coach A down there on the sidelines, but I didn't think it was likely there would be another Arcadia who coached football in the area.

"Yeah, I think that's his first name," Taylor replied,

studying me like she was hoping some scandalous news was to follow. "He transferred a few years back from some yuppie private school. Apparently there's some juicy reason why, but I haven't gotten the intel on that one yet. You know him?"

I sighed again. That seemed to be the appropriate response whenever Taylor was around. "He was the coach at my old school. Everyone knew Coach A," I explained, but that was all the explaining I'd be doing. Taylor and I were casual friends, but I'd never trust her with information I wasn't cool with the whole school finding out about.

"You went to that school?" She appraised me like it was positively impossible.

"Yep."

"And you transferred to Southpointe why?"

Keeping a straight face, I answered, "For the academics."

Not getting the irony in this, or maybe Jude was right and I was impossible when it came to the dry humor department, she grabbed hold of my arm again, frowning down at the sidelines. "With Sawyer out of the game and Lucas on academic probation, we are screwed."

I stared at the scoreboard.

"We're screwed even more," Taylor amended, grimacing at the scoreboard.

I really wished Jude would finish his manhunt and come

rescue me from Taylor and her nonstop drama-thon. I found him marching up the concrete stairs, aiming an empty water bottle at a boy who was scrambling as fast as he could go up the stairs. Jude arched his arm back and spiraled that bottle straight into the back of the guy's head. From a good thirty yards away.

I had an answer to everyone's problems.

"Excuse me, Taylor," I said, walking around her. "I've got to do something."

"Don't be gone long!" she shouted after me. "Homecoming royalty makes their debut during halftime."

I shot her a thumbs-up and jogged down the stairs. The game was still in time-out, while Southpointe's coaching staff scrambled to figure out which benchwarmer they'd make a quarterback, when I leaped over the fence. Shoving my way through nut- and head-scratching football players, I came up behind Coach A and tapped on his shoulder.

He didn't turn around at first; he was caught up in intense decision making with the rest of his coaching staff. So I tapped him again.

"Coach A!" I yelled over the noise.

"What?" he said, spinning around. The look of irritation on his face melted as soon as he saw me. "Lucy?"

"Hey, Coach A," I greeted, feeling like I should give him a hug, except that would only start a new rumor about me being some sort of teacher seducer or some crazy-ass shit like that. Coach A had been my brother's football coach since the seventh grade—he'd been like unofficial family.

"Lucy?" he said again, staring at me like I couldn't possibly be here. "What are you doing here?"

"I'm a student," I said, feeling the scar I liked to keep sutured closed rip open again. "I transferred this year."

"That's great," he said, waving off one of his assistant coaches. "But I meant, what are you doing here?" He motioned to the football field I was toeing.

"Oh," I said, glancing at Sawyer, who had his foot elevated. He was watching me, smiling his Sawyer smile, and waved. I didn't reciprocate, injured player or not. "I've come bearing a solution to your lack-of-quarterback situation."

Coach A smiled in amusement. "Of course you have, Lucy. Still trying to save the world?"

"Always," I said, "and in case you haven't noticed, it's working. The world is still here."

He shook his head, still smiling. "So what's your solution to my quarterback problem?"

"You know Jude Ryder?" I motioned up into the stands, where Jude was back in our spot and searching the crowd for me.

"Everyone does," he replied, looking at me like I'd gone bonkers. "And he was one hell of a football player until he started getting into trouble and got himself kicked off the team freshman year. How does Jude Ryder solve my problems?"

I didn't even pause. "Let him play QB," I said. I ignored Coach A choking on his own breath. "He's stronger than your two best guys put together, he's got an arm the Mannings would envy, and he's as accurate as a sniper."

Coach A's expression didn't change.

"I've seen him, Coach. He's the real deal."

He stayed quiet for a while, appraising me. He knew from experience I wasn't a putz when it came to football. I'd been to at least twenty games a year since I was a toddler— that wasn't what he was struggling with. It was the Jude part he was all bent out of shape about.

"Give him a shot," I said, not above begging. "It's not like you can lose any more than we already are."

"I gave him a shot, Lucy," he said, growing impatient. "And he blew it. In fact, I gave him another shot this year. I added him to the team roster when he guaranteed he'd stay out of trouble and show up for practice. Let's just say he couldn't live up to either of those expectations."

I swallowed. "Give him a second chance. Everyone deserves one."

Coach A muttered something under his breath.

"I'm going to lose my license over this, but what the

hell?" he said, sliding his hat off. "If the opposing team's coach is all right with me adding a last-minute player to the game roster, and seeing as we're having our butts handed to us, I don't see why he wouldn't be, I'll put him on the field." Exhaling, he raised a brow. "So, where is Southpointe High's newest quarterback?"

I shot him a smile, which he mirrored. "Right . . . ," I began, turning to survey the stands. However, a broad chest was blocking my line of sight. "Here," I finished, that warm, melty feeling picking up right where it left off.

"I turn my back on you for two seconds and you disappear on me," Jude said, his brow furrowed. "How can I look after you if I don't know where you are?"

"Look after me? Jude, we're at a high school football game." This whole protective thing had just risen to a whole new level.

"Exactly. There are at least three dozen ways a girl like you could get hurt at one of these things. If you want to go somewhere else, next time just wait for me and I'll go with you." His face was lined with worry, which worried me. This kind of territorial was a bit much. I was all for protecting your woman and all that credo, but I wasn't for you can't go anywhere, do anything, or think your own thoughts without my approval.

"Jude"—I grabbed the side of his arm—"chill. I was just catching up with Coach A."

"Now probably isn't the time to be shooting the breeze with Coach Arcadia, Luce," Jude said, glancing down at Sawyer, who was still watching us. Jude smiled like the devil to see Sawyer propped up on the bench. "It looks like the man's got to take care of some problems."

"His problems are taken care of now," I said, crossing my blanketed arms one over the other.

Coach A glanced up from his clipboard, assessing Jude and likely second-guessing his decision. "Suit up, son," he ordered, nodding toward the locker rooms. "I think I can stall the refs a few more minutes, but not much longer than that. They want to go home and get dry just as badly as the rest of us."

"Hold up, Coach." Jude raised his hand. "Why are you telling me to go suit up? I'm not one of your ass-slapping players anymore."

Coach A smirked at me. "You are now."

Jude was quick. "Luce?"

One word and he might as well have asked a dozen questions. The man had mastered the art of inflection.

Arching a brow, I waved an imaginary pom-pom. "Go, Southpointe."

NINE

There was nothing but an inch and a half of free space on the first bleacher. It would work. There was no way I was missing out on Jude jogging out of that locker room.

If he did.

I wasn't sure just how pissed he was with me for my latest bout of solve-the-world's-problems-itis, but if I had to guess, I'd say it was somewhere between ragin' Cajun and a rabid badger.

Squeezing in between two guys with bare chests and "Go Spartans" painted in blood red across their stomachs, which was now bleeding into their jeans thanks to the continued rain, I sucked in everything that could be sucked and hoped I could hold my breath for two and a half more quarters.

"Lucy!" a voice shouted over at me. "Lucy!" And again.

Try as I might, I could not escape the suffocating fog that was Taylor Donovan. "Get down here!" She motioned at me, waving at a space where she and her apostles stood clapping, kicking, and rah-rah-rahing.

Being front and center in a cheerleader sandwich wasn't my first choice, but it was better than my current situation. Half-naked boy to my right threw his arms into the air, yelling, "Go, Spartans!" and it was immediately clear he didn't believe in, own, or use enough deodorant.

Paint me crimson and gold and call me Go, Fight, Win Wendy—I couldn't get to those cheerleaders fast enough.

"What were you doing up there sandwiched between Dumb and Dumber?" Taylor asked, weaving her arm through mine. "You do realize you probably just made their night, because I'm certain that was the first time either of them has gotten anywhere near copping a feel."

"Eww." I shuddered. "Taylor, please check the visuals at the door. I'm totally creeping out right now."

"Well, you're lucky I saved you," she said, motioning at two other cheerleaders: Lexie and Samantha. "Besides, a girl like you belongs down here. I saw your tumbling routine in gym, and you've obviously done this before."

Of course Taylor would be the one person to catch a glimpse of my improv dance routine on the mats while I was waiting for everyone else to suit up for gym class. "I cheered at my last school," I said. "But only because they didn't have a dance team."

"Well, we have a dance team here, but that's just where the girls who are too fat or ugly to cheer go." Not even a smidgen of remorse in her delivery. "You don't want to join the dance team. You belong with us."

A few of the other girls circled around us and nodded their heads.

"Since Holly didn't come back this year, we've got an extra uniform, and we just can't form a proper pyramid without a tenth teammate."

"Thanks for the offer, Taylor, but really, I'm more the dance team type of girl. Plus, I heard Southpointe's has won some state champion—"

She lifted her hand to cut me off. "You're cheerleader material. You're gorge, you have experience, and ninety percent of the male student body is already jacking off to you." Another visual I really could have done without. "The other ten percent is still undeclared in the sexuality department," she whispered.

"There's a potpourri of reasons to join if I've ever heard some," I muttered, wondering if I was better off sniffing rancid armpits and getting "accidentally" felt up all night.

And that's when Jude came jogging out onto the field. I forgot about Taylor, and armpits, and the whole damn world. There was nothing but him. And gold spandex forming over parts that flexed and stretched and pulled and made me forget how to blink.

"Who, in all God's gracious green earth," Taylor said, leaning over the fence, "is that?"

Just then, he looked over, meeting my eyes, and the smile that broke over his face couldn't be disguised by the helmet's face guard. Extending his arm, he pointed at me the entire time as he jogged to where the rest of Southpointe's football team huddled at the twenty yard line.

"That, Taylor," I said, weaving my fingers through the fence, "is Jude Ryder."

"I knew there was a God," she breathed.

"Yes," I agreed, smiling as he squirmed in his spandex, "there most certainly is."

"So are you guys . . ."

"Taylor," I warned, spinning on her. Even if I hated to admit it, Taylor wasn't so bad. I couldn't forget that, despite all her elitist ways, she'd been the first person to reach out the manicured hand of friendship. People who didn't have a soul weren't the first ones to say hey to the new girl.

"What?" she said, adjusting the crown on her head. "Something is definitely going on with you two, and the only thing I'm more certain about than that is it's not just a friend relationship."

"We're friends," I said, because I didn't have any other title for what we were. We'd kissed in ways that were illegal in forty-nine states, we spent every free moment at school together, he looked after me, I watched over him, but we were, as far as I knew, in no way exclusive. I didn't have a claim to him, although I wanted that. But did he want the same?

"Honey, a girl can't keep a man like that as a friend. He's a lover or an ex-lover, but never a friend. Men like that weren't created to be a woman's friend—they were created to make a woman hit high C three times in a row."

Another colorful visual by Taylor Donovan, although this one I didn't mind as much. "Sorry, Taylor. I don't know what to tell you. I care about him. He cares about me. If that doesn't make us friends in your book, go ahead and label us whatever you like."

Her eyebrows went sky-high.

"Except for that," I clarified.

The buzzer sounded and the two teams lined up, Jude in the QB spot appearing like a giant playing a game with a bunch of munchkins. Snatching a pom-pom from Taylor, I lifted it in the air and shook the hell out of it. "Go, Spartans!" I yelled. "Come on, Ryder! Let's see what you've got!"

It was a long way off, and he was crouched in position, but I would have bet my worn-in pointe shoes a smug smile appeared.

"Hut. Hut. Hike!" the center shouted, hiking the ball back to Jude. You could feel the collective breath every single Southpointe fan in the bleachers took.

Jude caught it easily, and instead of throwing it a respectable twenty-five yards to get us a first down, he cradled that football into his side and ran. In fact, he sprinted, sprinted like he was running from his demons.

It was a long shot, hoping to run the football into the end zone when we were eighty yards back, but the only person who didn't seem concerned with that was Jude. He ran like he couldn't not finish in the end zone. He ran like no one could stop him.

And no one could.

Player after player from Cascade High tried to block him or tackle him. A few even tried to trip him or take him down by grabbing his face mask. None of them were successful. The ones who missed Jude's stiff arm were just swatted off like they weren't varsity-grade high school football players.

At the fifty, the crowd busted into a roar. Everyone was hooting and hollering and swinging their arms in the direction of the end zone. Beyond every law of physics, Jude's pace picked up.

By the time he hit the twenty, there were no more Cascade High players to stop him. They all decorated the Astroturf like a box of fallen toothpicks. Jude danced the last few yards into the end zone, shaking and shimmying in those gold spandex pants, eliciting an uptick in the female cheering.

Once in the end zone, he spiked the ball and then spun to face the crowd. Everyone was going crazy, like they'd just witnessed the birth of Jesus and the invention of electricity at the same time. Jude was a rock star, their savior, and they were paying him homage.

Not taking a few moments to bask in the glory of the eighty-yard run and one thousand people chanting his name, he loped over to the sidelines. Past Coach A, who was still frozen in place, past his players on the sidelines holding up their hands, and then over the cyclone fence in one seamless move.

He didn't stop until he was sweating and smiling in front of me. "Hey," he breathed, sliding his helmet off his head. The rain coming in contact with his sweaty forehead was steaming up the air.

"Hey," I replied, pretending we weren't the center of everyone's attention.

"Did you like that little run out there?"

I smiled as he slid his beanie around until it was in just the right spot. It was like some damn security blanket. "It was all right," I understated, lifting a shoulder.

"All right, huh?" he said, moving closer. In fact, so close our bodies couldn't have been closer unless we were buck naked. "That was a pretty clever move there, Luce. Volunteering me for the jerk-off team to get back at me for getting you voted an official Southpointe princess," he said, flicking my crown.

"It was clever, wasn't it?"

"It was a good one, I'll give you that," he said, rubbing the back of his neck. "But the hell of it is, Luce, that I never, ever let someone else get the last word in."

"Please," I said, making a face. "What are you going to do? Have me suit up and be a backup kicker?"

"No," he said, lowering his hands to my hips. My throat ran dry. "I'm going to do something much better than that."

"Oh yeah?" I said, watching his eyes swirl silver. "What's that?"

Lifting me above him, he winked. "This," he said, lowering me so my lips landed right on his. And whether it was his or mine that started to move first didn't matter, because it was apparent neither were going to finish soon.

Rain. Jude. Me. Kissing.

Stick a fork in me, because I was done.

"Mr. Ryder," a dulled voice cut through the din of noise exploding around us. "Mr. Ryder!"

Jude groaned against my lips, not letting me go when he turned to Coach A.

"Think you're about done here?" Coach A asked,

smirking. "We've got a game to win."

"I don't think I'll ever be done here, Coach," he called back, earning a few laughs from the bleachers and making me flush down to my toes.

"In that case, wrap it up and get your ass back out here," he commanded. "Starting quarterbacks don't make out with their girlfriends when they've got forty points to go."

"This one does," Jude whispered, lifting me up onto my tiptoes and kissing me again. "Wait for me after the game. I've got some unfinished business with you." Setting me down, he pulled the blanket tight around me again before leaping over the fence and jogging back onto the field.

I don't know how he was able to bound and sprint like that, because I couldn't move. What the hell had just happened? Whatever it was, I wanted to rinse and repeat until I took my dying breath.

"What. The. Hell."

My sentiments exactly.

Taylor marched up to me, arms crossed, and stare pointed. "Friends, eh?"

"Friendship is a pivotal element of our relationship." I was still breathless, but at least my speech patterns hadn't changed.

"Yeah, but not the defining element. Obviously." For whatever reason, Taylor seemed pissed. I guess she was going to revoke my pom-pom privileges.

"Oh?" I was back to one-syllable responses.

"Jude Ryder just kissed you in front of a gazillion people, and he didn't dispute it when Coach Arcadia called you his girlfriend."

Now that the aftereffects of the kiss were wearing off, reality kicked in, no thanks to Taylor. Jude might as well have posted our make-out moment to the internet, and he'd barely flinched when Coach A used the G word.

"I'm his girlfriend?" It was meant to be a question to myself, but Taylor didn't let it go unanswered.

"You're the first," she said, inspecting me curiously. "You lucky bitch."

TEN

That was all I could think about the next night, as I needed all my focus on getting ready for Homecoming—being Jude's first girlfriend. It had been a title I'd been over the moon to wear, but after I'd carefully agonized over it Friday night, as any self-respecting teenage girl would, now I wasn't so sure how I felt about being Jude's first.

Girlfriend, that is.

A guy like him, with a reputation like his, had likely spanned dozens of women. So none of them were his girl-friends. Big deal. They'd been intimate with him in ways I had yet to fathom. Knowing I wouldn't be the first, or the tenth, or—hold in the shiver—the hundredth, kind of put a damper on the whole first-girlfriend thing.

I wasn't naive enough to hope a boyfriend of mine

wouldn't have a history. Hell, I had a history that wouldn't exactly qualify me as shiny and new, but Jude's tag-'em-and-bag-'em reputation was well known across three counties and one state line.

Now, I was all for second chances. I was the second-chance champion. It had nothing to do with that. My concern lay in passing every single woman who gave him a suggestive smile or a once-over and wondering if she was one of Jude's once-upon-a-time conquests. He was allowed to have made mistakes and have regrets, but could I live with those and the consequences of them?

Letting the last hot roller tumble out of my hair, I realized there was only one way to find out. The only way for me to know if I could handle everything that came with Jude, his past, his seeming inability to talk about anything personal, his take-it-as-it-comes future, was to take it one day at a time. The only way to know if Jude Ryder was going to ultimately break my heart was to open it to him.

That epiphany should have been more terrifying than it was. Hell or heartbreak, I was in it all the way. All in, as I liked to say, because that was the only way to ensure a relationship had a fighting chance.

Checking my phone, I sighed my relief. I still had fifteen minutes to finish my makeup, get into my dress, and collect my wits, as they'd need to be to get through a night of being pressed up against Jude.

That's when the doorbell rang.

I let myself have a second of panic before scrambling into my robe and running down the stairs. Dad and Mom were out on a rare date night, thanks to me. I'd purchased a gift certificate to their favorite French café on the lake and a couple of movie passes to the Cineplex twenty minutes away. I'd even made reservations to ensure they'd be out when Jude showed up.

It was deceitful, and I didn't want Jude to think I was ashamed of him, but my parents were complicated people with memories that didn't allow for second chances. Plus, they were parents to a teenage daughter. My dad had once told me, crimson-red deep in "the talk," that with sons, all he had to worry about was one penis, but with a daughter, he had to worry about everyone else's. That little gem had stuck with me, probably because when I was twelve years old, I couldn't hear the word "penis" without breaking into a laughing fit.

I knew if Jude and I continued on at this rate, I couldn't keep them a secret from one another, but for tonight, it was the easiest solution to the situation that was Jude.

Pulling the door open, I tried not to gawk, but it was the only thing that seemed appropriate with Jude Ryder standing under the light of my front porch, dressed in a tux, a corsage box in hand, his trusty beanie in place. If anyone could rock the formal-meets-grunge trend—if one ever cropped up—it would have been him.

"I'm early," he started, "so I know I should blame it on losing complete track of time, but really I just couldn't wait to get here."

Stop staring, Lucy. Stop staring, Lucy, was my mantra, but it wasn't working.

"Okay, so don't take this the wrong way, because I'm enjoying the view," he began, raising his eyes to the ceiling, "I'm really enjoying the view, but I promised myself I was going to be one of those schmucky gentlemen all night, and you're not making my promise easy to keep."

My head was foggy, and I was still incapable of speech.

"Ah, hell, Luce," Jude cursed, wincing when he glanced over at me. "You forgot to tie your damn bathrobe."

I looked down. Nothing but a strapless bra, a matching pair of panties, and a hell of a lot of skin were on full display. Honest mistake? Maybe. Freudian slip? Positively.

"Sorry," I said, spinning around to properly cover myself up.

I heard his footsteps as he came up behind me. He brushed my hair away from my neck, and his mouth fell just below my jaw. "I'm not," he whispered, sucking the tender skin.

One touch, one kiss, and I was a mess. Right then, I

wanted nothing else but to twist in his arms and kiss him until Homecoming had long been over.

It was intoxicating and overwhelming. Deep within, I knew it was marginally unhealthy. A girl should not feel like being totally possessed by a man, but I did. A girl with goals and aspirations should not be able to forget about them the instant a man's mouth came in contact with hers. This was the first time I'd felt this way—felt even close to this way—and as exciting as it was, it was just as terrifying. My brain recognized this was wrong on some level, but my heart was convinced nothing had ever been so right. When it came to me, a tie always went to the heart, or at least it always had. I really hoped Jude Ryder wouldn't be the reason that would change.

"Get your dress on so I can go show you off," he said, pressing one final kiss into my neck before stepping back.

"Why don't we skip the dance?" I suggested, playing with the belt of my robe.

"Dammit, Lucy," he groaned, using my full name for the first time in a long time. "It's taking every last ounce of willpower I have to keep from throwing you down on the table and doing everything to you I've played out in my mind a thousand times," he said, waving his hands from me to the table to the ceiling. "But you're better than that. You deserve better than that. You don't deserve to be one of those girls screwed on her parents' kitchen table." He challenged me with his eyes. "So leave that robe in place and don't tempt me again."

I felt embarrassed and rejected, but special and flattered at the same time. It was a very confusing mix of emotions. "Sorry," I said again, shooting him an awkward grin as I approached the stairs.

"Hey"—he grabbed my hand—"don't apologize. I want you in every way a man could want a woman. I just don't want to screw this thing up, okay?"

"Okay."

"I'm in uncharted territory here, Luce. I need a little help." His fingers curved through mine.

"Me, too," I replied.

"Yeah, I suppose you do." He squeezed my hand before letting it go. "I'll help you out then, too. Now go get that sexy-ass dress on so I can dance with you all night."

"Fine, bossy," I said, making my way up the stairs. "Make yourself comfortable. I'll be down in five."

"Oh, and Luce," he called out, snapping his fingers. I looked back at him from the top of the stairs. "When it comes to underwear selection"—his eyes were gleaming—"you get an A."

As if I needed another confirmation, men were impossible creatures. Cinching my robe tighter, I said, "And when it comes to underwear removal, you get a sucks ass."

"Ooh, Luce," he said, grabbing the banister, "now that was a good one. Hanging around me has vastly improved your comedic delivery. Learning through osmosis."

I plunked a hand on my hip. "How can someone who knows what osmosis is be flunking most of their classes?" Jude was no dummy, but his grades were pitiful.

"Unequivocal talent, baby," he answered, grinning like the devil, "unequivocal talent."

I'd just slid my last earring in when I heard the familiar sound of tires crunching over gravel.

"Luce," Jude's voice carried up the stairs, "you expecting company?"

Grabbing my vintage cardigan from the bed, I rushed out of my bedroom, now hearing the familiar sound of the garage door retracting.

"It's my parents," I said, hurrying down the stairs.

Jude looked worried. "And they don't know I'm the one taking you to Homecoming?"

Pausing at the end of the stairs, I shook my head.

"And because I'm so good at guessing, I'd say they don't even know we go to the same school, do they?" he asked, trying to play it off like it was nothing, but to me, it felt like the worst kind of betrayal.

I shook my head again, not able to meet his eyes.

"All right, what's my exit strategy?" he asked, studying the room. "Front door, back door, or window?" He wasn't smiling, he was serious. Something broke inside my heart. I'd just become one of those girls who wanted to make Jude their dirty little secret.

"No exit strategy," I said, taking his hand and walking across the living room. "I'd like to introduce my date to my parents."

"This ought to be good."

"Yeah," I said sarcastically, "it'll be a blast."

"Any advice?" he said, shouldering up beside me in the kitchen doorway.

"Yeah," I said, watching the door from the garage open. "Buckle up."

"Who the hell's car is in the—" Mom came to an abrupt halt in the doorway. So abrupt that Dad bounced off her.

"Dad, Mom." I cleared my throat, putting on a face that said everything was normal. "You're home early."

"Your dad wasn't feeling well," she said in a clipped tone, leveling me with a glare.

I cleared my throat. "You remember Jude."

Stepping into the kitchen, she gave Jude that look. The same one she'd given him the first day she'd met him. The one that said, *Go back to whatever hole you came out of.* "One

141

has a tough time forgetting the face of a felon led off your property in handcuffs."

That flash of temper was begging to be taken off its chain.

"What are you doing here?"

Jude stepped forward. "Taking Luce to Homecoming, ma'am."

"No," she said, "you most certainly are not. Where *are* your friends, by the way?" she went on, peering over his shoulder like she expected to find them lounging in the living room. "Are they in the backseat, waiting to brutalize my daughter one more time? Or are they waiting in the school parking lot, ready to try ripping her hair out of her head again?"

Jude winced, looking down.

"Mom," I warned, "those guys were not Jude's friends. And cut out the parenting act. It's too little too late."

"Don't you dare talk to me that way, Lucille!" Mom shouted, pointing at me. "You are grounded until the day you move out of this house for lying to your father and me." She could really wield her index finger as a weapon. "And yes, those were"—she scowled at him—"are his friends. You chose not to read the police reports I've seen. Those boys and Jude committed their first crime together years ago. Drug dealing, wasn't it?" she said, not as a question to be confirmed or denied. "Jude and his friends all need to be locked up and have the key thrown away. They don't deserve to take good, hardworking girls with futures to Homecoming dances."

I lurched forward, something mean and loud on the tip of my tongue, when Jude pulled me back.

"I never said I did deserve that," Jude said, meeting my mom's eyes.

I could tell, from the blood vessels bursting in her eyes, that it was seriously pissing her off that Jude wasn't caving.

"And those guys never were and never will be my friends. If they ever find their way out of prison and I run across them, I will repay them every hurt they took out on Luce."

"How refreshing. The felon suggesting we repay violence with violence."

"Sometimes that's the only answer," Jude said, his fingers flexing in my hand.

Mom's face shadowed. "And sometimes that gets the people you love most killed."

Dad shifted behind Mom. I hadn't even noticed he was here. Shuffling around her, Dad tapped my shoulder in passing. "Good night, all."

It should have gotten old, mourning the person my dad once was and, at times, hating the shell of a human being he'd become, but it hadn't. He'd checked out of every facet of life, letting craziness and compulsion rule his few cognizant moments. You'd think I'd be used to it by now.

Mom steepled her hands over her face. "Lucy, time to say good night."

I grabbed Jude's arm, steering him toward the front door. I couldn't get out of this crazy house fast enough. "Good night, Mom."

"Lucille Roslyn Larson!" she shouted after us. "Get the hell upstairs right now. And you, Mr. Ryder, get the hell off my property before I call the cops." Her voice was less angry and more desperate now.

"No, Mom!" I shouted, letting my temper loose. "I'm going to Homecoming and I'm going with Jude, because I'm with him and he's with me and if you can't handle that, then say good-bye to the only child you have left!"

I'd stabbed her in the soft spot, and it registered immediately on her face. "That boy almost got you killed, Lucy," she said, her voice a whisper.

I was still every phase of pissed, so my voice was nowhere near a whisper. "This man also saved my life!" Throwing the door open, I practically lunged down the front steps with Jude's hand in mine.

"Lucy," she begged from the living room.

"I'll be home by one," I said over my shoulder, the anger

dimming to a dull roar now that I was certain I'd won the battle. But I was sure I hadn't won the war. There'd be hell to pay tomorrow morning, so I'd make sure tonight really counted. "Everything will be fine," I emphasized before rounding the corner to the driveway.

"When you say buckle up," Jude said, pulling a set of keys from his pocket, "you mean suit up for the damn apocalypse."

"Pretty much," I said, wrinkling my nose. "Sorry about that back there."

Jude waved it off, but he couldn't hide from me how much my mom's words had cut him. Just liked she'd hoped they would.

"No, those were awful, awful things to say to another human being," I said. "My parents, they're complicated people," I understated, not sure when or if I could ever explain the mess that was the Larson family.

"Luce," Jude said, stopping me, "I get what a piece of shit I am, and it's not awful or unfair or incorrect for people to call me out on what I am. But I'd like to think a person can change, and I swear to you I'm going to try to leave my piece-of-shitedness behind." His eyes were so earnest, I thought he was about to get down on one knee.

"Shitedness?" I repeated, nudging him. "That must be one I missed in Webster's."

"Nope," he said, "that's one plucked right out of Jude Ryder's urban dictionary."

"Nice," I laughed, tiptoeing across the gravel so that the stones wouldn't trip up my three-inch heels. "And in Lucy Larson's book of shitedness, you're nowhere on that list."

"That may be the most romantic thing anyone's ever said to me," he said, sliding his hand down my side. "Something about a hot woman in a damn fine dress lying through her teeth about me not being a piece of shit is a real turn-on."

"Glad I'm so . . ." And then I noticed the car parked in the driveway, and I stopped in my tracks. "What is that?"

I didn't speak boy, but I knew that gleaming silver coupe was fast, expensive, and would attract all cops within a mile radius.

"It's a car," Jude said, opening the door for me.

"Don't treat me like one of your one-night-stand girls."

"My God, woman," he said, leaning over the car door, "what does a man have to do to get a free pass from you?"

"I don't believe in free passes," I threw back. "I believe in honesty. I'm all old-fashioned that way."

"It's a '66 Chevelle," he said, shutting the door before I could ask any more questions.

"Is it yours?" I asked as he crawled into the driver's seat.

"Nope." He turned the key over, and the engine fired to life. "It belongs to a buddy of mine."

"A buddy at the boys' home?" I knew this line of questioning was making him tense, as his jaw could attest to, but I couldn't understand why.

"Does it seem like any of us have any family who gives a damn, jobs that pay a damn, or an inheritance worth a damn that would allow us to afford a ride like this?" Stretching his arm across my seat, he looked over his shoulder and backed out of the driveway.

Mom was staring at us through the living room window, for the first time ever seeming as lost as my dad was. Something heavy dropped in my stomach, something that felt a lot like guilt.

"Defensive," I mumbled, staring out the side window.

"Your parents pretty much called me gum on the bottom of their shoe. You failed to mention, or more likely chose not to mention, to them that I was your date tonight." Once we were on Sunrise Drive, he gunned the Chevelle. "I am the bad boy preying on the good girl. So yeah, I'm a tad defensive right now."

Not even a half hour into our first real date and we were already arguing. We were setting a wonderful precedent for whatever road our relationship was headed down.

Fighting back that knee-jerk reaction to volley right back, I took in a slow breath, then swiveled in my seat. "Listen, I'm sorry I didn't tell my parents about you. Really," I added when he made a face. "I didn't tell them not because of who you are, but because of who they are."

"Who they are?" he repeated. He didn't sound like he was buying it, but that was the truth.

"Yes."

"And just who exactly are they, Luce?" he asked, rolling to a stop at a red light.

"Sad, scared people who have lost a lot in life and are scared of losing more," I said, fiddling with the handles of my purse.

Hanging his hand over the steering wheel, he looked over at me. "And what happened in their white-picket-fence life to make them so sad and scared?" He was mocking us, mocking them, but he just didn't understand, and I was never in the mood to make someone understand what I didn't understand myself.

"Life," was the only explanation I had for him.

He huffed. "What a forthcoming, all-encompassing answer."

I was really having to work hard to keep my temper meter cool. "I learned it from watching you," I said, cursing the tears that were forming. I'd turned into a blubbering mess after meeting this guy.

The light flashed green, but Jude kept staring at me. Lifting his thumb to the corner of my eye, he let the tear run down his hand. "Shit. I'm such a jerk," he said as a car blasted its horn behind us. Raising his hand in the back window, Jude flipped off the car. "I'm sorry, Luce. I wanted tonight to be so great, and I can't seem to do or say anything right. I'm not mad at you, not even close. I'm mad at myself. I get why your parents don't like me, and I get why you didn't tell them about me. I get all of that," he said, hitting the dashboard. "I get that's the reality. I just wish reality would take a vacation, you know?"

Another horn blast, this one not nearly as polite. Punching the dashboard again, Jude rolled down his window. Sticking his arm out, he flipped the driver the bird again. "Blast your horn one more time and you'd better be ready to throw down, douche bag!" He was screaming, and oncoming traffic was stopping to see what the hell was going on. I scrunched down in my seat, wondering for the umpteenth time what exactly had happened in Jude's life to make him this way. So angry, so closed off.

Jude waited a few seconds, giving the driver the staredown, his muscles flexing in anticipation. Finally, he shouted, "Yeah! That's what I thought!" A handful of passengers were now sticking their heads out of windows, watching the two of us like we were menaces to society. I slid down farther in my seat.

He pulled his head back inside, rolled up the window,

and, looking both ways first, ran the once again red light.

Taking a breath, he glanced over at me, his face smooth. As if he hadn't just gone all Hulk at a stoplight. "You can ask me anything you want, Luce. I can't promise I'll answer every question to your liking, but you can always ask."

My first thought was that he must be on some serious meds and forgot to take his daily dose, but then I recognized this little pretending-nothing-had-happened routine. I was so familiar with this coping mechanism I could have written the psych book.

"What the hell was that?"

He drove into the high school parking lot and took the very last spot in the back corner. Staring through the window, he sighed. "That was me losing my shit. It happens a lot, Luce. I don't mean it to, and I don't even want it to, but ninety percent of the time, I can't control it."

There it was, that window of vulnerability, that so-honest-it-was-painful answer that reminded me why I was here, now, with Jude Ryder.

"I want to be a better man, but I don't know if I can be," he continued. "You need to know this if we're going to give this thing a go, because—"

And then I did something, depending on your views of the world, that was either very reckless and wrong or very situationally appropriate.

In one seamless move, thanks to my decade and a half of dancer's grace, I found myself straddling him, and before I could think twice about my actions, I pressed my mouth against his.

"Luce," Jude managed to murmur around my unyielding mouth.

"Shut up, Ryder," I answered, biting his bottom lip.

Giving up to the overbearing force that was me, his hands slid down my waist, settling on my backside. "Shutting up."

ELEVEN

"My God, woman." His breath was so labored it didn't really sound like him anymore. "Mercy."

"I don't believe in mercy," I replied, trailing my lips down his neck.

"Okay, I'm not going to screw you in the front seat of a car, and if you keep doing that . . . ," he said, trying to arch away from my lips. It was a failed attempt. "I'm going to be fresh out of willpower, so time for a change of scenery."

The door flew open, bringing a gust of cool air and the din of cliché high school dance music with it. I groaned.

He chuckled as he maneuvered me off his lap and outside the steamy car. "And I thought we men were horny bastards."

Adjusting my sweater, I ran my fingers through my hair. "So did I," I replied.

"Your corsage," he said, the whole half-hour make-out session filed to the back of his mind just like that. I was still breathing like a dog in heat.

Retrieving the plastic box from the backseat, he stepped out of the car. "Since your dress is black, I had the lady put some black-and-silver ribbon between the roses," he said, sliding the corsage on my wrist like it was one of the proudest moments of his life. "Do you like it?"

"Now that," I said, smiling down at it. He must have spent a fortune. Red roses streamed halfway up my forearm. "Is a corsage. Very nice, Mr. Ryder."

He beamed. "Why, thank you, Miss Larson." Holding his elbow out, he motioned at the gymnasium. "Shall we?"

I sighed. "Since you leave me no choice."

Covering my hand with his, he kissed the top of my head. "Not that I care or am complaining, but what was that back there?" I could hear the silly smile in his voice.

"Since when do guys need an explanation for getting to second base with a girl?"

"Since that girl was you," he said, his gaze holding me like I was something he'd lose if he looked away. I'd never been looked at that way. My whole life I'd waited for it, and here it was now, at age seventeen, in the high school parking lot of my new school, with a boy named Jude Ryder.

This, right here, was some powerful stuff.

Shoving the gym door open, he ushered me in. Some hip-hop song that was created and played only to give guys an excuse to hump a girl like a damn dog was blasting, and the entire gym appeared like it had been hosed down in Pepto-Bismol. The entire rainbow of pink was present: fuchsia in the balloons, tulip in the crepe paper, pastel in the cardboard heart cutouts, magenta in the spiral streamers twirling down from the ceiling.

This pink-drenched terrain was a clip stolen from my worst nightmare.

"Oh. My.—"

"Pink," Jude inserted, grimacing as he took in the gym.

Across the room, draped over some guy like a piece of Velcro, Taylor waved her arms at me. I almost shuddered again as I took in her fluorescent pink, heavily sequined, cocktail-length dress. Someone call the groupies from the Eighties Club, because this bitch just ripped off one of their dresses. My floor-length gown with a corseted bodice was tame in comparison to every other dress out there.

"Okay, hurry and dance with me before I make a run for it," I said, pulling on his jacket.

"Gladly," he replied, handing our tickets off.

Walking me onto the dance floor, he looked down at his feet and then up at me. "Okay, here's another little tidbit about me, since you say I'm not the forthcoming sort."

I raised my brows and waited.

"I'm not much of a dancer," he said, scratching the back of his neck.

"Like you can't dance or you won't dance?" I was familiar with both types.

"More like I've never danced."

"Seriously?" I asked.

"Seriously."

It was the first time I'd seen him unsure of himself. "Lucky for you, you brought a girl who danced before she walked."

He wrapped his arms around me and pulled me close. "Lucky me."

"Okay, I'm going to make this simple," I said, sliding my hands over his shoulders. "Just follow my lead and you'll be fine." Then, like the dance pro I was, I popped up on my tiptoes until I was at lip level.

"Maybe I've got this dancing thing down after all," he said, cinching me tighter against him.

"I'll be the judge of that," I whispered, pressing my lips into his, and just like that, we were the only people on the dance floor. The only people in the universe. Jude was the sickness I didn't want to be cured of. He was the intoxicant I never wanted to be clear of.

His hands cradled my face, and he kissed me harder. I

wanted to bottle that kiss and take a hit of it every hour of every day.

"Luce?" he said, running his thumb down my cheek.

"Yeah?" I said, burying my head under his chin.

"Your stilettos are piercing the hell out of my feet."

Peeking down, I saw that my feet were, in fact, covering his. Stepping back, I put my stilettos back on solid ground. "Whoops."

He just laughed. "Some dancer you are."

"Sorry I don't have much experience trying to teach someone how to dance at the same time he's kissing the wits out of me."

"Kissing the wits out of you, huh?" he said, tucking my hair behind my ear.

"Like you're not absolutely gloating."

The bump-and-grind song ended, and another started. Jude and I shuddered at the same time. "This music blows," he said, grabbing my hand. "And you look like you need some punch."

"I don't know about punch, but I need something," I said, bouncing my eyebrows.

"You"—he pulled me closer, speaking into my ear—"are making it exceedingly difficult for me to be on my best behavior."

Staring ahead, I tried to pretend his every touch wasn't

unraveling me. "Not my problem."

Winding his arm around me, he pulled me close. "It's about to be."

"Jude Ryder," words that were more slurred than spoken said from behind us. "If it wasn't so freakin' hot right here, I would have thought hell had frozen over. Jude I-don't-do-commitments-phone-calls-or-breakfast Ryder at a high school dance."

Spinning around, Jude kept me close to him. "Allie," he said, sounding like he'd just issued the anti-greeting.

"Oh, and by the way, it wasn't that great for me. And since I know you've been worrying nonstop about it," she said, propping a hand on her hip, "I found a ride home."

She so classically fit the mold for what guys seek out for a one-night stand, I almost felt bad for her. "Almost" ended when she curled her fingers around the lapel of Jude's jacket. My proverbial claws came out.

"What do you want, Allie?" He was losing patience, and I was all too familiar with how quickly the tracks ran out once he started down that road.

"There's a loaded question if I've ever heard one," she said, flipping her red-and-blond-streaked hair over her shoulder.

"Okay, I've been on this roller coaster of crazy before, and I'm getting off right now," he said, steering me away.

"Come on, I'm teasing," she laughed, grabbing his arm. "I just wanted to meet your new friend." She smiled at me all innocent-like, but I knew her game, and I wasn't going to be her pawn.

"This is Luce," he said, tipping my chin up with his finger and pressing the sweetest kiss I'd ever been given onto my lips.

"She'd have to be if you're with her."

That sweet kiss was all but eviscerated.

Jude's eyes flamed as he turned on her. "If you weren't a woman, sorry excuse for one as you are, I would teach you some respect, Allie." His voice was wavering with anger, he was so close to spilling over.

"Jude, stop," I ordered, stepping in front of him and pushing him back. "She doesn't know what she's saying—she's drunk."

"Watch who you're calling drunk, bitch," Allie sneered.

I wanted to turn around and slap her makeup-y little face so bad my hand was tingling, but for once in my lifetime, I wasn't the hotheaded one. I was trying to hold him back as he lunged forward again.

"No, she's not drunk," Jude said, pacing in place. "For once. How's that whole sobriety thing working for you, Al?"

She huffed. "Like you care. It didn't matter to you if I

was drunk or high or sober. Just so long as I was horizontal and accommodating."

Now this girl was getting to me. It had been bad enough for her to insinuate I was a loose girl, but now knowing she'd been intimate with Jude in a way I hadn't made me want to hit something hard. The closest thing, save for Jude, was her bony, sneering little face.

Taking a breath, I looked away from her and up at Jude. "Come on, let's just get out of here. She isn't worth it."

"And you won't be either come morning, sugar."

I shook my head at him, but he didn't take my not-so-subtle warning. Twisting around, he gave Allie a cockeyed grin. "There are two types of girls in the world, Al," he said, speaking so loudly this half of the gym could hear him. "The kind you screw and the kind you marry. That's just the way the world was made, so don't take it out on Luce that you're one kind and she's the other." Allie's face was flushing the color of her short streetwalker dress, and not the embarrassed kind of red, the livid, I-would-kill-you-right-now-if-it-wasn't-illegal kind of red. "Run along now and find yourself some other guy to screw so you can haunt him at every corner instead of me."

"Jude," I whispered. That slanted smile was still on his face, but his eyes were black. I hadn't known he was capable of delivering such cruel words, and if Allie hadn't spewed the mouthful of crap she had, I might have felt bad for her. "Come on," I said, pulling him away from one pissed-off ex-lover and a few dozen onlookers. "Let's go somewhere quiet."

I didn't let go of his wrist until we were out the gym door and halfway down a dark hallway, not trusting that he wouldn't head back to go another fifty rounds with Allie. When we were far enough away that we could hear ourselves talk over the music, I stopped. I couldn't get my first word out before he did.

"Luce, I know I said some things back there I probably shouldn't have, and I didn't treat a woman the way a man should, but I can't and I won't tolerate someone, male or female, talking about my girl like that." He stared down at me, his eyes asking for forgiveness as much as they weren't.

I only heard two words. "Your girl?" I repeated, because I needed confirmation.

Grabbing my face, he rested his forehead against mine. "My girl."

"And the expiration date on that title would be?" I asked, because I had to. He was Jude Ryder. Milk left out on the counter didn't expire as quickly as Jude's girls did.

"How about we take it one day at a time?" he replied, that warm breath fogging my mind again.

I wanted to kiss him so badly I had to fight every primal

instinct to keep myself from following through. I needed answers. "I thought a girl like me, the marrying kind," I began, raising a brow, "was entitled to more than just one day at a time."

"You are," he said, letting my face go and leaning against the opposite wall. "But I'm not."

Processing logical thoughts was easier with him four feet away. "Is that one of your go-to lines when a girl asks for something more than twenty-four hours of Jude?"

Tapping the back of the wall with his heel, he looked down the hall. "No, that's what I answer when a girl I'm falling hard for, the only girl I've fallen hard for, wants to be in a relationship with someone like me."

And we were back at the starting line. The whole Jude-doesn't-deserve-anything-but-pile-after-pile-of-shit thing was wearing on my last nerve. "You know, Jude, you're half as tough as you think you are," I said, "and twice as nice as you hope you aren't. So don't try to sell me the whole I'm-a-cancer thing again, because I'm not buying it."

His eyes were shining. "You're not, huh?"

"Nope. I've got you all figured out, Jude Ryder, and I expect someone like you to give someone like me more than just one day at a time."

"So what then? You want me to make some lame-ass comment that we'll be together forever? We'll take our dying breaths together beside each other in bed?" he said, his voice soft.

"I'm a realist," I said. "Lying and making promises about forever are almost as bad as one day at a time."

"So what, my sweet, beautiful, complicated Luce, do you want from me?"

I was staring at it, but I wasn't sure if I could have it. I wasn't sure if a person like Jude could ever be claimed. "That's for me to know and you to find out."

"Oh, Luce," he said, grimacing, "just when I thought you were getting better, you deliver a line like that."

"Ryder," I warned, "nice try attempting to divert this train, but I'm at the wheel, and this one's staying right on the tracks until you answer my question."

He hit the back of his head against the wall a few times. "Okay, so something between one day at a time and forever," he said, searching the ceiling for an answer that would appease me. "But you want an honest answer too, right?"

"Only you would have to qualify that," I groaned.

He nodded once. "How about," he said, rendering me witless with the look in his eyes, "I'll be here, each day and every day, as long as you want me to be?"

I finally got that whole "be still, my beating heart" line. "And that's the honest answer?"

Jude crossed his fingers over his chest. "Honestly."

"That's a damn fine answer, Ryder," I said, walking up

to him. It was a moment of intimacy and vulnerability, and passion was certainly there too, but all I wanted was to be in his arms. Mouths joined, hands exploring. Nothing else could have made the moment more consuming than it already was.

Tucking me close to him, his arms held me like they were incapable of letting go. "This is a damn fine response too, Luce."

I laughed into his shirt, wondering how a boy with his reputation could smell like soap and sunshine and could say the sweetest things I'd heard. That's when, as was becoming a pattern at Southpointe High, I had a revelation.

Our reputations weren't who we really were, they were what people told us we were. Some of us fell into that trap, while others fought their entire lives to break free of them. Jude was no more the bad boy with a dead-end future than I was the skanky slut everyone said I was. The difference between our assigned reputations was that Jude accepted his like it was penance for some wrongdoing.

"So you think you've got me all figured out?" he asked after a few minutes of silence.

"Pretty much."

Jude's head nodded above mine. "Okay. So when's my birthday?"

No idea.

"What's my middle name?" he asked. "What was the

name of my first pet? What's my GPA? How many stitches have I had? What size shoe do I wear?" he continued on, throwing out an unending stream of questions, none of which I knew and all of which had impersonal, one-word answers.

"So maybe we need to have a day of Q and A or something to get all the detail stuff out of the way," I answered, wondering how I could know so little of him, yet still feel like I'd never known anyone better. "But I know enough to know nothing you could tell me about yourself could change that."

"You don't know how much I wish that were true," he said against my head, running his fingers up and down the length of my back.

As I was debating whether to respond or just let that one hang in the air, a few couples came racing down the hall.

"Ryder, man," the guy in front called out, wagging his brows at the two of us pressed against the wall. "I thought the locker room was more your domain."

"Keep running, shithead," Jude growled, slapping the air behind his head. "Morrison," he said, grabbing the second guy running by. "What's going on? Your date's chasing you with a wedding ring or something?"

"A shitload of cops just showed up. They're searching the gym, and we've got something of a paraphernalia problem on us," he said, tapping his jacket pocket. "Might want to take the back way out if you have the same problem."

Jude's arms tensed around me. "Shit," he cursed under his breath. Shoving off the wall, he snagged my hand and began running. "Come on, Luce. We've got to get out of here."

My stomach dropped. No innocent man ran from the cops the way he was now. I couldn't believe it was drugs, because I'd witnessed enough stoners in the courtyard between classes at my last school to recognize the symptoms and Jude didn't have any of them, but I didn't have the courage to believe he was running because of something worse. I just let him pull me along, because running from the cops with him was better than being left behind.

Jude rounded down another hall, right as the doors burst open with a stream of flashlights and shouts.

"Damn it," Jude hissed, pulling me faster. I deserved some sort of medal or award for attaining the speeds I was in the height of heels I was wearing.

"Mind telling me what's going on?" I snapped as he shoved open a metal door. We were outside, close to the parking lot.

Jude's face was tortured. I'd never seen him so undone. "I have to go, Luce. And I can't take you with me."

I had tons to say, but the best I could come up with was, "They're here for you."

He nodded. "And if you're with me, they'll take you in, too."

I bit my lip, realizing I was about to be ditched on the sidewalk. "All right."

"Damn it, Luce, I'm sorry. I did something really, really stupid," he said, grabbing my arms.

I made a vow to myself I wouldn't cry. I forced myself to look up at him. "You'd better go then."

"Luce," he said, begging me for something I wasn't ready to give.

"Just go, Jude," I whispered.

He leaned in, wanting to kiss or embrace me, but I was not ready to be consoled.

"No," I said, stepping back. "Go."

His face broke, his eyes shadowing almost instantly. Backing away, he kept his eyes on me for another moment before turning and running like the devil had just arrived at Southpointe High.

TWELVE

*J*ude and the Chevelle had about a ten-second head start before a screaming line of police cars peeled out of the parking lot after him. I just stood there, frozen like a lawn gnome, watching the whole thing like it wasn't reality.

The man I thought I was falling for skidded out of the parking lot, hitting speed bumps so hard the Chevelle caught air, while a squad of police cars were hot on his tail—couldn't be real. I caught the shortest glimpse of him, and his face was eerily calm. The only way a person could be so calm was because situations like this were second nature to him.

A slew of officers burst through the door we'd just come out and ran right past me, having no clue I had just been with Jude.

"Suspect in stolen vehicle is heading north on Hemlock Avenue," the voice on the other end of the walkie said as the last officer rushed past me.

Theft. Car theft.

This was the straw that broke my back. I crumpled to the ground, wrapping my arms around my legs, and closed my eyes, praying not to wake up.

"So you didn't even make it through the night," a voice tsk-tsked as a flash of metallic red fabric came into view. "Let me guess," Allie said, smirking down on me, "in the janitor's closet?"

I so didn't need this shit right now.

"No? So the girls' locker room, right? That's a Jude favorite."

I was a tough girl, but tonight went beyond tough. I didn't have what it took to get past this mountain of crap.

"Okay, so the couch in the principal's office."

"Get the hell out of here," I said, into my folded arms.

"How does it feel? Being left on the curb like the piece of trash you are," she said, kneeling beside me. "At least when he was done screwing me, I got a few minutes of cuddling and a warm bed."

"Allie!" a voice shouted from behind. "The party at Morrison's is just getting started. You don't want to be late."

"Well, if it isn't Sawyer Diamond riding in on his white

horse." Allie laughed. Sawyer stepped around me, his jacket slung over one shoulder. "You hoping to score with Jude's sloppy seconds? Because I'd bet she's ripe for a rebound roll in the sack right about now."

"Damn it, Allie," Sawyer said, grabbing her elbow and steering her away, limping on his bad ankle. "You're a lot easier to be around when you're trashed, so be on your merry shot-slamming way."

"You're no fun," she said, trying to pull her elbow out of his grasp.

"Conner!" Sawyer yelled at a guy climbing into a truck whose bed was spilling over with students. "Got room for one more?"

"Does it look like I do, Diamond?" Conner shouted back, revving his engine. "There's only lap-sitting room."

"Perfect," he replied, handing Allie off to another guy in the bed of the truck. Neither one seemed to mind the lap arrangement.

"See you at Morrison's?" Conner called as he headed out of the parking lot.

"Maybe later," Sawyer said, tapping the truck bed as they passed by.

He came up to me and crouched beside me, placing his jacket over my hunched shoulders. "Lucy? Are you all right?"

Deciding between Sawyer or Allie was like choosing the lesser of two evils. "I'm fantastic," I answered, my head still curled into my knees. "Could you just give me some space, Sawyer?"

"No," he said, scooting next to me. "That's not going to happen."

"Okay, I asked nicely once, but I won't a second time," I said, heat trickling into my bloodstream. "Go. Away."

"Maybe you didn't hear me the first time. No."

Everything else had gone all to hell tonight, so why wouldn't I expect Sawyer to go with the hellish flow?

"If you're hoping for sloppy seconds, you can stop hoping now," I began. "If you're offering to be a shoulder to cry on, I don't cry. If you're here to tell me 'I told you so' or convince me of what a loser Jude is, save your breath. If—"

"Actually," Sawyer interrupted, "I just wanted to make sure you made it home safe."

Dead. Silence.

"Sawyer, I'm sorry," I said, feeling like a terrible human being. "I'm pissy and taking it out on you because you're the only one here to take it out on."

"I have three older sisters," he said, nudging me. "I'm used to pissy."

Tilting my head, I looked over at him. He was staring at me like we were good friends. I needed a good friend.

"Your date won't mind if you drive me home?" I asked, checking for some solo female floating off in the distance.

"I went stag," he said, popping his shoulders.

"Oh," I said. I didn't know much about Sawyer Diamond other than that he wasn't the kind of guy who went stag to dances out of necessity. "You did?"

"I was really hoping to take this one girl," he said, gazing over at me, "but she ended up going with some other guy."

I exhaled, staring into the parking lot. "Some other guy who ditched her because the cops were after him?"

"Something like that," he said, standing up. "Come on, let me drive you home so you can put an end to this night." He extended his hand for me to take, and it felt natural to accept it. Like I wasn't fighting every force of nature in this universe and the next to keep ahold of it.

Standing up, I dusted myself off and smoothed the wrinkles out of my dress. "I'm so relieved you came along and took care of the Allie situation, I could kiss you right now," I said, before realizing what I'd said and who I'd said it to.

Of course he couldn't just laugh it off or pretend he hadn't heard it altogether. "And I would happily go for it."

I tried laughing that response off, but the delivery was all wrong. It sounded more like the hysterics of the perpetually awkward.

Another few seconds of cringe-worthy laughter and

Sawyer tilted his head. "I'm just over here," he said, grabbing my hand and walking me across the parking lot.

His hand was warm and strong, but a little soft for a guy. Looking down at our entwined hands, mine appeared to fit perfectly in his, but it felt wrong.

Sliding up to a sleek white car, he opened the passenger door. I lifted my brows.

"I'm old-fashioned," he explained. "Don't tell."

"Plus, you had three older sisters," I said, getting into the seat.

"Exactly," he said before shutting the door.

"Where am I heading?" he asked as he climbed into the driver's seat and turned the key over.

"I live across the lake in Sunrise Shores," I said, trying not to think about what I'd been doing an hour ago in this same parking lot. I tried to swallow the lump choking up my throat as Sawyer peeled out of the parking lot, leaving behind a few good and a slew of bad memories.

"I'll take one hot fudge sundae with extra fudge and two cherries on top." Sawyer looked across the seat at me, jacking his eyebrows.

"That will be six fifty-eight at the first window," the speaker crackled back.

"Really, I'm not hungry," I said as Sawyer pulled

forward. I couldn't imagine eating right now.

"You don't have to be hungry to enjoy the healing qualities of a mound of ice cream and a river of fudge," he said, pulling out his wallet. He handed the cashier a hundred-dollar bill, and she glared at him like there was no greater offense in the land of fast food.

"And here I'd been under the mistaken belief that ice cream made you fat," I said, trying to pretend that Sawyer's attempt to cheer me up was working. Nothing, not even a VIP pass to Disneyland, could leap over that hurdle.

"Nonsense," he said, handing over a bucket-sized sundae. "Ice cream makes any situation at least fifty percent better." The cashier handed him a spoon, which he jabbed into the mound of whipped cream, waiting for me. Cars were lined up behind us, but he obviously wasn't moving until I took a bite.

I rolled my eyes and dug in. It was just a spoonful of whipped cream, with a smudge of fudge, but Sawyer was right. I felt better, not jump-out-of-your-seat-and-raise-your-hands-to-the-heavens better, but enough so it counted.

"Better?" he asked.

I nodded slowly. "Better."

"Well, my mission is done here." With that, Sawyer punched the car into gear and pulled out of the drive-in like we were cruising down Rodeo Drive.

I dug into the ice cream, glancing over at Sawyer. He noticed.

"What's on your mind, Larson?" he asked, trying to sound like he was talking to one of his buddies, but he wasn't looking at me like I was one of his buddies.

"You don't want to know," I answered around a mouthful of ice cream.

"Sure I do."

I took another bite so I could come up with something tactful to say. Yep, nothing was coming to mind.

"What I meant by 'you don't want to know' is that I don't want to tell you." Why did I have to be so bluntly honest?

"Oh," he said, heading down Sunrise Drive. "Moving on, then."

He was silent for another mile or so. Any other high school student would have pressed for every last detail of tonight's drama fest. Another point for Sawyer. He'd scored a lot of them tonight, and I started to realize I'd been quick to judge him, like everyone else had judged me. He wasn't the cliché jock-slash-prep. I mean, he did play sports and wear a lot of name-brand polos, but he was also thoughtful and kind and helped a girl out when no one else would.

Sawyer Diamond was in danger of being labeled a good guy in my book.

We pulled into my driveway another minute later, and

I was surprised to find I'd finished almost half the tub of ice cream. I'd be dancing my ass off tomorrow morning. Literally.

"Thanks for the ride, Sawyer," I said, swiveling in my seat. "I'm sure there are about a thousand other things you'd rather be doing on Homecoming night, but it means a lot to me."

"Right now," he said, unbuckling his seat belt and leaning toward me, "there's nowhere else I'd rather be."

I forced myself not to roll my eyes at that line. One point forward, one point back for Mr. Diamond.

"Good night," I said, reaching for the handle.

"Hold up, Lucy." Sawyer's hand grabbed mine. "I've been going back and forth the whole drive here on whether to say anything to you, but I wouldn't be a very good friend if I didn't." He took the melting vat of sundae from me and set it on the backseat floor. "I know you like Jude, and maybe that's in the past tense after tonight."

That pit in my stomach returned, ice cream be damned.

"Sawyer," I began, wanting to stop him because I wasn't sure I wanted to know everything that was Jude, because then I might not have any excuses to stay with him.

"He's not the right guy for you, Lucy," he began, but something about the look I gave him or the anger starting to radiate off me stopped him.

"I'll decide who is and who isn't right for me, Sawyer," I said, making another push for the door.

He didn't let my hand go. "No, wait, don't leave like this, Lucy," he said, taking a deep breath. "You're right. I have no business telling you what to do or who to stay away from."

Damn straight, my inner voice replied.

"But do me this one favor. Next time you see Ryder, if there is a next time"—Sawyer paused, looking like he was fighting a battle he was about to lose—"ask him about Holly."

That prickly feeling was my hackles standing on end. "Holly who?"

"That's Jude's history to tell you about, not mine."

And women were supposed to be infuriating creatures? It was time for another census. "Then why did you bring her up?"

"Because you have a right to know what you're getting into."

I knew I had the right, but I wasn't sure it was one I wanted to claim. There was nothing else to say. "Good night," I said, stepping out of the car. He let me go. "Thanks again for the ride."

He beamed that ultra-white Sawyer smile. "Thanks for letting me give you a ride," he said. "I'll see you Monday?"

I slid into my sweater. "Unless the West Coast falls into the ocean."

"So, all natural, personal, and economic disasters aside, I'll see you on Monday?"

"Just get the hell out of here, Diamond," I said, covering my smile as I shut the door.

Flipping a salute, Sawyer turned around in the driveway and waved as he pulled out.

I watched his car go until its taillights were eaten up by the night, trying to decide how I felt about Sawyer. By appearance's sake, he was a shoo-in for the young-man-of-the-year award, but something else, something I couldn't yet pinpoint, made the hair on the back of my neck stand on end when he was around. It was nothing more than an instinct, but it was something I couldn't ignore.

Wondering why I was standing in the middle of the driveway contemplating anything about Sawyer Diamond at midnight, I gave my head one good, clearing shake and turned to go inside.

One light still burned in the living room. I winced as I opened the front door. Of course it would be Mom, hovering over her laptop. Her shoulders lifted when the screen door closed behind me.

"Hey, Mom," I said, because the quicker I got this started, the quicker it could be over.

Swiveling in her chair, she removed her glasses and looked at me. Really looked at me, like she hadn't seen me in years and was trying to memorize the face of the seventeen-year-old Lucy.

"Was that a different boy who just dropped you off than the one who picked you up?" There was no anger, no ice in her voice, just wonder.

I nodded, sliding out of my heels and kicking them to the side.

"And the reason for that is . . . ?"

I didn't have an answer. Not for her, not even for me, but she waited.

"I don't think I even know why yet," I answered, heading up the stairs. I wanted nothing more than to throw on some pajamas and sleep the whole night away.

Mom bit her lip, doing that debating-something face. "Did he hurt you?" she spit out, appearing almost as scared of the question as she was of my answer.

Again, no easy answer for this, but I knew what she meant exactly. "Of course not," I replied.

"Lucy," she said, standing.

"Mom, I know I'm in huge trouble," I said, resting my hand on the banister. "I know I'm grounded until the day I turn eighteen for lying to you and running out tonight, but right now I just want to go to bed and forget tonight ever happened. Okay?" For the third time tonight, I felt close to tears. That was unacceptable.

"Okay," she said, sitting back down, "but I meant what I

said, Lucy. You can talk to me if you need to."

"Yeah, okay. Thanks," I said, shuffling up the stairs. I missed the days when I could knock on my brother's door and he'd be there to offer words of wisdom or a shoulder to cry on. I needed both right now.

"And Lucy?" she called after me. "You're grounded all right, but only until the end of the week."

For the first time in a long time, I felt like my mom and I had just had a constructive conversation.

THIRTEEN

I dreaded stepping foot into Southpointe's halls Monday morning—what rumors had flared over the weekend, what truths were confirmed, and what new reputation would await me. I'd managed to remove the memories of Saturday night and the anxiety of what would happen today, since I'd spent the entire day in the dance studio yesterday. We're talking sunrise to sunset, an all-day dance-a-thon. Yet again, dance had provided a shelter from the storms that followed me at every turn in life. However, the dance studio couldn't save me today. Right now.

That might be the reason I stayed locked in the Mazda after I pulled into my parking space. I convinced myself I wasn't cowering, just enjoying the last few songs of my favorite CD, but the fact I'd shoved my black cat-eye sunglasses on and stayed hunched down seemed I was cowering at best.

I knew the first bell was going to ring soon, because the parking lot was mostly full of cars and empty of students, but I still couldn't pry myself from the safety of my car. I'd prepped myself an entire day for this moment, stepping out in front of everyone who'd know what happened Saturday night, head high and confidence higher, but it wasn't working. Confidence was a hard thing to muster when you'd been ditched at the curb by the resident bad boy.

Again contemplating the pros of homeschooling, I started the car up again, concluding that today qualified as a sick day. I couldn't think of a time I'd felt more under the weather.

Checking my rearview, I put the Mazda in reverse, finding myself hoping to catch a glimpse of someone I shouldn't. Someone who was likely pacing in his cell. Then something flashed in my peripheral vision, followed by a knock on my window.

There stood Sawyer Diamond, smiling at me like it was any Monday morning, holding a bouquet of flowers. He waved. "Where do you think you're going?"

I rolled down my window. "Anywhere but here."

"Reason being?" he asked, handing the flowers to me through the window. It was a mixed bouquet wrapped up with butcher paper and twine, purchased at one of those fancy boutiques. They were beautiful, but I wasn't sure I was ready to accept flowers from Sawyer.

"I'm contemplating shooting for the stars and becoming a high school dropout," I said, staring at the school. "I hear there's a great beauty school downtown."

Sawyer chuckled, leaning into my door. "There is, actually, but that's for girls who get knocked up or can't tell the back from the front of their pre-algebra book."

"Sounds perfect," I said, gripping the steering wheel, trying to pretend a couple of girls rushing by us weren't whispering to each other about me. It wasn't easy, given they threw at least four sideways glances my way before they were out of sight.

"Come on," Sawyer said, leaning across my lap and snatching the keys. "Time to get to class."

"Give me those," I ordered, trying to grab them.

"You can have them back after sixth period," he said calmly, pocketing them. From the gleam in his eyes, I couldn't tell if he was more excited about the possibility of me reaching for them or about holding me hostage here all day.

"Sawyer," I groaned, calculating how long it would take me to walk home. "I don't need this right now."

"Yeah, you kind of do," he said, swinging my door open. "I've watched one too many girls' lives derail thanks to one upstanding citizen"—I glowered at him through my cat-eyes—"who shall not be named," he edited, holding out his hand. "I don't want to watch another."

"Everyone is going to be talking about me and staring at me and whispering about me. I need to be in a better state of mind to handle that kind of ridicule."

He grabbed my hand in his and squeezed. "No, they won't," he vowed. "I won't let them."

"You won't let them?" I repeated, looking down where his hand wrapped around mine. If there could be a complete opposite to what it felt like when Jude held my hand, this was it. "What are you, the godfather of the Southpointe Mafia?"

"My ancestors were like Mennonites or something, so we're not big into the whole Mafia thing," he said, reaching across my lap and grabbing my bag. "But give me a little credit. I've built up a lot of clout at this school over the years." Giving my hand a tug, he motioned toward school.

"Let me guess, it's your boyish good looks and smile," I said, sliding from my seat and slamming the door. I couldn't believe I was being coerced into attending class by Sawyer.

"My family owns a nice place down by the lake, and I've thrown some killer parties over the years."

"Ah," I said, as a few guys greeted Sawyer across the parking lot. He waved, continuing on. "Nothing like the lure of alcohol and no chaperones to make you a god in the world of teenagers."

"Precisely," he laughed, pulling the door open for me. After weaving through the metal detectors, Sawyer stayed right with me, heading down the hall with me. "I thought you had student government first period," I said, as a few more students passed by us, high-fiving Sawyer and barely taking note of me. It was like he was some personal cloaking device.

"I do."

"So why are you coming with me to literature?"

"Because I want to," he said without pause.

It was a little odd, Sawyer sticking to me like glue, bringing me flowers, the whole bit, but I felt steadier with him by my side, more grounded. And I needed to feel grounded to get through a day like this.

"And Mr. Peters is going to be cool with you sauntering into class and hanging out like you own the place?"

"I don't think he'll mind."

"Really?" I said, stopping outside the classroom door.

He gave me a sheepish grin. "My dad's on the school board. My grandfather was before that. My family's dug six feet deep into this school."

Unbelievable. "Well, then," I said, sweeping my hand through the door. "After you."

Sliding through the doorway, he plucked my hand from my side and towed me in. Everyone in class stared at us like they weren't quite sure what was going on. Sawyer surveyed the room, nodding his head at a few students. Before we'd passed the second row of desks, half the class had already shrugged it off, and the other half stared another second and got back to pulling their textbooks out. What the hell kind of influence did Sawyer have here at Southpointe, and how could I pull something like this off?

"Hey, Mr. Peters," he greeted as he led us to a couple of seats in the back of the room. "I'm going to sit in this morning."

The way Mr. Peters's eyes fell on me, I knew even he was aware of what had transpired at Homecoming. Then he nodded at Sawyer.

"I hope you'll enjoy the finer points of literature, Mr. Diamond," he said, turning to the board.

Sawyer glanced back at me, his eyes alight. "Oh, I will, Mr. Peters," he said. "I will."

The next three periods went the same way, although I called "no way" on Sawyer when he tried coming with me. It wasn't because I wasn't thankful for everything he'd done, how he smoothed out what should have been a hellish day, but I couldn't carry him around like a security blanket all year long. He gave me the glimmer of confidence I needed to get through the rest of the day. He even quoted to me on our way to second, "No one can make you feel inferior without your consent." Before rolling my eyes, I reminded myself he was just trying to help.

I wasn't totally immune to sideways stares or hushed voices, but they were a fraction of what I'd anticipated, and I knew that had to do with Sawyer. I was in his debt but didn't know if that was a place I wanted to be.

Taylor looked like her head was about to blow up by the time I meandered to our table in the cafeteria. After ignoring her first five calls on Sunday morning, I'd just switched off the phone. I wouldn't be able to dodge her inquires any longer.

"Did you drop your phone in the toilet or something?" she asked before I even sat down.

"My battery died and I couldn't find my charger," I said, smiling all innocent-like at her. Was it still considered lying if it was done to keep blabbermouths like Taylor in the dark?

Her face changed—she actually bought that one. "You poor thing," Taylor said, resting her hand on my arm. "As if your weekend needed to get any worse."

I mm-hmmed through a sip of orange juice, chalking another lie up on the wall of shame.

"Okay, where do we start?" she said, scooting closer. Lexie and Samantha dropped their celery sticks and leaned across the table.

I just wanted to get this over with. They wouldn't relent until they'd sucked me dry of information, and I knew if I didn't give them what they wanted, lies would be created to fill in the gaps.

"Where do you want to start?" I asked, popping the top back on my OJ.

"Did you know he'd stolen the car?" Taylor whispered, looking conspiratorially around the table.

"Of course not," I answered, offended until I realized they were disappointed with my answer. In these girls' books, I would be at least one or two shades cooler if I'd been in on or gone along with the whole vehicular theft thing.

"Have you talked to him since?"

It hurt thinking about him; it hurt even more admitting I hadn't heard from him.

"Nope."

Taylor and her apostles appeared disappointed again. "The buzz around here is that he was chased down by, like, a hundred police cars, returned the car to its owner, then walked right into the downtown precinct and turned himself in," Taylor spewed, waving and shaking her hands so manically I scooted a few inches back. "What did you hear, Lucy?"

"A whole lotta nada," I answered, already exhausted from the grand inquisition, and we were only three minutes into lunch hour. We were just getting started.

"So it's true he just, like, left you behind?" Lexie asked, chewing the end of a carrot stick. These girls ate more damn raw vegetables than a family of rabbits. As a dancer, I'd seen my fair share of raw veggies, but I liked to mix up my diet with an apple or a granola bar or something of substance.

"Yep," I said, praying for some kind of distraction. "It was tragic."

"How did you get home?" Lexie said, waving her carrot.

I was about to answer "a car" when Taylor smiled over at me, arching a brow. "I heard you rode shotgun in a certain BMW 325i."

"I don't even know what that means," I said, glancing behind me again. Still no one coming to my rescue. Hell, at this point in the questioning, I wouldn't have cared if it was a masked madman carrying a chain saw over his head.

"Sawyer drove you home?" The half-eaten carrot dropped from Lexie's hand.

"Yeah?"

Pushing out of her chair, Lexie glared down at me. "Why, Lucy Larson has certainly made the rounds around Southpointe, hasn't she? Not bad for the new girl." She spun and marched out of the cafeteria.

"Don't worry, she'll get over it," Taylor said, waving her hand in the air. "She and Sawyer dated on and off for a couple years and had a nasty breakup a few weeks before school started."

"Two years?" I said, having newfound respect for Sawyer. A two-year commitment to the genius that was Lexie Hamilton should have guaranteed him a seat among the gods. "She hates me. She's going to hate me for a long, long time."

Curling her finger at me, Taylor leaned in. I didn't move any closer. "Lexie hates everybody. Just don't tell her I said that."

"How nice for her," I said.

"Wow, Lucy Larson," Taylor said, pulling out a compact from her purse. "You somehow manage to tame the untamable Jude Ryder, short-lived as it was, then move right on to Southpointe's most eligible bachelor and coveted husband-to-be. You are officially my hero."

Samantha giggled. "Are you taking on any apprentices at this time?"

"Only the morally handicapped," I muttered, as Taylor powdered her nose and Samantha sipped diet pop from a straw. I was surrounded by sweater-set, peaches-and-cream, future Stepford wives. What the hell was I doing? We all had our place in the world, and that was all fine and good, but mine was nowhere near theirs. I liked substance and, lightning strike me down, sincerity. I got a whole lot of neither in this circle. Sure, they'd befriended me when no one else would, but it wasn't thanks to the goodness in their hearts. It was because they saw me as a pawn in their climb to the top.

I was a rung in their ladder. A stone to pass over.

"Sawyer frickin' Diamond," Taylor sang, shaking her head. "Unbelievable."

"I am, aren't I?"

I don't know which of the three of us jumped more, but Taylor's powder shattered when it hit the floor, so she won some sort of prize.

"God, Sawyer," Taylor said, picking up the shattered triangles of powder. "Don't ever sneak attack a bunch of girls in a huddle unless you want to get an elbow in your balls."

He tapped his head. "Duly noted."

"What do you want?" Taylor asked, melting a bit under his smile.

"I came to borrow Lucy." His hands rested on my shoulders. "You girls don't mind, do you?"

"That depends," Taylor said, watching Sawyer's hands on me. Her eyes read juicy gossip.

"On what?"

Taylor slid me a loaded look. "On what you came to borrow her for."

"A man's business is his own," he replied, pulling my chair out.

"Except when it isn't," Taylor said under her breath, before whispering in my ear, "I expect a full report."

Popping up, I waved to Taylor and Samantha and turned to Sawyer.

"Get me out of here," I mouthed.

He grabbed my hand and led me out of the cafeteria. "Come on."

If this was what having everyone's scandalized eyes on me felt like, I never wanted to run for office. I didn't get what was the big deal with Sawyer and me walking together, but Southpointe High was rumor central. The gossip from this ordeal ought to get the student body through the week.

Once we were free of the cafeteria, I exhaled. "Thank you."

"You looked like you were in physical pain back there," he said, leading me down a quiet hall. "I had to save you from that."

"I'm glad you did," I said, checking for anyone who might start a fresh round of rumors. "Why did you?"

Leaning into a wall of lockers, Sawyer tucked his hands in the pockets of his jeans. "I wanted to apologize," he began, taking me by surprise. "I shouldn't say anything to you, good or bad, about Jude. Whatever relationship the two of you have is none of my business. I'm sorry I tried to make it mine."

The apology took me off guard, but hearing Jude's name affected me more. Every time I heard it, another dagger was twisted into my heart.

"I'm not sure if there ever was a relationship," I admitted, "and if there was, there isn't anymore."

It should be because he'd stolen a car, or he'd been arrested more times than I could count on two hands, or because he personified everything we girls were taught to stay away from since we were grade schoolers. But it wasn't for any of these reasons. I knew Jude and I had no relationship because if he had indeed turned himself in, he hadn't bothered to call me first. Not to check to make sure I'd made it home safe or to explain what the hell had happened Saturday night. If we had anything of a relationship, Jude would have cared enough to contact me, but he hadn't.

"I'm sorry, Lucy," Sawyer said.

"No, you're not," I said, laughing about the fact that Sawyer was the one I'd opened up to about Jude, but I knew it had something to do with the way his face was always warm and his eyes were never judgmental.

"I'm sorry for you and the pain this has caused you," he said. "But I don't feel sorry for Ryder. He can kiss my ass the next time I see him."

Another dagger right through the left ventricle. "I'd like to see that."

"Stay tuned," he said, looking off into the distance, "you just might. Jude Ryder might finally get a dose of his own medicine before we all head off to college and he stays behind as a waste-of-space lifer."

FOURTEEN

The third week of school passed by ten times less dramatically than the first couple of weeks. In fact, I felt like I was settling into a pattern of normal when I worked my way through the metal detectors Friday morning. I was getting As in all my classes—kind of hard not to when one times one equals one and spelling words like "question" and "mystery" were as hard as my senior year got. Mom liked to be dramatic about my grades, but really she was just comparing my As and Bs to my brother's once-upon-a-time A-pluses. As if I needed any more guilt in my life.

I'd also joined the dance team, ignoring Taylor's warnings that my popularity would drop by at least 50 percent, and joined the Environmental Club, which she said would drop my popularity by the other 50 percent.

I was now zero percent popular. Go, me.

I didn't think now was a good time to announce I was planning on chairing the big dinner gala the school hosted every spring to raise money for the local library. That might have earned me banishment from the lunch table in the back corner.

I'd also managed to put up some boundaries between Miss Taylor and friends—which they, on most days, tried to respect. Flying in the face of everything that made sense—had been a bit of a trend as of late—Taylor had endeared herself to me. Beneath that veneer was a girl who was smarter than she let on, cared more than she dared to show, and had a wicked sense of humor begging to be set free. I found myself looking forward to our daily back-and-forth. I might have even worn her down enough to attend an Environmental Club meeting, assuring her a 50 percent cut in popularity wouldn't be the result.

To top everything off, Mom and I had even had a couple of other mostly amiable talks. The only thing that remained unchanged: every day after school, I rushed to the studio and lost myself in dancing until dinnertime.

Life hadn't felt this normal in years, and while I'd mourned normal for so long I should have been reveling in it, I wasn't. I knew that had something to do with a certain someone I still hadn't heard from, and a certain someone I should avoid from here until the grave, but as I'd learned the hard way, the heart wants what the heart wants. I wanted Jude.

Much like a parent won't let a child have a second piece of cake because it's not what's best for the sweet-loving, impulsive child, I couldn't let my heart have what it wanted most because I knew it would lead to its destruction.

"Good morning, beautiful."

I elbowed Sawyer as we settled into our morning routine. "Go away, ugly, and don't come back until you come up with a better line."

"Just you wait, I've been working on a few, and I think you're going to be rather impressed come next Monday," he replied, handing me the morning mocha he'd started bringing me a few days ago.

"Unlikely," I said.

"You calling me ugly every morning might actually bruise my delicate ego if I wasn't sure you were only teasing," he said, nodding his head at a couple of his football teammates as they passed by.

"Or if you weren't positively certain you weren't ugly."

"Are you saying you think I'm hot?" he asked, grinning a wicked one over at me.

"If that's what you heard, you need a couple of hearing aids," I said, taking a sip of coffee. "I was merely confirming you are not, in fact, ugly."

"I think that's the worst compliment I've ever been given," he said, slinging an arm around me and pulling me in.

And the whole easy relationship Sawyer and I navigated most of the time ended, like it always did, with an awkward embrace.

"How's the ankle, Diamond?" a voice called out from behind us. A voice that froze my feet to the ground, but melted me in every other place.

Coming around us, Jude crossed his arms, glaring at Sawyer's arm hung around me before turning to me. At once, my breathing became irregular and painful.

Lifting a shoulder, Sawyer glanced down at his wrapped ankle. "It'll heal up all right."

Jude's eyes didn't leave mine. "I was talking about your other ankle."

Sawyer paused, clearly thrown off guard. "It's fine," he answered.

"Do you want it to remain that way?" Jude asked, stepping forward, still watching me. Other than a bruise shadowing his cheekbone, he looked the same. I don't know what I expected, but it just seemed like a person who'd spent almost a week in prison would come out looking different. But maybe for someone who'd been to jail a grand total of thirteen times now, it was just another day in the park.

"You've got your arm on something of mine," Jude said, his eyes flashing.

"I believe that property changed ownership when you left it high and dry curbside." Sawyer tried to cinch me in closer, but not before I weaved out from under his arm.

I leveled a glare at Sawyer first before spinning around and giving Jude the same. I had not worked my ass off for the grades I had, or worked summer days waiting tables, or paved my way as my own woman to be reduced to some object two jealous boys could fight over.

"I am not a piece of property," I said, pointing my finger at Sawyer. "I am not yours," I said, then met Jude's eyes. "And I am not yours."

Saying that the first time around was infinitely easier. "Now both of you leave me the hell alone."

I brushed past Sawyer, shoving the mocha back into his hands—I didn't want anything from him—before weaving through the crowded hall, trying to calm my heart. For the first time this week, it felt warm.

And I didn't want to accept the reason why. I could feel Jude's eyes all the way down the hall, and even after I rounded the corner, I could still feel his watchful gaze on me.

I was tempted to skip first period. I was more tempted to skip the whole day, but I didn't. I picked myself up by my bootstraps and reminded myself I wasn't going to let two boys, mainly one boy, reduce me to one of those girls who flushed her life down the toilet. I was strong, I knew how to overcome, and damn it, I was better than that. And even if this was something of a stretch, I was going to adhere to the "fake it till you make it" policy.

I couldn't focus. I might as well have skipped first period. By the time the bomb-siren bell went off, I hadn't taken any notes on *Oliver Twist*. Oh well, I'd read it two years ago and gotten an A on my paper then.

As I gathered up my books, I noticed everyone looking at me as they headed out the door. It was enough to put me on alert for what awaited me on the other side of that doorway.

The classroom had emptied—even Mr. Peters had left—before I worked up the courage to shoulder my bag.

"Hey, Luce." Jude took a couple of steps inside the room, closing the door behind him.

I hated myself for wanting him to come wrap his arms around me and tell me everything was fine, that there was nothing we couldn't overcome, and that last weekend had been some terrible misunderstanding.

I was a dreamer.

"I'm not talking to you," I said, trying to walk by him,

but he stepped in front of the door.

"And why's that?"

Glaring up at him, I crossed my arms. "Don't you pretend like nothing happened. You know why I'm not talking to you now or why I won't talk to you ever again."

"Uh, Luce," he said, leaning against the door, "you're kind of talking to me right now."

I wasn't in the mood to be trifled with, not even by Jude. "I'm not talking, I'm a note below screaming, and I'm only not-quite-shouting at you long enough to let you know I'm finished with our pathetic excuse for a relationship," I said, having no designation to assign what had been ours. "I'm finished."

Looking down, he searched the ground, stalling. "You're finished?"

"Yep," I said, trying to sound like I couldn't care less.

"Does this have something to do with Diamond?" Fury etched its way into his face. "Because he's not the kind of guy you should be spending any amount of time with."

"No," I said, trying to shove him away from the door. "It has to do with you."

"Let me explain," he said, gripping my arms.

I snapped away from him. "You could explain yourself until you're blue in the face, but there's nothing you could say that would make me change my mind."

The muscles in his neck popped to the surface. "So you've finally decided to take my advice and keep the hell away from me?"

"Finally," I said, my throat tightening around the word.

He nodded, sliding his beanie down over his eyebrows. "Good," he said. "It's for the best anyway."

Just as I was starting to believe my hurt couldn't ache any more.

"Then I guess there's nothing else to say," I said, waving him away from the door.

He didn't budge. "Yes. Yes, there is," he said, his eyes the color of pewter. "I still owe you an explanation."

"Thanks, but no thanks," I said, trying to slide past him. "I'll be on my merry way."

Jude's hand flexed over the door handle. "Not before I explain what happened on Saturday."

I was close to breaking, close to letting him back in. I wasn't sure whether it had something to do with the way his eyes looked lost or the way I felt lost, but I was sure I couldn't let him back in.

"I don't need an explanation, Jude!" I said, shouting up at him. "I was there. I got to see the whole thing firsthand. As far as I'm concerned, whatever relationship we had is over, and I'm done talking, screaming, and listening to you, so save your breath, because I'm done wasting mine on you."

This time, when I shoved past him, he didn't stop me. And still, some part of me wished he would.

Jude shadowed me all day, which meant everyone stared like I was some circus freak, and everyone steered clear of me and my six-foot-two, two-hundred-pound shadow. He didn't say anything else, but it was clear he wanted to, and it was also clear he was waiting for me to make the first move. I hoped he enjoyed waiting a lifetime.

I snuck out of sixth a few minutes early, racing to my car, exhaling only once I had cleared the parking lot without a towering shadow in my rearview mirror.

I obviously needed to revamp my life, but for now, only one thing was capable of helping me escape. Lucky for me, the dance studio was empty when I arrived. It was the same place I'd learned to dance. I'd gone from a tutu-twirling toddler to a competent dancer with her sights set on the best dance schools in the country, all thanks to the work ethic I'd picked up from my father, the grace my mom swore I got from her side of the family, and the saintlike patience of Madame Fontaine.

She opened the studio thirty years ago, turning a condemned building in the historic district into the most celebrated studio in the area. It wasn't anything fancy, nor did she take on a lot of students, but Madame Fontaine had turned out her share of prima donnas. She was a legend in the dance world, well known for her chew-'em-up-and-spit-'em-out attitude, but to me, she was a saint.

She was the only person I could talk to during a time in my life when no one else was capable of talking. When I told her I was contemplating quitting dance five years ago, she threatened me with life and limb. Thanks to her, I stuck with it, working through the pain, and soon found dance was not only masking the pain, but healing it. Dance saved me in ways my parents, doctors, and even I couldn't.

Sticking my head in the office, I found it, like the rest of the studio, dark and empty. A tray of dried fruit was saran-wrapped on her desk, topped off by a pale pink note tented over it that read *Lucy*.

Sliding an apricot from under the wrap, I grabbed the note.

> *Since I know you forget to eat an after-school snack, here's an attempt at nutrition. Don't tell anyone I've gone soft in my old age. Work hard and dance harder.*

And there was Matilda Fontaine, the legend. Homemade dried fruit topped by a work-your-toes-till-they're-raw threat.

Working my toes, feet, legs, and mind until they were

raw was exactly what I needed. I didn't bother to change out of my leggings and cashmere tunic; I just bobby-pinned my hair back, tied on my pointes, and rushed through a few basic stretches. Sliding Tchaikovsky into the stereo, I cranked up the volume and was mid grand jeté before the first note vibrated the mirrors in the studio.

As a rule you didn't screw with, dancers always warmed up pre-setting-the-dance-floor-on-fire, but my heart had been beating double time since nine o'clock this morning. I wasn't only warmed up, I was warmed out.

I danced until the sun set and the sky grew dark. I danced until I tore through the same CD three times. I danced until I'd chugged down two liters of water. But no matter how hard I danced, or how intensely I concentrated on perfecting each and every step, I never stopped thinking about Jude.

The room went silent for the fourth time as Tchaikovsky's finale to *Swan Lake* drew to a close. I was drenched, out of breath, and sore from my neck to my toes. It was a good day of dancing.

As I reached for another liter of water, a low whistle echoed across the room. Even when it was a whistle, I knew his voice.

"God, you're beautiful," he said. "A man could live a full life watching you dance."

"I was wondering how long it would take you to find

me," I said as Jude came out of the shadows of the office. He'd aged a decade in six hours. The hollows under his eyes were a shade shy of black, his olive skin had gone sallow, but it was his eyes that had aged the most.

"Only about as long as it took me to walk from school to here," he answered, taking up the doorway.

"I've been at the studio for a good six hours." I took a long drink, then let myself collapse on the floor, settling my back against the mirror wall.

"I've been here almost as long," he said. "But I didn't want to interrupt you, so I just made like a good Peeping Tom and checked you out through the window." He grinned, scuffing his boot into the doorjamb. "Plus, I was a little frightened of what you might say or do if I did interrupt you."

"Ah," I said, folding my upper half across my legs to stretch muscles that were about to snap. "There's the truth. Finally," I muttered just loud enough so that he could hear me.

"I need to tell you a lot more truth, Luce," he said, looking the most lost I'd seen him. It appealed to my already-Jude-friendly heartstrings, and before I knew what I was doing, I patted the patch of wood beside me.

"I need to stretch, and it sounds like you need to talk," I said, forcing myself to stretch so far it felt like I was about to break. "Let's get this over with."

He crossed the room, his body relaxed, but his face wary. "I meant what I said. That was the most beautiful thing I've ever seen," he said, sliding down beside me. "I didn't know you were so damn talented. You're going to be the star of some bigwig ballet production, where millionaires pay, like, a thousand bucks for a front-row seat," he said, while I tried not to smile at his obvious ignorance of ballet lingo, "or some crazy shit like that."

I laughed as I straightened and crossed my left arm in front of me. "I think you're right. I'm quite certain my life is destined for plenty of 'crazy shit,'" I said, elbowing him with my other arm.

"You and me both, kiddo," he said, tilting his head up. "But me for real and you just as a figure of speech. Your name's going to end up in lights, and mine's going to be replaced by a number on some warden's list."

Stretching the other arm, I inhaled, trying to muster up all the anger I'd had for him just hours ago. I couldn't do it. "Haven't you ever heard the saying that your past doesn't have to dictate your future?"

He opened his mouth; nothing came out, so he closed it again. Seeing Jude tongue-tied made me smile; it somehow made him less intimidating.

Finally, he said, "That's some stinkin' smart shit." He hung his arms over his knees. "Who said that?"

Folding one leg over the other, I shrugged. "I did."

"You are one smart little senorita, you know that, Luce?" he said, appraising me with warm eyes. "Not only is your name going to be in lights, you're going to have, like, three acronyms after your name: Lucy Larson, MD, PhD, and some other smart fill-in-the-blank *D*."

"Enough with the flattery, Ryder," I said, wiping my forehead off with the back of my arm. "You've got some explaining to do. Some honest explaining to do," I added.

"Yeah, I do," he said, thumping his head against the mirror. "Why is the truth so damn hard to admit?"

"Because it's honest," I said.

"So damn smart," he said under his breath.

This man was the god of dodging the topic. Too bad for him he was dealing with the queen of seeing through a man's shit.

"Ryder." I turned his face toward mine. I leveled him with a no-nonsense expression. "Explanation." I leaned in, lifting my brows. "Now."

"Bossy, too," he muttered.

Since playing nice was getting me nowhere, I elbowed him in the ribs and decided to get this conversation ball rolling. "So you stole a car?" How could I sound so casual talking about this? Only one answer to that riddle: Jude Ryder.

"I prefer the term 'borrowed,'" he said, clasping his hands together.

"I suppose most felons do," I said, biting my tongue two words too late.

"No, you're right," he said, trying to comfort me after my flash of bitchiness. "I am a felon. A repeat felon. And if I was eighteen, I would have been locked away for at least a solid month, not just a few nights. It goes on my record as car theft, but I did, in my mind that night, borrow the car, Lucy."

I inhaled patience. This was new conversation territory for me, and I was running low on sympathy. "Explain to me why, in your eyes, you borrowed a stolen car."

He shifted in his seat. "The Chevelle was parked in my buddy's garage. Damon dropped out of Southpointe after his junior year and opened up his own garage. He specializes in rebuilding old cars, like real piecers, and turns them into beauties doctors and lawyers pay a hundred grand for," he said, getting all animated. "You should have seen this one El Camino that came in once, it was a real hunk of junk, not even good enough for scrap metal, and Damon—"

"Jude," I stopped him. "It thrills me to see you've got a passion in life other than women and being the honorary president of the Bad Boys Club of America, but I don't have long before my parents start blowing up my phone if I'm not home."

"Sorry," he said, cracking his neck. "So I do side jobs for Damon from time to time. I've got a knack for getting underneath the hood of a sexy-ass machine and making her purr."

I bit my lip to keep from laughing. "I bet you do."

"Ah, Luce," he said, curling his nose at me. "You have a sick, sick mind. You know that?"

"I learned from the best."

"Ouch," he said. "But deserved."

"Very," I added.

"So someone had just dropped the Chevelle off for a full-body detail job. Damon left town for the weekend to visit his girl, so he left me in charge."

This was where I began to wince, because I began to see the picture in the connect-the-dots he was drawing for me.

"Saturday came and Damon was gone, the owner wasn't expecting the car back until Monday, and the keys were still in the ignition," he said, taking a breath. "And me, being the morally corrupt idiot that I am, I saw an opportunity I couldn't pass up."

"If Damon was visiting his girlfriend and the owner wasn't planning on picking it up for a couple days, how did the cops find out you'd taken it?" I asked, feeling sympathy trickling back into my heart.

"Because I didn't follow my number one rule of always

expecting the worst." He sighed, rubbing his forearms. "Damon's girl chose Saturday night to break up with his sorry ass, so when he got back to the garage and saw the Chevelle was missing, he assumed it was stolen and called the cops."

"Wait," I said, feeling a little numb. "Why would Damon head to the garage at ten o'clock on a Saturday night?"

"He lives in a loft above the garage," Jude answered, staring straight ahead.

"And the cops found the car, and they found you, and you got arrested."

"Pretty much."

"But didn't you get to tell your side of the story?" I asked, taking my time untying my pointe shoes because I needed something else to focus on. "Didn't they understand that it was all just an honest mistake?"

"I took a car that wasn't mine, Luce," Jude said, his voice quiet. "From where the cops are standing, that's not an honest mistake. Plus, they called the owner, and the prick is so pissed, he's threatening to sue Damon. Over nothing more than a few miles on one of his six cars he never even would have known was missing if Damon—" Cutting himself short, he punched the floor with his fist. "If *I* hadn't taken the car in the first place."

"God, Jude." Again, I had no other words.

"I know. I know," he said. "So, not only have I jeopardized my buddy's business he's worked his ass off to make into something, I added another mark on my two-page record, and I'm likely out of a job too."

I didn't know how to solve any of those problems, and I was the master at problem solving. But I was coming up with a whole lot of nothing. "Can't you get a new job?" I asked finally.

He laughed. "I live in a boys' home, and I have the record of a seasoned criminal. I can't even get hired on as a burger flipper. I worked off the books for Damon because I don't exactly pass background checks, and the state says the boys' home provides for all of our needs, so technically we can't get paying jobs until we leave." Grabbing one of my pointe shoes, he admired the pale ribbons, running them through his fingers.

"If you ever need something, money for whatever," I said, clearing my throat, "I've got some money saved up from waiting tables during summers. You could have some whenever—"

Jude lifted his hand. "Luce, thanks, but no thanks," he said, closing his eyes. "That's sweet as hell of you to offer, but I'm not taking money from anyone, least of all you. I'm not a charity case, and I don't take handouts."

"I never said you were."

"No, you didn't," he said, opening his eyes and staring

straight into mine. "But everyone else has."

That put a ball in my throat I couldn't swallow. Clearing my throat again, I said, "What did you need the money for? Are you saving for college or a car or something?"

He rolled his eyes at the mention of college.

"Or are you blowing it all on bubblegum?" I asked, leaning into him.

"That's more my style, but no. I have responsibilities, you know? Things that need taking care of."

I didn't know, but I wasn't sure I was ready to know about Jude's responsibilities. "Things that I need to take care of, and before working for Damon, the only job I could find was drug dealing." He waited for my reaction.

Outside, I gave him nothing. Inside, I was falling apart. Jude had quite possibly the biggest heart I'd found in a man. He also had the longest rap sheet I had yet to encounter in a peer. He was the classic example of good intentions running amok.

I leaned my forehead into my bent knees. "Why did you take the car, Jude?" It wasn't something I'd meant to say out loud, just an internal why-is-the-universe-so-unfair? musing.

"Come on, Luce," he said. "I couldn't show up at your front door with nothing more than my two feet to get us to the dance."

"Why couldn't we have doubled up with another couple

then?" I said, rubbing the arches of my brutalized feet. "Or why couldn't we have taken my car? You could have driven." I was now even more pissed at the whole situation.

"Because I'm sick of being a leech on society, on everyone around me. Because I'm tired of taking handouts, and I'm tired of the pity in the faces of those who give the handouts. But really, most of all, because the girl I was taking out deserved the best," he said, sliding down past my legs and pulling the foot out of my hands. "Let me do that," he said, his hands swallowing up my whole foot as they gently worked the muscles.

"Jude, I'm not the girl who wants or needs the best. I'd be over the rainbow with 'above average' or 'meets expectations' as long as the guy I had was the best."

He continued to massage my feet like he was capable of crushing them if he wasn't careful. "You kind of drew the short straw on that one."

I kept quiet because I didn't want to give away everything I still felt for him. I still wanted Jude like I'd never wanted anything before, but I didn't want to be left in more pieces than when I started.

"And just so you know, since I know those shitheads are all saying I left you behind because I was done with you, or I didn't want you slowing me down, or at least a dozen other BS explanations, I left you because I didn't want you with me if I got caught," he said, his shoulders tensing beneath his gray thermal. "I didn't want them to try to label you an accomplice or anything." He looked up at me with that fervent expression of his. "So that's it, that's the truth. Don't let those jackasses try to twist it around to make you feel bad, okay?"

I should have felt better, knowing he hadn't abandoned me like last week's garbage. But I felt guilty knowing I'd bought into that theory. Jude deserved to have at least one person on his side, and that person should have been me.

"Hey, Luce," he said, rubbing his hands over my other foot. "Okay?"

I closed my eyes, because that was my last defense against tears. "Okay."

"Luce?" he asked. "Shit, don't cry. I'm not worth it, not worth even thinking about crying."

I took in two slow breaths before opening my eyes. "I'm not crying," I said, trying to convince both of us. "I'm just frustrated. And I get all watery-eyed when I get frustrated. But for the record, you are worth crying over."

He studied me another moment before turning his attention back to my feet. "Why are you frustrated?"

"Pick a topic, any topic, and there's a pretty good chance I'll be frustrated about some element of it."

"That was a nice attempt at being vague, Luce, really it

was," he said, one side of his mouth lifting, "but why are you frustrated, in particular, right now?"

To answer this honestly would require a multipronged, daylong explanation, which would leave me transparent and exposed in every way a girl dreaded most. So I went for the least complicated answer. "I'm frustrated with noon to midnight of last Saturday. The whole damn day and everything that could have gone wrong that went wrong," I began again, trying to put a stopper on the verbal explosion. "I'm frustrated because I don't understand why everything that could go bad did, and I'm frustrated because I don't understand why you took that car in the first place."

"I took that car," he said, "and I would take a hundred more, because even though you say you don't want the best, I want to give you the best."

"Why, Jude? Why are you so damned determined that I need to have the best?" I asked, leaning forward.

He raised his shoulder, his eyes cast down. "Because, Luce. Because you're the most important person in my life."

And that was the tipping point. I couldn't hold the damn tears back. A person he'd known only a few weeks, a person who'd turned her back on him when he needed a friend most, a person who had convinced herself and was still trying to convince herself that he was not the man to fall for. And I was the most important one to him.

"I don't deserve that title," I said, playing with the sleeve of my tunic.

"Why?" he asked, lifting my chin. "Because you finally accepted what a cancer I am and feel guilty for it?"

My eyes flashed. "No."

"Then why?" he asked, nothing antagonistic in his voice, just curiosity.

"Because you and I have too much bad history to make a good future."

"Shit, Luce." His forehead lined. "Weren't you the one who just said your past doesn't have to dictate your future?"

I'd never felt like such a hypocrite. My shoulders sagged from sheer mental and physical exhaustion.

"Or does that go for everything but me?"

Jude's life had been filled with enough crap, he didn't need any more from me, but I just couldn't do this. I knew, with absolute certainty, I'd come out in worse shape than I'd gone in if I let Jude into my life the way he wanted to be.

"Jude," I said, biting my lip. "I just can't. I can't do this."

His expression darkened. "I know I don't deserve a second, or third, or whatever-the-hell-this-is chance, but you and I have something special, Luce, and you know it. Give me another chance, one more chance, and I'll walk a line so straight people will think I've been possessed." God, I wanted to look away from those eyes, but I just couldn't.

"One more chance. Not because I deserve it, but because we deserve one."

If the first tears I'd cried in years were any indication of our future together, that should make my decision easier. "I can't," I whispered.

"Why? Because you can't or you won't?"

A lie was going to be the only hope I had of convincing him I wasn't fighting every urge to be with him. "Because I just don't want to be with you, Jude." The words flamed my throat.

His face fell for barely a second before it sharpened. "Bullshit," he said, shaking his head at me. "I'm so used to dealing with liars I know a lie's coming before a person opens their mouth."

I was the worst bluffer around and Jude was the best caller around, which meant I wouldn't get away with anything. Reason number one thousand and one why Jude and I would never work. "I'm not exactly your garden-variety thug, thief, or dealer. I don't lie through my teeth, so you might want to recalibrate your BS detector."

His eyes stayed trained on me, unblinking. "Fine. Convince me then. Convince me you don't want me like I want you."

He was not going to let this go; he was not going to let me go so easily. It was as romantic as it was infuriating. "I've said everything—"

"Screw words," he interrupted. "I don't believe what you've said. Convince me through action."

That whole breathing thing was getting hard to do again. "Do I want to know what that means?"

Then, without warning, he pulled my calves, sliding me across the floor toward him. He leaned into me, his eyes shifting down. "Kiss me," he said, his mouth so close to mine we almost were kissing. "Convince me I'm nothing but some random boy you've left in the past."

I had one more no in me, and then I was toast. "Not a good idea," I said, my voice shaky.

His jaw tensed as his arms wound around me. "Damn it, kiss me, Luce."

So I did, and the moment my lips touched his, that ache I'd felt all the way to my bones the past week evaporated. Just like that.

Pressing into me, Jude lowered my back to the ground, his mouth never leaving mine. His weight rested over mine, grounding me, keeping me from falling apart. This only made me kiss him harder.

"Shit, Luce," he breathed, when my hands slid up his shirt, gripping into his back.

And then his hand was under my sweater, lifting it higher, exploring the parts of me I needed him to. Sitting up just enough, I lifted my arms in the air, waiting for him to take it off. He managed to remove it with one hand and in about one second before he pinned me to the floor again.

We were close, one word from me standing between me and him going all the way. He was ready, and I'd been ready since the day I first saw him. I wasn't thinking about our past when his hand slid underneath my bra, and I wasn't thinking about our future when his mouth took its place; I wasn't even thinking about the present—I was living the present.

His mouth moved to my neck while his hands traveled beneath the elastic of my leggings, pulling them lower. I lifted my hips to make the job easier.

"Are you sure?" he said, planting a patch of sucking kisses at my hairline.

I'd never been more sure about what he was asking about, but a hint of reality wedged its way into my head. Reality really sucked sometimes.

"Wait," I said in between breaths, wanting to strap a piece of duct tape to my mouth immediately after.

His body tensed over mine, his hands stopping right away. But his mouth took a little longer. Finally, moving his face over mine, he gave me a tortured smile. "Okay," he said. "Waiting." I could hear his silent questions, they were written so expressively on his face. *Why?* and *For how long?*

Kudos to Lucy Larson for being able to render a reformed ladies' man witless.

"It's not because I don't want to, because I do," I said, my heartbeat still pounding about a monkeyload of beats per minute. "I really do, but I don't want our first time to be on a wood floor when I'm all stinky and sweaty and wearing shamefully boring underwear." This was why you never left the house without some jaw-dropping, man-catching undies strategically in place.

Smiling down at me, he kissed my nose. "Some other time," he said, pulling my leggings back around my waist.

"Any other time," I emphasized, convinced that stinky, sweaty sex with Jude on the floor I'd danced across for fifteen years was better than delayed sex. I was just about to tell him this when he sat up, pulling me with up with him.

"By the way, you failed the convincing-me test." He grabbed my sweater and pulled it over my head.

"Was that before or after I removed my sweater?" I said, adjusting said sweater into position.

He gave me a cool look. "Before."

"Just checking," I said, pulling the sleeves up over my elbows, because making out with Jude Ryder was all kinds of hot, not excluding body temperature. "So was that a first?"

"I'm going to ask for further clarification on that before I tie my own noose answering it," he said, his pupils still dilated, still excited.

"Was that your first time with a girl in a ballet studio . . . ," I began, "and getting denied?" I smiled, taking a gulp of water.

"That was a first," he said, pulling me into his lap.

"At least I've got one of them," I teased, resting my arms over his.

He didn't speak until I met his eyes. "You've got all my firsts," he said. "All the ones that matter."

I pressed a kiss into his mouth.

"But Luce, I need you to promise me something," he said, his face wrinkling. "If I ever mess things up again, whether it's a misunderstanding, or shit luck, or I just do what I was created to do and screw everything up"—he paused, exhaling—"I want you to promise me you'll leave. Drop me like a bad habit and don't look back, because God knows, it can't be me who walks away, since I'm incapable of it."

Reality, if you're listening, bite me.

"You won't," I said, willing or wishing it to be true, probably both.

"I know. But I'd feel better if you promised," he said, running the back of his hand down my cheek. "That much more motivation to not mess up."

"Okay," I said, already regretting the words before I spoke them. "I promise."

FIFTEEN

"Are you going to get in trouble?" I whispered across the seat. Why I was whispering in my own car, I don't know, but something about the dark, utilitarian building dictated hushed voices. "Don't you guys have some kind of curfew?"

"Don't you?" Jude teased, leaning across the console and tickling my side.

"Yeah, I do," I said, jolting away from him. "And I'm past it. Plus, I'm grounded and not really minding the whole rules of being grounded. So I'm extra grounded now."

"You were at your dance studio," he said, clearing his throat, "perfecting your moves. How can your parents punish you for that?"

"You're every kind of twisted," I said, shoving his arm before glancing back at Last Chance Boys' Home. Nothing about it seemed welcoming or warm or conducive to nurturing young boys into men. It seemed like the kind of place you used to dare your grade-school friends to go up to on Halloween and ring the doorbell. "You sure you're not going to get in trouble?" I glanced at the time on the dashboard; not quite midnight, but close enough to count.

"Not as long as I use the back window and don't get caught," he said, reaching for the handle.

"Jude?" I said, winding my fingers around the steering wheel, searching for the right words.

"Yeah?" He let go of the handle and turned to face me.

"Just because I want to really try to make this whole thing work—"

"So do I," he added.

"I just want to lay everything out on the table now before we go any further." I was nervous, and when I got nervous, my voice got all high.

"What do you want to know?" he asked, guessing I wasn't wanting a life story, but fishing for something specific. He was right.

Taking in a breath, I pressed on. "Is there anyone from your past who could potentially come between us?" I said, peering over at him. "Anyone in your life I need to know about?"

Jude tilted his head, puzzled. "Are you talking about a girl?"

"Not specifically, because I don't know or want to know the girls of your past—I just need to know if there's one you still have any kind of ties to." I'd tried to flush Holly's name from my brain all week long, but I was a woman; we didn't just forget the names of our man's ex-flames.

"Hey," he said, lowering his head until his face was level with mine. "There's you, Luce. Only you. And don't let anyone, most of all yourself, convince you otherwise."

Everything inside me sighed with relief. "Okay, thanks," I said, unwinding my fingers from the wheel.

"Anything else you want me to lay out on the table?"

Staring over at him, I wet my lips. "Nothing other than me."

His eyes widened in surprise before he could recover. Chuckling, he said, "Anytime, Luce. Name the time and place. I'll supply the table."

"Make sure you disinfect that sucker first," I called after him as he swung the door open. "I don't want to catch whatever's been laid out on the table before me."

Pausing with his hand on the door, he suddenly threw himself back in the car. His mouth was on mine before my heart could react and then, once it was trilling at flying speed, his mouth left mine. "Just you, Luce. No one else. There never has been."

"That sounds like a convenient case of selective memory," I said, wishing he'd stay here and finish what he'd started.

"I try to only keep the happy memories," he said, exiting the car. "If that's what you call selective memories, I'm good with that."

"Me too," I replied after he'd left, watching him disappear into the dark.

It was becoming a familiar sight. One light burning in a window late at night, my mom's silhouette behind it. I was either in deep shit or deeper shit coming home this late at night on the second-to-last night of my weeklong grounding sentence. Grabbing my bag, I shoved out of the Mazda and marched up the stairs, not even attempting to mask my footsteps.

I wasn't sure what to expect when I walked through that front door; knowing what to expect from Mom was kind of like flipping a coin. In the morning she might be cold, removed, and act like I was the bane of humanity, and by evening she could be baking cookies and asking if I'd learned anything interesting in class that day.

For years I'd been able to predict her; I always knew what to expect and could tailor my life around that. Now, I couldn't. As a teenager, one of a race who thrived on manipulating the routines and regimens of their parents so they could get away with all forms of hedonism, I should have been devastated beyond repair. But I wasn't. Seeing the pieces of my mom from my childhood come back together made me feel like maybe there was hope for our family after all. Maybe we could get back to what we were, never forgetting, but moving on.

It was a childish wish, but I held on to it.

Opening the door, I paused in the doorway, not sure whether Mom was going to scold or smile at me. She did neither. Her attention was focused on her laptop and nothing else.

"Hey, Mom," I greeted, dropping my bag on a nearby chair. "I'm off to bed."

"Lucy?" she said, sounding confused. She glanced at me and then the clock on the wall behind me. Her eyes bulged. "Are you just getting home?"

Great. She had just turned into my dad. Didn't have a damn clue what was going on in her household, but was cordial enough not to raise her voice.

"Yeah," I said. "I was at the dance studio, practicing a new routine. Time totally got away from me. Sorry." I was ashamed enough to hang my head. Lying was not something I wanted to list as a top skill on my résumé and darn it if each lie wasn't making me a more proficient liar.

"Oh, I see," Mom said, shoving her glasses on top of her head. "That's all right. Just call next time you're going to be home so late, okay?"

"Yeah, sure," I said, grabbing a couple of bananas from the fruit bowl because I was, for the first time in a week, hungry. "Night, Mom," I said, charging up the stairs.

"Lucy, wait," she said, taking something from her desk and crossing the room. "This came earlier today." She was grinning. Grinning. My mom had smiled before, but I couldn't recall a time she'd grinned.

When I saw the stuffed manila envelope she was holding, I understood why. My knees buckled right before I collapsed on the stairs.

"Marymount Manhattan," she said, holding it out to me with both hands like it was an offering.

I'd been waiting for this for months. Well, I'd been waiting all my life. One letter would determine whether I could live the dream I'd always wanted.

"This thing is pretty thick," Mom said, extending it closer, "and my psychic abilities are telling me this is a welcome packet. So tear this sucker open and let's celebrate."

Marymount Manhattan. Dance. Dreams. Future. It was one envelope-rip away. But I wasn't ready for it.

"Thanks, Mom," I said, grabbing the packet and running up the stairs.

"You're not going to open it?" she asked, gaping at me like I'd caught a nasty case of crazy.

"Not now," I said, yawning. "I'm exhausted and would

probably fall asleep before I read the first paragraph. I'll open it tomorrow."

"Lucy?" Her voice was tight, worried.

"I'm good, Mom," I said. "I swear. I'm just beat. I promise you'll be the first to know once I open this baby up." I waved the packet at her.

"All right," she said, followed up with a have-it-your-way look. "Sometimes I just can't figure you out."

"That makes two of us," I mumbled, running all the way to my room.

The packet haunted me from my desk all weekend long. Mom didn't push the issue, and I just couldn't find the balls to open some damn letter. I didn't even mention it to Jude when he called first thing Saturday morning. I'd wanted to get together that night again, maybe dinner and a movie, or maybe picking up right where we'd left off in the ballet studio, but apparently, other than school-related functions, weekends at a boys' home were synonymous with work.

So in between fighting an internal battle in my bedroom, I took a few walks and gritted my teeth and danced through the pain I'd inflicted Friday night. Monday morning couldn't get here fast enough.

I parked the Mazda and was all clear through the metal detectors ten minutes before class began. The halls were empty save for a few zero-hour students and tired-eyed teachers. I knew better than to expect Jude this early before class, but it didn't stop me from swinging by his locker to make sure. My frown was just forming in front of his empty locker when a strong hand grabbed mine and began leading me down the hallway. I didn't need to identify the gray thermal or the worn beanie to know whose hand held mine.

Jude didn't say anything, he didn't even glance back at me; he just powered through the hallway, shoving us into a dark room at the end of the hall.

"Good morning to you too—" But my words were cut short as he pushed me up against a wall, his hands and mouth landing on me like they'd been starved all weekend.

I kissed him back, winding my arms around his neck. And then, because close wasn't close enough, I put my dancer's strength and flexibility to good use and leaped up, winding both legs around his hips. He groaned, pressing me harder against the wall, his mouth moving in and over mine with such fury I couldn't breathe. I didn't care. In fact, passing out because Jude Ryder had been kissing the breath out of me sounded like something to add to the life goal list.

Right when I was certain this was it, this was the time and place we were going to go all the way, his mouth slowed at the same time as he lowered me to the ground. Now was not the time for slowing down, not when everything was quickening in me, about to explode if we didn't keep going.

I groaned when he pressed one final kiss into my mouth.

"Good morning," he said, beaming like an idiot.

I groaned again when he took a step back.

"I missed you too."

I tried to scowl at him, but apparently it was a physical impossibility when the person who'd just kissed the living breath out of you was grinning in front of you. "You're mean."

"I know," he said, brushing my hair back, "but the image of that got me through a long weekend. I needed that."

"You'd been dreaming this up in your mind all weekend?" My stomach managed yet another flip-flop.

"That was all I thought about."

Double flip and flop. "Did it meet your expectations?"

"Exceeded them," he said, leaning in. "But in my dreams you were wearing this short schoolgirl skirt and nothing underneath." I felt his smile curve into place as he kissed my neck.

"Tomorrow's another day," I breathed, squeezing my legs together in agony. "Keep dreaming big."

"Can do," he whispered into my ear before sinking his teeth into my lobe.

"Don't swallow my earring," I said, my breath all ragged again. "I hear sterling silver can really upset a stomach."

"No earring here," he said, piercing another gentle bite into my ear.

I groaned again, but this time it was the frustrated kind. "Then it must have fallen out while you had me pinned against a wall," I said, sending him a look as I dropped down to the floor, running my hands along the carpet.

"Are you sure you had one in?" he asked, scanning the floor above me. "I don't remember seeing one."

"I think you skipped through four senses this morning and barreled on through to touch." I looked up at him, sitting up taller on my knees to take in more of the carpet. Class was about to start any minute, and I'd cordon the entire room off before I left my favorite silver hoop behind.

Walking closer, he continued scanning the floor with me. "That does happen to be my favorite sense, by a landslide."

"No kidding?" I said sarcastically, ready to get down on all fours and inspect the carpet a centimeter at a time.

"Oww!" I howled, snapping back up on my knees, hoping a chunk of hair hadn't just been ripped out.

"Luce, wait. Don't move," Jude said, gripping my head in place. "Your hair's caught on something."

I tried pulling in the opposite direction, but my hair was stuck good. "It's caught on your buckle," I said.

"Stop moving," he said, holding my head in place. "You're only making it worse."

I pulled back again, this time grimacing. "Stop telling me what to do and start untangling it then," I said, laughing despite the pain.

He laughed, trying to cut it short, but he couldn't stop.

"You're enjoying this, aren't you?" I said, peeking up at him through a tangle of hair.

"I wish I could say I wasn't, but I'd be lying," he said in between his laughter.

"You're so obnoxious," I said, grabbing his hips and bracing myself for hair extraction.

Right as I was gritting my teeth, about to whip my head back, the door whined open, the overhead lights flashing on right after.

"Dude," a voice said, stopping short in the doorway.

Another boy popped his head inside. He lifted a cell phone and pointed it where I kneeled in front of Jude, my hands on his hips, his hands on my head, and a flash went off. "This is so going on the internet."

Our picture went viral, amassing about ten thousand hits all before the lunch bell rang. Two sophomores had their phones snapped in half and would never dare pass Jude alone in a hallway again, but otherwise Jude managed the unthinkable and kept his hellfire temper caged.

I was so impressed that he didn't nose-dive into a record-setting explosion that I managed to stay pretty Zen with the whole of Southpointe, not to mention the rest of the country, getting an eyeful of our photo shoot. I didn't even feel the urge to defend ourselves or explain what had actually transpired before I wound up on my knees in that risqué position because, well . . . no one in their right mind would believe the truth.

So I endured yet another flood of stares and whispers, girls gaping at me like I was the red light hussy spawn of the devil here to decimate the world, and guys gawking at me with dilated eyes and tipped smiles, like they were imagining me on my knees in front of them. The girls I got. They were just worked up because if I'd done it once, what was to stop me from blowing their boyfriends in the bio lab? I got that kind of disdain because I was a girl. However, the guys were just horn dogs, salivating to hump whoever and whatever they could. A couple of the repeat offenders I flipped off in passing.

"Hey, Morrison!" Jude slid into line next to me, hollering at the guy who was staring at me in a familiar way. "Turn your eyes unless you want to lose them."

Morrison tilted his chin at Jude. "Ryder, you are one lucky son of a bitch."

The urge to throw my container of yogurt straight at Morrison's smug face arose, and it was almost impossible to resist.

Jude moved in front of me, pressing me behind him with his forearm. "If you're referring to the fact that my girl-friend is an intelligent, classy, sweet, righteous girl, you'd be right," he said, squaring himself at Morrison, "but if you're referencing anything less than honorable, then you might want to make some adjustments to your college applica-tions, because I don't think Arizona State's going to want you if you can't run the ball."

Morrison flipped Jude a salute and spun around, as his trio of friends heckled him.

"Lace-curtain bastards," Jude muttered, glaring at the back of their heads. "I hear any of them running their mouths or see them looking at you again, and I'm going to show them how we do things at the bottom-feeder level."

Shoving my way around him, I turned on him. "Does that sound like someone who's committed to staying on the good side of the law?" I asked, shuffling a piece of pizza onto my tray. "Does that sound like someone who promised their . . ."

"Girlfriend," he filled in the blank, winding his arms around me.

"Their girlfriend they wouldn't do anything to mess this

up? Because going to jail for attempted manslaughter might be considered messing up to some people."

"Woman," he exhaled, resting his cheek against mine, "you are busting my balls. In every way."

"What was that promise you were about to make me about not touching Morrison and his bunch of half-breeds?" I said, paying the lunch lady, who wasn't even trying to mask the judgment in her eyes. Someone else had seen our photo.

"Fine," he relented, steering me toward the courtyard. He'd either read my mind or felt the same way I did: tired of the looks and sick of dodging questions. "I won't touch the Jerk-off Jockeys." Grabbing the door handle, he swung it open for me. "But I can't promise I won't pay someone else to touch them," he added as I passed by.

I jabbed him in the stomach.

"I found your earring," he said, pulling my silver hoop from his pocket.

"Where was it?" I asked, taking it and sliding it back into place.

"Tucked inside my boxers."

"How the hell did it wind up there?" I asked, going all soft thinking about his boxers.

"Don't know," he said as we walked about the mostly empty courtyard, "but let's just say I was close to becoming pierced. Down there."

I laughed, giving the missing earring a pat. She'd had a better morning than I had. No one glanced up at us as we walked across the grass and settled at an empty table. It was a cool day, the kind where you wished you'd packed a sweater, but as Jude hung his arm around me, I found myself hoping I'd never have to pack a sweater another day in my life.

"Girlfriend, huh?" I said, setting the pizza in front of him.

"Girlfriend," he stated. "No question mark."

I smiled into my tray. "What number does that make me?"

He sighed. "One. And only. I told you before, Luce. You're my first and, God willing I don't screw this up, my last."

It was a good thing I hadn't just sunk my teeth into the apple in my hand, because I would have choked on it. It should have freaked me out beyond repair, my boyfriend who'd been to jail three times as many times as we'd been on dates, tossing "forever" into normal conversation, but it didn't. He wasn't saying marriage tomorrow and a baby the day after; he was saying someday, maybe. And someday, maybe sounded appealing to me in ways it shouldn't to a seventeen-year-old-girl with dreams of a bright future.

"How many girls have you been with, Jude?" I said, asking the positively worst question a girl should ask a guy like

Jude. I was hoping for a number less than fifty.

He lowered the slice of pizza before taking a bite. "Enough to know when something special comes along."

"And if you were to quantify 'enough,' that number would be . . ." I dropped my apple too. With this kind of conversation circling about, decreased appetites were an expected side effect.

"Luce, I don't want to talk about my past anymore. I don't want to hash out over and over again how many times I've screwed things up," he said, his hands curling into fists. "I know you girls have some sick fascination with knowing the name, time, and how we screwed the girls before you, but I'm not giving that to you. It was a lot, probably even a lot more than the number you've got in your head"—my stomach dropped—"but I didn't love a single one of them, and not a single one of them loved me either."

"Sounds romantic," I muttered, shoving my tray away.

"You're the one who wanted to know," he said, straddling the bench to face me. "Listen, with a guy like me, don't ask questions you don't want to know the answers to, Luce, because I'm going to do my damnedest to be honest with you. Don't delve into my past unless you want to come out on the other side wishing you hadn't."

I'd learned that a while ago, but how could you have a relationship with someone you didn't know on a past, present, and future tense level? "So if you didn't care for any of them and none of them cared for you, why did you"—every term bouncing to mind was just wrong—"do it?"

"You want to know this?" he asked, challenging me with his eyes. "You really want to know this kind of stuff?"

I nodded once, because I was a stupid girl.

Jude's nod echoed mine. "For me, it was an escape. A way to forget my life was shit for a little while. And for the girls," he said, lifting his shoulders, "they were hoping to piss off their mayor and doctor parents when they discovered their precious daughters were screwing the quintessential bad boy. That, or they just were really hot for me and wanted to know what I was like in the sack." His smile curled up on one side, which I put to a quick end as my elbow connected with his stomach.

"This isn't funny," I scolded, scowling at the picnic table because it was impossible to scowl into his face.

"Sorry, sorry," he laughed, rubbing my arms. "Sometimes the only way I can get through reminiscing about my shitty life is through humor," he said, tilting my face upward. "But the humorless, honest truth is that I didn't care about them, and they didn't care about me." He stared hard into my eyes, and he couldn't stare at me the way he was now and not be honest.

"Okay," I said, relieved this topic was officially off the books now.

"And if it helps you to know, the sex was unfulfilling and unsatisfactory."

"It doesn't help, but thanks for the footnote," I said, snatching my apple back up.

"You know, it seems like you and me are either kissing the shit out of each other or discussing topics that are better kept in the graves they were buried in," he said, biting into the pizza. "Why can't we just have normal, everyday conversation?"

I thought this over while I crunched into my apple. "You're right," I said. "How can you be my boyfriend if I don't know your political views, or what you think about the weather, or what you thought of the last movie you saw at the theater?"

"Point taken," he laughed, chugging an entire can of pop in five seconds flat. "Screw the everyday crap. And the rotting corpse topics too. Just keep kissing me, or whatever else you might have in mind," he said, wagging his brows, "until you've stockpiled enough crazy on my brain shelf I can't talk straight anymore."

"That sounds like a fulfilling relationship," I said, turning and straddling the bench to face him. Since we weren't ones for the lighter points of conversation, might as well delve into one of the deeper areas that had been plaguing me. "Why do you like me, Jude? Really? In the looks department, I'm the ordinary to your extraordinary. In the personality department, I'm the girl who puts on a tough act but fights off just as many insecurities as the next girl. In the future department, I just want to set the world on fire with my dancing. I don't have aspirations of becoming the first woman president, or finding a cure to childhood diabetes, or unveiling the formula for fusion. So why does a guy like you go for a girl like me?"

I could tell from his expression that he didn't understand what I was saying. "Luce, are you kidding? What do I see in you? Please. What do you see in *me*?" he answered, shaking his head. "And if you must know, it's not one thing I can put my finger on, it's a bunch of little things that add up to a whole lot of amazing."

"Specific," I mumbled.

He threw his hands in the air in exasperation. "Fine, if you want me to pinpoint one of the many reasons I like you, here's one," he said, staring at me. "I knew if there was ever a girl who could love me, warts and all, it would be the girl who went to the pound and adopted the ugliest, meanest piece of crap she could find." My heart swelled, my smile following. "All because she believed that under every rough exterior was a soul begging to be loved and accepted."

Still smiling. I'd probably still be smiling into sixth period from his words.

"Good answer?" he asked, knowing it was.

"Not bad," I understated.

"Dare me to continue? Because I will sit out here with you all afternoon and sing your praises if you need any more convincing. All. Day. Long."

I scooted closer, dropping my hands to his knees. "Nah," I said. "How about you just shut up and kiss me already?"

"Sounds like a plan." His mouth was so close to touching mine I could already taste it when a backpack slammed down on the table across from us.

"Hey, Lucy."

"Lord help me."

Jude's and Sawyer's sentences overlapped as they both turned to each other.

"Ryder," Sawyer said, sticking out his hand. It hung there awhile before Sawyer stuck it in his pocket. "How's it going?"

"It was going fantastically."

I nudged his leg with mine in warning. So far, Sawyer was playing fair.

"Of course," Sawyer said, looking between the two of us. "Sorry for interrupting you two. I just wanted to say something, and then I'll leave you to it."

"Well," Jude said, tying his arms around me. So territorial. "Say something."

Sawyer smiled. "I didn't want you to get the wrong idea if

you heard about me taking Lucy home after Homecoming. I saw a friend who needed help, and I helped her. I know she's your girl, Jude."

"So does that mean you'll stop staring at her every time you see her in the hall?" Jude asked, drilling Sawyer.

"I'll try," he said, stretching his neck. "She's a beautiful girl, Ryder. You're a lucky man."

"Don't tell me what I have like I don't know it," Jude said, his arms stiffening. "And if you think I'm letting you anywhere near Luce after what you've done, you've got another think coming."

"Jude," I warned.

"Wow, easy, big guy," Sawyer said, lifting his hands and walking backward. "I didn't mean to offend you, just wanted to say my piece and get to lunch." Glancing at me, his smile tipped higher. "See you in fifth period, Lucy."

I shot him a wave as he shoved through the door.

"I didn't think I could hate that shithead more, but I should've known a dick of that degree has no hate limit." Jude glared at the door Sawyer had walked through.

"Has anyone ever mentioned you might have anger issues?" I said. From the flash of hatred in Jude's eyes, you would have thought he'd never loathed anyone more.

Jude's face softened just barely. "Only a few dozen times a year since puberty."

Curling my fingers through his, I took another bite of

apple. "What has Sawyer Diamond done to make you that pissed every time you see him?" I said, crunching apple bits. "Because other than having an overinflated sense of self and a smile so white it doesn't register on the color palette, he doesn't seem like that bad of a guy to me."

Jude spun on me, his eyes bleeding to black. "Sawyer Diamond is what happens when God turns his head for one second. A guy like that doesn't deserve second chances, or mercy, or understanding, especially from a girl like you, Luce, because he will twist that into something he can use to manipulate you." His hands braced around my arms, holding me tight. "I want you to stay away from him, Luce. Don't talk to him, or look at him, or acknowledge him in any way. You got me? Because he can deny it all he wants and pretend he's a cheerleader for you and me, but he wants you so damn bad he's probably in the guys' room jacking off right now."

"Ew, Jude," I said, making a face. "Gross."

"Just stay away from him, Luce," he said. "I've known that dick for ten years now, and I can tell when he's up to something. And he's up to something."

The lunch bell rang. We both groaned, tossing our half-eaten lunches into the garbage. "I have three classes with the guy. How am I supposed to stay away from him?" I asked, while Jude wrangled up our bags and slung them over his back.

"I want you to kick him in the nuts every time you see him," he said, not a trace of teasing in his voice, "and after a few of those, he'll stay away from you."

"Now why didn't I think of that?" I said, thumping the palm of my hand against my forehead.

"Because you're sweet and innocent and don't know about sinister things like deflecting dirtbags," he said, opening the courtyard door for me. "Leave the dirty work to me, Luce. You stay your sweet self."

"And nut kicking isn't considered dirty work in your world?"

"If it's Sawyer Diamond's balls we're talking about kicking," he said, grimly grinning, "he deserves it and more."

SIXTEEN

A few weeks passed, and the photo worked its way to the bottom of the drama pile as the talk of the town shifted to Southpointe High's newest quarterback.

Jude had single-handedly turned a historically cursed team into the top-ranked team in the conference. We were at four and one, and the one loss happened during the first game of the season before I forced Jude into joining. Pulling only about a million strings, I'm sure, Coach A was able to keep Jude from getting suspended, or even serving a few game suspensions thanks to his "stolen" car escapade. That might have had something to do with me cornering him in his office one day and pleading with him to give Jude another second chance. Just as I was about to give up on Coach A, he sighed. "I can't refuse a request from the sister of my once-upon-a-time all-star," he relented.

I'd repaid his leap of faith by baking him chocolate chip cookies every day for a week. From the way Jude played, I almost sensed he was paying Coach A back in touchdowns and wins for believing in him. All was right in the universe again, short-lived as I knew it would be.

I told Jude I expected half his earnings when he was a big-time NFL quarterback. He said I could have it all. The ironic thing was that the day after I'd said that, Coach A was given the heads-up that a crap load of scouts would be at Thursday's upcoming game. All the guys on the team were bragging about it, but everyone knew the only reason a dozen scouts would be in attendance at a Southpointe game was due to one Jude Ryder.

"Aren't you a vision in gold sequins and crimson sparkle," a voice I'd been avoiding said as the rest of the dance team and I were taking the field for the halftime performance.

I exhaled, looking for Jude. He towered over a huddle of seemingly tiny high school boys, completely in the moment.

So I replied, "Hi, Sawyer." I could've sounded more enthused, but I'd avoided him for a reason. If Jude said he was someone to steer clear of, that meant he was someone to steer clear of.

"What?" he said, sliding up to me. "Was that an actual

verbal response? Couldn't be."

"You're reminding me why I've been verbally absent around you," I said, stretching my dance top lower. Like most high school dance teams, Southpointe's ascribed to the less-is-more motto of dance wear, and up until Sawyer's eyes slid down me, I hadn't minded the lack of cover.

"Sorry," he said. I took a step to the side. "My ego's not used to this kind of rejection." He crossed his arms, inspecting the field as the teams lined up. I took another step to the side in case Jude glanced up before the hike. I knew he'd march right off the field midplay if he saw Sawyer sidled up against me. "How's Jude?" he asked tightly.

I glanced pointedly at Sawyer's jersey tucked into his jeans, then at the place he occupied on the bench. "Kicking ass."

Sawyer laughed, glancing at the scoreboard. "I can see that. From the looks of it, if he keeps dominating the rest of the game, he's going to get about twenty football scholarships tomorrow morning." Looking up into the stands, he focused on the clump of scouts. A dozen had grown to two dozen, and not a single one of them had taken their eyes off Jude tonight. They were drooling for him, and I was so damn proud of him, I'd made special arrangements for tonight. Much to my dismay, Jude had insisted we take things slow these past few weeks, but with the lingerie I'd picked out and what I had in mind, he'd swear off slow for good.

I forgot Sawyer was there until he cleared his throat. "I've missed you, Lucy."

Damn, I didn't need this right now. The dance squad was getting ready to hit the field, and I was pretty sure Jude had just caught a glimpse of Sawyer beside me. I weaved farther into the cluster of my dance mates.

"Why are you avoiding me?" Sawyer asked, sliding right up beside me again. "What did Ryder tell you to make you turn anti–Sawyer Diamond?"

I'd resisted for three weeks, but I was coming very close to following Jude's words of advice and kicking him in the balls.

"I'm avoiding you because Jude told me to, because he said you're not someone I should be hanging around," I said, feeling no need to explain myself to him, but it felt good to shout a little at him.

"You do everything Ryder tells you to do?"

Okay, now I was seething. Implying I had no backbone and did my boyfriend's every bidding flicked my temper switch to the on position.

Turning on him, I took a step into him and then another, until he was backed up against the fence. "Listen to me, you arrogant ass," I said, resting my hands on my hips so I wouldn't slap him. "I'm avoiding you because I don't like you. I don't like the way you leer at me, or the way you smile at me, or the way you have this sense of entitlement. I don't like the way you saunter down the school halls like you own the place, and I really don't like the way you throw corn kernels at the band table every day. You're pretentious, and sneaky, and rude," I said, ready to fire only about a hundred more insults when I heard the buzzer announce the end of the quarter. "And ugly," I added, knowing this was the one that would sting the most for a guy like Diamond.

"You asked him about Holly yet?" Sawyer said suddenly, pushing off the fence and stepping toward me.

I stepped backward. "I don't need to," I said. "I trust him. Trust, Sawyer. You might want to look that one up in the dictionary and give it a shot one day."

"And maybe you and your trust should follow him one day to a derelict trailer down in SouthView Park," he said, ambling back to the bench. "You might find Jude's the one who needs to look up 'trust' in the dictionary."

I waited until Sawyer turned before plopping onto the grass. I couldn't breathe. I couldn't move. And I had to dance lead in a brand-new routine in three minutes. I was pissed at myself for letting Sawyer get to me, and I was even more pissed at myself for letting him drop that seed of doubt in my mind again. I could trust Jude. I did trust him.

So why did I feel my heart in my throat? Why did my stomach feel like it was about to explode? Why did I hate the name Holly on principle alone?

The dance team was making a circle around me, everyone kneeling around me, asking if I needed some water. I shook my head, watching Jude lead the team off the field. I could trust that man. I was falling in love with that man.

Like he could read my thoughts, he looked over just then, his eyes falling on me, a smile already in position until he saw my face. He stopped abruptly as a wave of players passed him. The smile faded from his face as he jogged across the field toward me.

Not now, not now, I told myself. Halftime, when he had twenty of the best coaches in the country here watching him, was not the time to bring up Holly. Later, after the game, so I could put the Holly ghost that haunted me to rest.

"Luce," he said, sliding his helmet off. "Are you all right?" Lifting his hands, he ran them over my face.

No was the honest answer, but yes was the answer I needed to give. Perhaps I needed to review the finer points of trust too.

"I'm fine," I said, resting my cheek into his hand. "Just a little light-headed. I forgot to eat dinner again." I rolled my eyes like I was hopeless.

"Somebody get me some water!" Jude shouted. "And a granola bar or something!" He kissed me softly. "Dammit, woman, you mean too much to me. Eat, okay?"

I nodded, taking the Styrofoam cup from someone's hands.

"I've got a defensive line that needs a tongue-lashing, so I better get going." He kissed my cheek and stood up.

"And a couple dozen scouts to impress," I added, taking another sip.

"That's already been taken care of," he said, snapping his helmet back on.

I smiled. "All right, cocky, run along. I'll wait for you after the game. I've got something planned," I said, lifting my brows.

He stopped, glancing back, his face unreadable. "Hey, Luce, rain check on tonight, okay? I'm sore as all hell already, and I'm going to be lucky if I can make it home upright. Tomorrow night?"

That stomach-exploding feeling peaked. "Don't you need a ride?"

"Meyers offered to drive me home," he said, looking down the field. "That way you won't have to wait for me and listen to a big baby crying for ice and painkillers."

I couldn't talk.

"I gotta go, Luce," he said, jogging backward. "I'll call you tomorrow." As he headed for Southpointe's team tunnel, he called over his shoulder, "Your turn to kick some dance ass on that field, Luce. Don't let me down."

I bent my head over my knees. "You neither."

SEVENTEEN

T was staging a stakeout on my own boyfriend. So much for the trust I was so confident I had in him a couple of hours ago. I was becoming so up and down, so hot and cold, I bet I could have been declared certifiable. It wouldn't have been a first occurrence.

Southpointe, as anticipated, obliterated the top-seeded team in the conference, making Southpointe, for the first time in its history, number one. Jude came back from halftime like a twenty-four-point lead was inexcusable, widening that gap by another twenty-one. It was like watching a team of gods play a team of mortals, Jude playing the part of Zeus.

I'd managed to suck it up and dance my ass off during halftime before running to the girls' locker room and changing so I could blend into the herd of raving fans in the bleachers. I knew he was looking for me, even hurt I wasn't down on the sidelines cheering him on, but I was in no mood to cheer. Not even in a mood to pretend to cheer, and I couldn't give him any reason to suspect something wasn't right.

I couldn't have him checking over his shoulder for his girlfriend, identifying her crouched down and hoodie up behind the wheel of her car. Because then, like the good, trusting girlfriend I wasn't, I couldn't tail him to see where he was really headed tonight.

It was nearing the hour mark following the end of the game, when almost all the players' cars were long gone, when he emerged from the locker room. Scottie Meyers wasn't with him. He was alone.

People preach to you about pivotal moments like this one. Moments where you have two options, and one choice. One path to head down with no turning back. Choice numero uno: I could jump out of my car, run and throw myself in his arms, and keep playing the fool. That was appealing on just about every level.

And choice numero dos: I could stay put and follow him to wherever he led me, hopefully getting to the bottom of this whole Holly situation or discovering Sawyer was a lying sack of shit. This choice didn't appeal to me at all, but it was the one I had to make.

Because I wasn't one of those girls who could turn a blind

eye while their boyfriend skirted around town. Because I wasn't one of those girls who thought trust was a conditional, open-to-interpretation thing. I was one of those girls who needed to know if my boyfriend was screwing some ex-flame behind my back so I could wind up miserable, heartbroken, but at least informed. I guess.

Jude skipped the parking lot, weaving through the weeds. Heading south.

As in SouthView Park.

Wherever he was going, he was traveling on foot, so that meant tailing him in the Mazda would be impossible.

So I peeled out of the parking lot, heading for the place that he was most likely headed and the place I most wanted him not to show up at.

I didn't know the way to get to the trailer park. It wasn't exactly my summer hangout, but a few wrong turns followed by a few more right turns and the help of one gas station employee, and I was pulling into SouthView Trailer Park, where, according to the sign, THE VIEW'S BETTER DOWN HERE.

It wasn't a big park, only two rows of trailers taking up a quarter mile or so of road. There was no view I could see, unless you counted the rusting walls of your neighbor's trailer, and there wasn't a single pot of flowers or one hanging basket to be seen. I noticed because this was the first year we hadn't had flowers on our front steps. People who were

253

worried about paying their electric bills and were putting ramen noodles on the table didn't buy flowers.

I parked in a spot where the streetlamps wouldn't shine on my car, hoping he hadn't beaten me here. Hoping he wasn't going to show up at all, because if he did, if I had to watch him shimmy into some other girl's trailer late on a Thursday night, I'd know the truth. I'd know everything I'd believed we had was false. I'd question any and all love I'd experience in the future.

Despite knowing better, I held on to one last hope that I was wrong and Jude wasn't going to come knocking on Holly's door.

One minute later, I watched a familiar body cut through a couple of trails and lumber down the weed-lined driveway in my direction. He passed beneath the streetlights, flashing light, then dark, clutching a couple of clear plastic bags.

He was almost at the end of the road, the Mazda was only a couple of trailer lengths away in the dark, when I realized he wasn't here to make a trailer visit, he was here for me. He'd caught a glimpse of me weaving around town like a woman on a mission and somehow followed me here and was going to talk some sense into me. I didn't care about the questions he'd ask or the explanations I'd have to give, because he was here for me. Sawyer could shove his trust nugget up his ass.

I was remembering how to smile as Jude passed the last trailer. I was about to open the door, tackle him to the ground, and kiss the sense out of him. He cut a sharp corner around the last trailer. He leaped up the stairs of the rust can in front of me, and tapped on the door.

My heart broke.

I couldn't breathe as I waited for that trailer door to open.

The door screeched open, illuminating Jude in soft yellow light. I told myself that he wasn't the man I was falling for. A girl, right about my age, appeared in the doorway wearing a pretty summer dress and a prettier smile. She kind of looked like me, but her hair was shorter.

She threw her arms around Jude and he did the same, lifting her off her toes.

This was not happening; it was a dream, a nightmare.

The air in the car started to suffocate me. I lowered the window, sucking in mouthfuls of cool air.

"You're late," the girl said after Jude lowered her down. I knew in my heart she was Holly.

"Walking a few miles on foot after playing the late game can make a man late," he said, leaning back into the stair railing. "I made it, though, didn't I?"

Holly rubbed Jude's arm, admiring him like he was the sun, the moon, and the stars. I knew that look of admiration, and after tonight, I never would know it again.

"You always do," Holly replied, flashing a coy grin. "How was the game?"

"Good," Jude answered. "We kicked Valley's ass."

"Valley needs to get their ass kicked," she said, sliding out of her sweater. Both arms were covered in intricate tattoos, from her wrist to her shoulder. It would have made me feel better if she was tipping the ugly scale, but she wasn't. She was better-looking than me. "I wish I could have come, but that's a whole lotta drama I'm not ready to deal with yet."

"Yeah, it's probably for the best."

Then a cry cut through the door, disrupting the quiet night. A cry that made the pit in my stomach expand.

"*Un momento*," she said, lifting a finger and disappearing into the trailer.

Jude stayed where he was, staring up into the night sky, when suddenly, he tensed. Shoving off the railing, he glanced to the side, then the other side. He was just about to turn around, and I was about to get the hell out of there, when Holly reappeared in the doorway, holding something in her arms.

A baby.

This was the part where I knew I should jump out of the car, march up those dilapidated stairs, and give Jude Ryder a piece of my mind and the back of my hand. But I didn't, because I realized Holly and the baby had been around long before me. They'd had the claim to Jude before I'd even known I wanted one.

"Isn't this guy supposed to be asleep by now?" Jude said, making a funny face at the baby. The baby squealed in delight, flapping his little hands.

"Teething," Holly said, sighing.

"Trade me," Jude said, dropping the bags at Holly's feet and holding out his arms. She handed the baby over, and he stopped crying immediately as Jude started bouncing and patting his back.

"Thanks for picking up diapers and formula, Jude," she said, picking up the bags. "I was getting dangerously close to tearing my sheets into makeshift diapers."

"Of course," Jude said, kissing the top of the baby's head. "Anytime."

"I don't know what we'd do without you," she said, looking at the baby, something sad in her voice.

"You'd be all right, Holly," he said, making another face at the baby. "But I'm glad I'm able to help."

"Well, are you going to sleep out on the porch?" she asked, propping a hand on her hip.

"I'd rather not." He smiled.

"Well, get in here," she said, stepping aside. "I've got plans for you tonight."

"Boy, little Jude," he said, holding the baby in front of

him, "your mama sure is bossy."

Holly sighed, grabbing Jude's arm and pulling him in. He shut the door.

I needed to get out of here. I needed to go home. I needed to forget about Jude. I needed a good hard cry to get him out of my system.

I waited a few more minutes, turning the key over in the ignition when a light went out in a back room. I was not going to be there when that trailer started rocking.

I tore out of the trailer park, the roads leading home blurry because I couldn't contain my tears. So Sawyer was right and I was wrong. I couldn't trust Jude, and I never should have. Jude himself had warned me about himself, but I wasn't smart enough to listen.

My boyfriend, my ex-boyfriend, although I wasn't sure if I could even call him that, had a second life stuffed away in a crummy trailer. This shit did not happen in real life.

My hands were shaking over the steering wheel by the time I got home. The cabin was dark, and it was the first thing that had gone right in the past hour.

I was through the door and up the stairs in five seconds flat. I slid into my bedroom noiselessly, grabbed the shopping bag with the garments I'd intended to put on so Jude could take them off, and chucked it in the garbage can. Flopping on my bed, I knew if I took my finger out, the dam holding back the flood would shatter. I couldn't decide whether I needed to let myself go or if I needed to keep myself together.

Jude was the kind of guy who'd I'd thought deserved a second chance, but after what I'd learned tonight, he didn't seem worth the effort anymore.

I sat up in frustration, and something on my desk caught my eye. A yellow envelope that had remained unopened. Until tonight.

Snatching it off my desk, I tore the packet open. My future seemed easier to accept now that it was so bleak right now.

I held the top sheet in front of me, scanning the all-important first paragraph. My breath caught as I sank to the floor.

EIGHTEEN

A few hours of sleep had flipped my emotion meter from anguish to anger. I woke up Friday morning ready to give Jude hell. I had to remind myself as I got ready for school that I hated him, but I hoped that after enough reminders, it would become second nature. I threw on a sundress, one that I realized later was awfully similar to Holly's, and grabbed a sweater out of my closet for good measure.

Mom was already gone, and Dad was thirty minutes deep into *Sergeant Pepper's*, so it made getting out of the house speed-bump free. During the drive to school, I rehearsed what I was going to say to him. What words would do the most damage, what expressions would show me at my most incurably pissed.

I was sure I had it all down pat until I pulled into my

parking spot, only to find someone standing on the patch of grass in front of it, waiting for me.

Jude waved, grinning at me. A man shouldn't be able to grin like that at a girl he was cheating on.

I had a moment of getting choked up, looking at what I was about to lose, but I quickly reminded myself he wasn't mine to lose in the first place.

I took a deep breath, and then threw the door open.

"You look nice," Jude greeted.

"Don't look at me that way," I said, slamming the door. "Because you won't be peeling off this dress."

His face pinched with confusion, the smile fading. "Did someone wake up on the wrong side of the bed?"

"At least I didn't wake up in the wrong bed." I came around the front of the car, crossing my arms.

"Luce," he said, pausing. "What the hell are you talking about?"

"Don't play dumb with me," I warned, "and don't try to make me out to be dumb. You fooled me for a while, good for you, but not anymore."

"Hey," he said, lifting his hands and walking toward me. "What's the matter? Why are you so upset?" He tried wrapping his arms around me, but I shoved him away.

"I can answer both those questions with one word," I said, glowering at him. "Holly."

His eyes widened for the shortest second. "What about Holly?"

I huffed, trying not to meet his eyes. I could achieve a higher degree of anger if I didn't look into them. "I've arrived at my own conclusions about Holly, but why don't you tell me your story? Because I'm sure it's an interesting one."

He wrapped his hands around his neck, tilting his head back to survey the sky. "Holly is my friend."

I laughed. "A friend who invites you into her trailer with a baby on her hip? A friend who greets you with a cute little dress and spreads her legs for you later? After the baby's tucked in, of course."

"You were there last night," he said, almost to himself. "I had this feeling, like you were right there. Turns out I was right." He looked straight through me.

"Yeah, damn right I was there last night," I said, "and I saw everything."

"And why were you there?" he asked, staying calm. "Why did you follow me?"

"Because someone had been telling me for weeks now that you and Holly were having this thing behind my back, but I ignored it because I thought I could trust you." I paused, biting my tongue because I was too close to crying. I couldn't let him see how he had hurt me. "Boy, was I never so wrong about anything in my life."

"Let me get this straight, because you're talking like a crazy woman right now and I'm having a tough time following." Jude exhaled. "Someone told you Holly and I were getting it on behind your back? Someone told you where she lived and where I was banging her brains out?" he asked, shifting his weight. "And you believed them?" His voice wavered, like he was hurt, but he didn't fool me. This kind of man had perfected his acts, all his acts, in order to juggle multiple women.

"I'm glad I did," I answered. "Turns out I was right." The parking lot was filling up, and we were catching more attention than I wanted.

"Who told you about Holly?"

"That doesn't matter," I said, glaring at a group of girls trying to get within hearing distance.

"Trust me, when it comes to Holly, it does matter." He was defending her, to me. I needed to get angrier.

"Sawyer told me, okay?" I said.

Jude's face shadowed, his jaw straining. "Sawyer Dickhead Diamond told you I was cheating on you with Holly." He paused, swallowing. "And you believed him?" His face was etched in pain.

I bit my cheek and nodded.

"Why didn't you just ask me?"

Why hadn't I just asked him? It was a question I hadn't

asked myself yet, and it was one I couldn't answer. So I made something up. "Because you would have lied."

His eyes closed, his head sagging. "So you trust Sawyer more than you trust me?"

Yesterday, that would have been answered with a "Hell, no," but today I wasn't sure. One sad nod was all I was capable of.

"Then I guess there's nothing left to say," he said.

"Oh, there's plenty more to say," I said.

"Sounds like there's just one thing to say," he said, shifting his weight, staring at me like he didn't recognize me.

I knew that was where this whole thing was leading, but I wasn't ready. I couldn't say it yet.

"Don't worry about me, babe. I've seen so many backs walking away from me that this is old hat," he said, shrugging like this wasn't killing him like it was killing me. "Say it," he said, his voice shaking.

I bit my cheek. I wanted answers, explanations.

"Say it!" he yelled, charging forward, the sinews of his neck bursting through his skin.

I swallowed and closed my eyes. "Bye, Jude." Turning away, I walked across the parking lot, warning myself not to look back.

I rarely heeded my warnings, as this whole Jude mess had proven.

Glancing back, I found him standing in the same spot, frozen in place. And then he turned and walked away.

The excited buzz of a Friday morning echoed down the hall when I weaved through the metal detectors. Everyone acted like nothing had happened, like my world hadn't just fallen apart.

I stood there, unable to move. Students shuffled by me, some ignorant, and others staring at me like I was an exhibit at the zoo.

"OMG, Lucy!" Taylor said, popping up beside me. "What happened with you and Jude? Did you guys break up? Did he drop out? He just walked off the school grounds and kept going. What is going on?" she asked, shaking my arm. "Lucy." She snapped her fingers in front of my face. "What is with you?"

I was suffocating, really suffocating. I'd had asthma as a child, nothing real serious, but I outgrew it before middle school. Or I thought I'd outgrown it. My lungs felt like deflated balloons, and my breaths came out in short, panicked bursts.

I needed a way out.

A hand grabbed mine from behind, spinning me around. "Let's get you out of here," Sawyer said, pulling me under his arm and guiding me to the door.

"Sawyer, what the hell's going on?" Taylor shouted after us.

"Put a clamp on it, Taylor," he muttered, shoving the door open.

The fresh air helped right away. My breathing slowed as my lungs filled to half capacity. A tear finally slipped free.

"I've got you," Sawyer said, squeezing my arms as he led me to his shiny white car. He helped me into the car, snapped my seat belt into place, and reclined the seat.

I covered my eyes with my forearms, letting another tear escape.

Sawyer crawled in beside me, fired the engine, and flew out of the parking lot. He rolled down my window, allowing another rush of air to fill my lungs. I was almost breathing normally again.

"Thank you," I said after a while. I didn't know where we were going, I was beyond caring, but I didn't care as long as it was in the opposite direction of Southpointe.

"Yeah," he replied, "it was kind of the least I could do, since I was the one responsible for you feeling the way you are."

"How are you responsible for me feeling like crap?"

"Because I was the one who told you about Holly," he said, cutting down a gravel driveway.

I stiffened at the name. "You weren't the one screwing her."

Sawyer chuckled tightly. "Not that I recall."

We rolled to a stop. "Are you busting into Bon Jovi's or something?" I asked, gawking at the McMansion in front of us. It was on the lake, but unlike the other cabins, this was a cabin on steroids.

"This is my place," he said with a shrug, shoving open the door.

I didn't move; I hadn't anticipated Sawyer would take me to his place. This didn't feel right—showing up at another guy's house during school hours, thirty minutes after I'd broken up with my cheating boyfriend. If this got out, in addition to the slutty girl known for giving a guy head in between classes, I'd also be labeled a rebound opportunist.

"Don't worry, my parents aren't home," he said, mistaking the apprehension written on my face.

The fact that we were totally alone in this mini hotel did not ease my mind, but I didn't want to stay in his car all day and I wanted to return to school even less, so I stepped out and shut the door.

"So this is your place?" I said, using my hand to shield my eyes to take a closer look. "Then your dad's Bon Jovi?"

Sawyer laughed. "Nope. My dad's not nearly that cool. He just owns a few car dealerships in the state."

That explained the fancy car Sawyer drove.

"Come on," he said, tilting his head toward the house. "Let's get you some ice cream therapy, and then we'll talk."

"I can guarantee, even if that whole house is filled with ice cream," I said, following him, "it wouldn't be enough therapy to cure me."

"How about I'll pick up where the ice cream leaves off?" he said, grabbing my hand.

Because I didn't know which other way to go, I went along.

NINETEEN

"Your ice cream's melting," Sawyer said, contemplating the bowl between us.

I slipped my toes deeper in the sand, wrapping my arms around my legs. "I told you inside, I'm not in the mood for ice cream."

"Something so bad ice cream can't fix it?" he said, tossing a rock into the lake. "Okay, let's talk."

"Not in the mood."

"Of course you're not," he said. "That's why you need to. Once you get it out of your system, you'll feel better."

"I doubt it." Talking wouldn't change what I'd seen.

"Let's give it a shot. I'll even get the conversation ball rolling." He slid his sunglasses on top of his head and took a deep breath. "I'm guessing this has something to do with Jude and Holly?"

Hearing their names together was ten times worse than just hearing her name. "Is this the part where you sneer I told you so at me?" I snapped. "Because I'll save you the trouble." I looked over at him. "Yeah, you were right. You told me so. Jude's still with Holly." That lump in my throat returned. I was so sick of it I wanted to reach down my throat and manually remove it.

Sawyer sighed, shaking his head. "How did you find out?"

"I followed the bastard to her trailer park last night. She has a baby, Sawyer," I said, grabbing a rock and hurling it into the lake. "They have a baby together, and he didn't feel the need to mention any of this to me." My voice was breaking, and the tears were finally flowing. "They have a cute, teething, precious little baby and he didn't tell me." Each word was its own sentence, since I was doing the sobbing-while-trying-to-talk thing.

"Ah, hell, Lucy." Sawyer draped his arm over me. "I'm sorry. This is exactly the reason I tried to tell you early on about her, before you and Jude got too involved. I knew it would tear you up when you found out."

"I trusted him, Sawyer," I cried. "I trusted him. And he lied to me. What kind of screwed up is that?"

He slid my wet, matted hair behind my ear. "Some people just thrive off manipulating others, you know? We search for some deeper, honorable explanation, but some people are just messed up."

"Well, you were right. And I was wrong. Jude and I are finished," I said, getting ahold of myself. "That's a chapter in my life I want to close the book on and never open again."

"Sounds like you need a fresh start," he said, dropping his arm now that the only effect of the hysterics was a red, puffy face.

"I'll take two," I said, wiping the mascara likely smeared beneath my eyes.

"I know this might seem sudden, but hear me out," he began, twisting in the sand to face me. "The Sadie Hawkins dance is next weekend, and I've already told three girls no because I lied and said I was already going with another girl."

He was right. This was about a hundred miles per hour too fast. "Sawyer," I warned, about to stand up.

"Wait," he said, grabbing my knee. "Just hear me out on this before you say anything."

I sat back down and waited.

"So now I'm in a jam because if I don't show up, these three poor girls will know I gave them the brush-off, and if I show up with some other girl, they're going to know I lied."

"Wait," I said, narrowing my eyes. "Who exactly did

you tell them you were going with?"

I already knew the answer. "You," he said, having the decency to look ashamed.

"Sawyer," I groaned, rocking in the sand. "My life is complicated enough without you making it more so."

"I know and I'm sorry, but here's part two of you hearing me out." He took in a breath and squared his shoulders. "I like you, Lucy. More than I should, and a hell of a lot more than you like me. I've been biding my time, waiting for you to wake up and smell the Jude heartache, and now that you have, I know at least half a dozen guys are going to be standing in line at your locker tomorrow morning." He paused, judging me for my reaction, but I still wasn't sure how to react. "Would you do me a favor and just give me a shot? One shot, and go to Sadie Hawkins with me. I swear I'll behave like we are nothing more than friends, and maybe, if you feel the same way, we could figure this thing out together."

Every acceptable response escaped me.

"For me, Lucy? Just this one thing, and if you still feel the way you do now, I promise I'll leave you alone." For the first time, Sawyer's bronzy skin didn't appear so golden. He was pale, and scared, and vulnerable. "I don't want to live my life with regrets, and I know I would regret it every damn day of my life if we didn't at least give us a chance."

My life had officially just become a daytime soap opera.

Because Sawyer was a friend, and had had my back from the very beginning despite me going off on him on numerous occasions, and because I felt indebted to him, I said, "Fine. We'll go to Sadie's together."

"We'll have a blast, I promise," he said. "And I can assure you, I don't have any love children I'm keeping a secret."

I leveled him with my glare.

"Sorry," he said, "that was in bad taste."

"Exceptionally."

He grabbed my hand, his fingers weaving through mine. "Let's give this thing a shot, Lucy. Nice and slow and see what happens."

"Nice. And. Slow," I reiterated, because I knew Sawyer had it all on paper. He was what drove women to cat-fight and to drink and to swoon. He was just the vanilla version to Jude's chocolate. He had it all: looks, money, personality, but he didn't have one thing yet. And that was my heart.

"We'll walk before we run," he said, squeezing my hand.

TWENTY

awyer and I walked right through Sadie Hawkins. Were still walking into November and pushing a twelve-minute-mile jog by December. By Sawyer's standards, I was fairly certain he was ready to run, maybe even go the distance, but I wasn't anywhere close to that.

Sawyer wouldn't be my first, but I also knew I didn't want him to be my last, so then, what was the point? I didn't get into bed with a guy just because we'd reached that stage in our relationship. It had to feel right; I had to be able to see myself with him months or maybe even years down the road.

I might be Sawyer's girlfriend, but I pictured someone else's face when he had me pinned against a couch. I saw another face when I looked at him. Period.

I know that Jude skipped a few days of class after our parking lot explosion, then showed up for his next football game and hadn't missed a day since.

I saw him every day in the halls and a couple of times around town, but he didn't see me. He hadn't spared one glance my way since that day, and I never knew that kind of rejection could hurt the way it did. I reminded myself every morning what he'd lied about, what he'd failed to mention, and every night I wound up thinking about the way his eyes would lighten right before he kissed me.

I'd been to every football game of the season. At the home games I was expected to be there because the dance team performed during halftime, but I traveled to the away games too. I let everyone assume I was there to support Sawyer, who, even after his ankle healed, never returned to the starting quarterback position. However, if anyone had been watching me, they would have seen who my eyes lingered on. And it wasn't my boyfriend's jersey number who I silently cheered for.

Jude Ryder took up residence in my soul, and I couldn't find a way to evict him.

So I threw myself into anything and everything that would keep my mind off Jude. Dance was the obvious first choice, but when I wasn't dancing, I was filling my free time walking dogs at the nearby shelter, or attending meetings and functions for one of the half-dozen clubs I'd signed up for. It didn't make a difference. Even dance couldn't erase Jude from the forefront of my mind. He was always there.

The song on the radio came to an end, that damn song that made me all nostalgic and longing for Jude.

"I'll fix you," I said, shutting the radio off.

And then, not at all in slow motion like movies make it seem, a piece of scrap wood bounced off the back of some ramshackle truck, landing in my lane. The Mazda smashed over the shard of wood, and almost immediately I felt it.

"Damn it," I cursed, not able to understand how a sliver of wood could bring down a two-ton moving piece of metal. Nature was fighting back against industry, one tire at a time.

And then a familiar rubber-flopping-against-metal sound echoed through the cab.

"Double damn," I said, knowing I had a spare in the back, but that was all I knew about changing a tire.

Pulling onto the shoulder, I scanned up and down the road, hoping to find some kind of auto-anything-shop. Someone must have been smiling down on me, because not even fifty feet away was a sign that read Premier Auto Repair in front of a blue-and-gray painted building with three open bays.

"Thank. You," I offered up to whoever was listening.

I coaxed the Mazda forward, cringing as the flop-flop-flopping got louder. I really hoped my entire wheel wasn't going to fly off, but if it was, at least the professionals were close by.

A man in his midtwenties, sporting a bowling shirt, walked out of one of the bays. Waving his hand, he motioned me over, pointing at the empty first bay.

A nearby auto shop and a helpful employee. I'd just gotten a call from the miracle network.

Once the Mazda was inside, I got out, wanting to inspect the damage.

"Let me guess," the guy said, wiping his hands off with a cloth. It didn't look like it did any good. "The other guy won." Crouching down to inspect my wheel, he shook his head.

"Sharp projectiles hurling themselves into soft, man-made materials generally do," I replied, kneeling beside him.

"Words to live by," he said, slapping the tire and standing up. "Let's get this taken care of for ya, honey."

"Thank you," I said, standing. "No rush, but any idea how long this might take?" I'd been on my way to the dance studio, hoping to get a full Saturday of dancing in before I was expected to be manning the money box at the lasagna feed the dance team was hosting tonight to raise money for new uniforms, but it seemed as if my plans might be changing.

"You'll be in and out in a jiff, hon," he said, motioning to someone inside the office area. "I'm going to put my best man on it."

And then, inexplicably, goose bumps rose over my arms, and everything around me got warm and bright.

"Hey, Jude," the guy called, "get your ass out here and help this cute little thing."

I could see him through the back windows, his back to the garage, talking on the phone with someone. He hung up the phone and turned around. I'd never before seen a smile disappear so fast. It was a world record, thanks to me.

Then, squaring his shoulders, he marched out of the office, coming around the back of the car.

"What's the problem, Damon?" Jude asked, staring at the car, refusing to look at me.

"Girl had a run-in with a nasty piece of junk," Damon shouted over, his head hidden in the hood of the truck next to us. "Fix whatever needs done. It's on the house."

"Oh, that's not necessary," I said.

Peeking his head out, he looked at me pointedly. "Yeah, it is."

I would have gone back and forth a few more rounds with him, but when Jude breezed by me without so much as a hello, I knew my fight was needed elsewhere.

"Hey, Jude," I said, walking a few steps toward where his back was to me, inspecting the tire.

Shoving into a stand, he walked by me, lips sealed shut and eyes dead ahead. He popped the trunk open and pulled the spare free.

"You've really got this whole silent thing down," I called after him. "Good for you, you've proved your point that you absolutely disdain me"—"disdain" might have been a tad generous for the way Jude ignored me—"but you're really not going to say hi?"

Pausing at the end of a bay, he grabbed a lever. "Hi," he said with no inflection. "Now scoot the hell back so I can get your tire fixed and you can be on your way."

Wow. It was worse than I thought. Jude didn't disdain me—he hated me. However, I didn't hate him, and I wasn't going to pretend I did.

"I heard you got a full ride to just about any university of your choice," I said, hollering over the lift as the Mazda went up.

Watching the car, he responded with a shrug.

The lift shuddered to a stop, and Jude marched for the flat tire. He looked over at me where I was leaning against the wall and glanced away about as fast. "I'm sure those are just rumors. If I get picked up by one of the top football universities, I'd probably just wind up on the bench or getting injured playing with guys a hundred pounds larger."

I couldn't stop the smile that surfaced. Jude was talking to me again. "Was that just a full sentence directed at me?" I asked, tipping my ear.

Hoisting a tool off a bench, he began ratcheting off the lug nuts. "Actually, that was two."

"And what have I done to deserve two complete sentences from you?" I didn't care.

"You're talking to my good side," he said, looking over at me and giving me just barely, but enough of a smile.

I never imagined I'd be thankful for a flat tire, but I added it to the list. "I didn't think you had one."

"I don't," he said, removing the last lug nut. "But damn if one doesn't try to emerge every blue moon." Hoisting what was left of the tire and wheel from the axle, he hefted it on the ground.

Damn if he wasn't the sexiest thing I'd seen in a long time. Maybe ever.

"How have you been?"

"There's a loaded question," he said, cocking a brow at me. "How's the prick known as Sawyer Diamond?" he asked as unemotionally as Jude was capable of when he talked about Sawyer.

"Did you just answer a question with a question?"

Rolling the spare around the side, he glanced up at me

again. This time for a whole second longer. "I just canceled out your question with one of my own. You don't want to answer my question any more than I want to answer yours," he said. "So we're square now."

The man had the most messed-up sense of fair and square.

And, because I was the idiot I was, I broached a topic that I already knew wasn't going to fly well with him. "Jude," I began, staring at my hands, "I'm sorry for everything I said and did."

His body was already tensed as he lifted the spare onto the axle, but it flexed at least 50 percent more. "Can you be any more vague?"

I wasn't going to get defensive. I wasn't going to get defensive. "Was that a request or a jab?" I got defensive.

"If you're thinking about bringing up certain topics," he began, tightening a lug nut like it had done him a world of wrong, "then it was both."

Swallow pride. Apologize. My internal dialogue was having to guide me through this. "I'm sorry I followed you that night to Holly's." I swallowed—something about that name just didn't feel right. "And I'm sorry I went off on you the next morning."

"I don't care about any of that," he said, clenching his jaw.

"You don't?" I crossed my arms. "Then why are you still

so damn pissed at me you're about to blow your lid?" Being someone prone to bouts of temper overload, I could spot another's tics from ten paces.

Jude exhaled, leaning his forehead into the tire. "Damn it all to hell," he muttered, banging his socket wrench on the metal cart behind him. "Because," he began, shifting his eyes over at me, "because you took his word over mine."

That rendered me speechless. In all my midnight over-analyses, I'd never arrived at this conclusion. "And I was wrong to?" I said slowly. "Because it turned out Sawyer was right."

"He was right about what?" Jude said in a tone that was way too controlled.

"You and Holly." Man, I hated saying her name. I was done. She would now be referred to as the tramp who shall not be named.

"Me and Holly, eh?" He fastened another lug nut into place. "So you didn't think to ask me about her before you decided to stage a stakeout? You didn't choose to trust me over him? You believed that piece of shit over me. A guy who lies, cheats, and is no good for someone like you, Luce!"

"Jude," I sighed in frustration, taking another deep breath to stay calm. He wasn't getting it, or I wasn't getting it. One of us was definitely not getting it, and neither of us was speaking the same language. "It turns out I had no reason to trust you."

"And you know this for a fact because?" he asked, fastening the last nut into place. I wasn't ready to say good-bye. Being near him and arguing was better than passing by him and being ignored.

"Because I saw you, Jude," I said, wondering how much I needed to spell out for him to get it. "I saw you with Holly and"—I swallowed—"and the baby. I saw it all."

"You saw me with Holly and the baby," he repeated, nodding his head with each word. "And that's why you can't trust me?"

This should be more obvious than it was to him. Unless cheating behind one's girlfriend's back had become a morally accepted practice recently. "I think that pretty much sums it up," I said, wondering if I was missing something. Something so obvious I was overlooking it.

"Well, there you have it," he said, striding to the opposite wall. "We're at an impasse again. Neither one of us trusts the other." Pressing the lever, he lowered the Mazda to the ground.

I didn't want to go; I wanted to figure out what the hell was going on between us. "I get you're still pissed at me and I'm still a little pissed with you, too," I said, following him around the back. "But do you think we can get over it and be friends again?"

He laughed one low note, heaving the flat tire into the trunk.

"I miss you, Jude. I miss having one friend who actually has my back and isn't throwing daggers at it when I turn around."

He stopped, keeping his back at me. "Sorry, Lucy. You and I can't be friends." Shouldering by me, he went around to the driver's door and opened it.

"Since when do you call me Lucy?" I asked, feeling a new depth of heartbreak.

"Since we stopped being friends." He craned his neck to the side, motioning me into the car.

I wouldn't be herded. I planted my feet and crossed my arms. "You can't make that choice for the both of us," I said, glaring at him. "You don't want to be my friend, fine, that's real big of you. But you can't tell me I can't be your friend. So go screw yourself and deal with it." Hello, temper, nice to see you raising your ugly head again.

His face didn't even soften like it used to when I went off on him. "People like you and me cannot be friends, Luce," he said, staring at me like he used to, "and you know it too."

"What do I know?" I asked, waiting. And waiting. "Come on," I said, marching toward him. "What do I know?" Because, for the umpteenth time, I didn't have a clue.

His lips tightened as he tried to slide aside. I didn't let him. I blocked his path, shoving him back. "Come on, Ryder. What the hell do I know?"

His eyes blazed, meeting mine. "You can't be friends with the person you were meant to spend your life with," he said, his eyes darkening. "So get on with your life and leave mine the hell alone." Nudging by me, he stepped out of the garage and kept going.

What I regretted most, more than anything I'd already screwed up, was that I didn't go after him.

TWENTY-ONE

*E*very day of the rest of the school year, I regretted letting Jude go that day at the garage. I regretted not chasing after him and holding him captive until he explained exactly what the hell he was trying to say. In concise, detailed sentences a woman could decipher.

The months that followed our cryptic conversation left me wishing for the silent treatment back, because now when Jude passed me in the hall, he was no longer intentionally ignoring me. It was as if I didn't exist.

I'd gone from someone he despised to someone he didn't notice.

I turned eighteen and was going to graduate next week. In the fall, I would be a freshman at Marymount Manhattan. It was a time to celebrate, to let down my hair and look back at the past with nostalgia and forward to the future with hope.

I felt like some lost ship in the night, at the very core of me where things like right and wrong, truth and love existed. I knew why.

"I'm calling time-out on your zoning-out bouts tonight, Lucy," Taylor shouted at me over the speakers blasting some song about summer and friends and partying. "Tonight is about nothing but having a killer time and being in the moment."

Sage words coming from a girl who mainly talked about her bright future. "And by that you mean getting smashed and making out with the first piece of ass you see, in the moment?"

Taylor groaned. "And I thought I was a cynic."

Turning the volume down, I pulled up the top of the dress Taylor had stuffed me in and tugged the bottom of it down. Now it covered half of my boobs and most of my ass. "Sorry. It just comes naturally when you've dressed me like a cheap hooker on her way to work."

"You're wearing pearl earrings, for crap's sake, Lucy," she said. "Last time I looked, hookers didn't wear pearls."

"Fine," I said, checking my reflection in the mirror for the third time. Could she have added another coat of mascara before my eyelashes snapped in half? "A hooker on her way to church."

Taylor laughed, staring over at me when we hit a red

light. "Jewelry, huh?" She gave me a scandalous look. "Somebody must have been very good, or very naaauw-tie, to get a pair of pearl earrings for a graduation gift."

"Your depravity never ceases to astound me," I said, sticking my tongue out. "And the earrings were a graduation gift from my parents, not Sawyer."

Thank God he hadn't given me any jewelry yet, because I was about three commitment levels below jewelry.

The light flashed green, and Taylor gunned her little Volkswagen off the line. "You only have yourself to blame for that. Guys get jewelry for girls as a reward for them putting out. It's a simple fact of life."

"Again, you are depraved," I said, rolling down the window. Where I really wanted to be was at the studio, preparing for the next four years of dancing with and against the best. I didn't want to be crammed in a small car with a high school drama vixen, heading to a graduation party where alcohol would be in endless supply and inhibitions would be in no supply, suctioned into a dress that made a Hollywood socialite look like a prude.

"Since I'm seeing no diamond pendants or gold bracelets on you, I'm taking it you're still cock-blocking Sawyer into a coma?" The shit this girl came up with. It might have been funny if it wasn't so sad.

"None of your business."

"So, no," she assumed, whipping the car down a gravel road.

"So, hell no," I edited, since she was going to draw conclusions whether I validated them or not.

"Why not?" she asked as we bumped over the potholes. "You guys have been 'seeing each other' since Sadie's and an official item since winter formal. Are you guys taking it slow or some stupid shit like that?"

"I'm taking it slow," I said as the party grounds came into view. I was familiar with the place, the mansion on the lake. Sawyer's parents were out of town at some auto auction, so he'd decided to throw the most epic graduation party that would go down in the books. His words, not mine. From the end of the road, the Diamonds' place appeared like it was crawling with ants. Drunk ants.

"And Sawyer?" Taylor asked with pointed inflection.

"Sawyer's a guy. Since when have any of them been up for taking things slow in that department?"

"Since never," she said, answering perhaps the most rhetorical question known to woman.

Finding a vacant spot on the grass, Taylor cut the ignition and dabbed on another coat of lip gloss. The satellites were going to be able to pinpoint those lips if she added another glob of that sparkly, shiny goop.

"Taylor, I'm not really feeling this right now," I said,

grabbing her arm. "Let's get in and get out. There's going to be nothing but wasted wannabes in there looking to get laid."

Peaking her brows at me, she smacked her lips. "Exactly."

"I feel this is the time I should discuss the correlation between girls with low self-esteem and guys who use this to their advantage," I said, shoving out of the car and jacking my dress down. The more I pulled it down, the more my boobs came popping over the top.

"What's your point, Debbie Downer?" Taylor said, weaving her elbow through mine.

"Don't be a statistic," I said, flashing an exaggerated smile at her.

"And let me discuss the ramifications for girls who don't put out for their fine, rich boyfriends heading to college in Southern California in the fall," she said, pulling me toward the house, which rumbled with music.

"This ought to be good," I muttered.

"They wind up dried-up, bitter, old hags with a herd of cats and nothing but cobwebs between their legs."

Hanging my head back, I groaned. "Add twisted to depraved and I think we've got Taylor Donovan pigeonholed."

We weren't even on the front lawn and already a cacophony of catcalls and whistles were foghorning at us. "One hour," I said, feeling generous, "and we're out of here."

"Three hours," Taylor countered, giving some guy draped over the front stairs a smile that made me blush. "And don't forget you're my DD tonight, so no skipping out."

I was all for playing chaperone and DD for my friends to make sure they made it through the night safe and in one piece, but I wished I had pawned Taylor off on someone else tonight, because getting through three hours of everyone partying while I felt like the anti-party was going to mean bloodshed.

"It's about time the party showed up," Morrison shouted over the music at us, running his eyes down the two of us like he was using his hands.

"It's officially started now," Taylor replied, feeling like the belle of the ball from the stares we were getting. I suppose when you showed up to a party with inebriated guys rocking a scrap of fabric and a heap of makeup, ogling was par for the course.

"What's your poison, ladies?" Morrison asked, weaving toward the bar area set up on Sawyer's mom's Italian buffet. She would bust something if she saw what was littered on it right now.

"Make it a screwdriver," Taylor yelled over at him.

Morrison's mouth curved up. "I believe I can accommodate that request."

And I still had to put up with two hours and fifty-nine minutes of this hedonism. Looked like someone was going to spend their time down on the hopefully vacant beach.

"Lucy?" Morrison called.

I was smart enough to know you didn't take an open drink from a guy, most of all someone like Luke Morrison.

"I'm good," I said, shooting him a thumbs-up. Leaning into Taylor, I said, "Be good and call me if anyone tries something. I'm getting some fresh air."

"Somebody better try something on me," she replied, putting on a smile as Morrison made his way back to us with a drink in hand.

"Statistics," I said, heading for the back door. "Don't become one."

"Don't become a cobweb-growing old hag!" she shouted after me.

Winding my way through the maze of students in the kitchen, I shoved a couple making out to the side so I could open the refrigerator. One can of pop was stuffed behind all the beer, and that's what the designated driver snatched.

"Hot dress, Lucy!" someone yelled from somewhere in the kitchen. I didn't bother with a response.

"Sawyer's looking for you. Something tells me he's going to be a happy man when he finds you!"

I couldn't get down to the beach fast enough. It was quiet

and almost vacant save for a couple doing the nasty in Mrs. Diamond's lounger. The night was warm, and the water was so still it almost seemed like I could walk out on it without falling beneath the surface.

I slipped out of Taylor's nude sling-backs and walked to the end of the dock. I was going to have my own little party right here. Just me and Mr. Lemon-Lime. I cracked open the can and took a sip. What the hell was wrong with me? When had the girl who used to love being the life of the party become the girl who found a quiet little corner to sulk?

Like most of the questions I posed to myself these days, it always came down to the same answer. The same name.

"Not really my scene either."

I jumped so hard I managed to spill lemon-lime soda all over Taylor's very inappropriate dress. It would be the last time she'd lend me something from her wardrobe, and that made me rather happy.

"Yeah, me neither," I said, wiping the beads of pop off the champagne-colored shiny material. "Obviously."

"Nothing's obvious about you, Lucy Larson."

Those words, and that voice, very much got my attention now I wasn't enraptured with pop removal. Even her voice was sexier than mine.

Holly was wearing a dark pair of skinny jeans and a white T-shirt. I didn't know whether to offer her a seat or bail into the lake and swim for the opposite shore. I didn't know what she knew, if she knew anything at all about me and Jude, and I sure as hell didn't want to round-robin our relationships with Jude together.

In the end, I decided to be civil. "Hey, Holly," I said, "pull up a chair."

She'd obviously sought me out. This wasn't some happenstance meeting. She had something she needed to say. I wanted to get this out of the way so I could continue to fail at trying to move on with my life.

She sat down, setting her red plastic cup to the side, and rolled up her jeans. "I thought I'd have a tough time getting you alone," she said, dipping her feet in the water and scooting closer. "I hear you've become Southpointe's 'it' girl this year."

I didn't want to think about who she'd heard that from.

"If you mean 'it' girl in terms of the one who's had more rumors and half-truths shot at me than an entire club of strippers, than yeah, I guess I did wear that sash this year." I was sounding a little more defensive than I wanted, but I was having a conversation with the girl who my ex-boyfriend had a love child with.

She nodded, staring at the lake. "Sorry I didn't get a chance to hand that crown over personally. My reign ended last year after I dropped out."

I didn't know what to say. I wasn't ready to sympathize with her and I should have been able to empathize, but I was coming up short in that department.

"Is Jude here?" I asked, immediately wanting to whip myself for asking. If she didn't already believe I was a desperate loser, that question just nailed it.

"Not sure," she said, taking a drink from her cup.

"Home with the baby?" It was an honest question that came out sounding every kind of bitchy.

"No." Holly stiffened, her bright-blue eyes flashing. "My mom's babysitting tonight."

"Holly, I'm sorry," I said, wishing now I had stayed inside so I wouldn't be having this conversation from hell. "I'm not trying to be a bitch—"

"It just comes naturally?" she filled in, giving me a fake smile.

"I deserved that."

"Yep," she agreed, taking another sip.

We were silent for a while, for so long I wasn't sure if she was waiting for me to say something or if she was having a tough time getting out what she wanted to say.

So I blurted something neither of us was expecting. "Is he a good dad?"

She seemed as surprised by my question as I was. "I'm sure he will be someday."

A nasty case of realization whiplash hit me. "Wait," I said, turning toward Holly. "Did you just say 'someday,' as in not present day?"

She bit her lip, thinking something over. "I don't know how much of this I should be the one to tell you, but—"

"Tell me everything," I interrupted, scooting closer. "Because no one else will."

She looked at me under her lashes. "That might be because you drew your own conclusions before asking questions."

I'd held the same breath now for a solid minute.

"Are you ready to ask questions now?" she said, leaning back on her hand. "The right questions?"

I nodded.

"Ask away," she said.

Did I want to go down this road? Did I want to have assumptions confirmed or denied at this stage of the game? When a face eclipsed my thoughts, one with a long scar and silvery gray eyes, I had my answer. "Is Jude your baby's dad?" Might as well get the first one out of the way.

"No."

Oh my God. The guilt was as sudden as the relief. "Do you and Jude have some sort of relationship together?"

"Yeah," she answered, taking a sip. "He's been my best friend since we were in first grade."

Again, I wanted to slap myself across the face at the same

time I wanted to jump and scream for joy. "And that night I followed him to your place," I said slowly, trying to process everything. "He brought diapers and formula, and you said you had big plans for him and you hugged." I was reliving the scene, but seeing it with different eyes. Eyes that were less likely to draw conclusions without asking questions.

"And I thought Jude had trust issues," she muttered, gawking at me like she wanted to wring my neck. "I called him earlier that day because I was out of money and the baby was going to be out of food and diapers in about twelve hours if I was lucky. Jude's been a support from the very beginning, since little Jude's real father wants nothing to do with him."

I swallowed, remembering the things I'd thought and the things I'd said to him that morning after. I understood why he'd ignored me the way he did now.

"We hugged because, come on, we've been best friends our whole lives." Holly was counting things off on her fingers, looking at me like this was a childish game. "The plans I had for him that night including fixing up a crib I'd found at a yard sale that day, and yes, he did stay the night," she said, arching a brow. "On the couch, in case your jump-to-conclusions little mind's already going there."

I let everything Holly said sink in. "Why didn't he tell me about you?" I whispered. "Why didn't he deny everything when I approached him the next morning?"

She dipped her toes in the water, skating them across the calm surface. "Because I asked him not to tell anyone about little Jude. He knows who the father is, and the piece-of-shit father knows, but I didn't want anyone else to know the real reason I dropped out of school. The rumor spreaders at Southpointe would have had a field day with that juicy tidbit," she said, smirking. "And only Jude can speak for why he didn't tell you the truth about us that morning. Maybe because you wouldn't have believed it even if he did tell you."

All I could think about was the look in his eyes that morning I confronted him, telling him I trusted Sawyer over him. The pain and betrayal that darkened his face. "I'm the worst person in the world," I said, more to myself than anything.

"I thought that too the day Jude came to me, looking like you'd just pulled the heart out of his chest, and told me what happened," she said.

"I get it now," I said. "I get why he hates me." I deserved to be loathed. After everything I'd been through with the populace of Southpointe judging me and jumping to absurd conclusions, I'd done the same thing to Jude. I'd become what I'd hated to the person I'd loved.

Holly chuckled; it was dark and throaty. "You really

are a clueless bitch, Lucy," she said, dumping the rest of her drink into the water. "Jude doesn't hate you. That man, against everything he knows and everything I tell him, he still loves you."

There was only one explanation. I'd just crossed into an alternate universe. "He still loves me?" I whispered.

"Still and always will," she said, shaking her head.

I needed to get up and find Jude. I needed to apologize and beg his forgiveness and find out if what she was saying was true, because even though I'd tried to bury it six feet deep, I still loved him too.

"Thank you, Holly," I said, finally meeting her eyes.

"I didn't do this for you. I did it for him, so no need to feel all indebted to me." Holly didn't spare my feelings.

But I was grateful to her, the girl I'd assumed was Jude's lover, the girl who was, in fact, his best friend, the girl who had set all the facts straight.

"Holly," I asked, setting my pop to the side. "Who is little Jude's dad?"

She gasped, like I'd caught her off guard. It wasn't any of my business, and I was expecting her to tell me to go screw myself when she sighed.

"Well, if it isn't two of the most lovely ladies to have ever graced the halls of Southpointe High."

Sawyer's voice cut down the dock, making me groan and

Holly go all stiff and silent. The dock creaked beneath his feet as he came toward us, dressed in his standard flat-front khakis and name-brand polo.

"Hey, beautiful," he said, bending down to kiss me. His breath was rank with alcohol and cranberry juice. "And Miss Holly," he said, staring down at her. "Always a pleasure to be in your company. How's the little bastard"—he covered his mouth, his eyes amused—"I mean baby?"

She bolted up, glowering at him. "You'll never know as far as I'm concerned," she said, shoving him aside. She raced off the deck and disappeared into the crowd.

"You might want to be mindful of who you hang around with, Lucy," Sawyer said. "Girls with her reputation don't help girls with your old reputation."

"Sawyer, we graduate in a week. I'm not concerned about my reputation," I said, getting up because I didn't like the way he was leering down on me with that drunk smile. "And that was a shitty thing to say to Holly. Where do you get off calling her baby a bastard?"

Raising his cup, he said, "Takes one to know one. It's in the kid's blood." Taking a drink, he drained the cup and tossed it into the lake.

"Nice," I said, crossing my arms. "Aren't you in fine form tonight?"

"I'm just wound so damn tight, Lucy," he said, pressing

into me and tightening his arms around me, molding his hands around my ass. "I need a release." Sliding my hair over my shoulder, he ran his lips over my collarbone. "And from the way you're dressed for me tonight, something tells me you're finally ready to help me with that."

"What the hell, Sawyer," I said, shoving him away, harder than I'd planned, but not as hard as he deserved. I don't know if it was the alcohol or my superhuman strength, but Sawyer stumbled back, right into the black lake.

"Damn it, Lucy!" he yelled, kicking to the surface.

"Have a nice swim," I said, stomping down the dock.

"Lucy! Get back here right now!" he yelled, making a raucous splashing through the water.

"Have a nice life, jerk-off," I said to myself, grabbing Taylor's shoes and heading for the house.

The party had grown, and it was now standing room only. People could be amazingly creative when there wasn't a spare surface to spread over. I was about to grab Taylor from Morrison's lap so I could get her home and tear the town apart searching for Jude when something too tempting to ignore jumped to mind.

I wound, dodged, and leaped over bodies as I went up the stairs to the second floor. Sawyer's room was at the end of the hall, probably the only room in the house that wasn't being used, since Sawyer had a key lock installed to keep parents out and horny teenagers from shagging on his bed when he threw these kinds of parties.

However, as his girlfriend, he'd entrusted me with the location of the spare key, probably hoping I'd one day lock myself in there as a birthday surprise. I'd never been happier I'd said no to a good-looking guy before.

Getting on my knees, I crouched beneath the bench at the end of the hallway, sliding the key out of its location. Getting up, I clicked the key over in the lock and opened the door.

"I thought you'd never ask," one of the defensive linemen slurred, staggering up to me.

"Yeah," I said, sliding behind the door. "I could never get that drunk." Slamming the door shut, I locked it and ran to Sawyer's bathroom. Standing in his room, fresh from dumping his sorry ass, I couldn't recall what I'd seen in him. Surely something should pop to mind after spending almost six months with a guy, but there was nothing.

Nothing but a stream of regrets and relief that I'd figured it out sooner rather than later.

I pulled the hand towel from the metal ring and slid the bottom drawer of his bathroom sink open. I didn't have to fumble around the mass of male hygiene products to find what I was searching for. It was right on top.

Rushing out of the bathroom, I went to his desk and

grabbed a pen and a sticky note and wrote my parting words. I wasn't even trying to stifle my smile. I rolled up the towel before laying it down on the center of his bed, then propped the lubricant next to it and stuck the note over the almost empty bottle. I stepped back, admiring my handiwork.

Sawyer was going to lose it whenever he sobered up enough to read words again. I wished I could see the look on his face.

I was turning to leave the room for good, when I heard the door whisper open almost as quickly as it closed. Sawyer was dripping wet, key in hand, smirking at me like I'd just tripped his trap.

"Did you miss me?" he asked, locking the door behind him.

Other than being a horny bastard, Sawyer had never done anything to make me feel threatened or unsafe or scared. I felt all those things now. I'd also never seen him so rip-roaring drunk. Sawyer Diamond wasn't only a mean drunk, he was a dangerous one.

"What's this?" he asked, crossing the room toward his bed. "A present?"

I didn't reply—every instinct in my body was firing, telling me to get out of this room. I slowly started sidestepping my way for the door.

Sawyer peeled the note from the bottle, and his eyes

squinted. "Have fun releasing yourself," he read, a slow smile stretching over his mouth. Dropping the note onto the bed, his head whipped to where I was making my way toward the door. "Oh, baby, I plan to."

It was right then, the look on his face even more than his words, that kicked my adrenaline into high gear. I gave up on slow and sprinted toward the door. I wasn't fast enough.

"Where are you going?" Sawyer said, grabbing me from behind. Damn, he was strong for a stumbling drunk. The icy swim in the water must have sobered him up. "You just got here."

"Let me go, Sawyer," I warned, trying to free my arms where he'd pinned them at my sides.

"Or what?" he taunted, dragging me back to his bed. "You going to cry to your could-care-less bitch of a mother, or maybe your wouldn't-know-if-the-room-was-burning-down father? Or maybe all your friends who were mine before they were yours?" Reaching the side of the bed, he threw me down on the mattress, hovering over me. "Be a good little bitch and behave." He looked meaningfully at his nightstand, where I knew he kept some kind of handgun. He'd explained it was to ward off intruders, but apparently it was also handy to threaten a girl into doing whatever he wanted. "Or I'll have to make you."

"God, Sawyer. Who the hell are you?" I said, grabbing

the bottle rolling on the mattress and lobbing it at him. "You really had everyone fooled, didn't you?"

"Not quite everyone," he said, stretching his wet shirt above his head and tossing it into the corner. "Holly and Jude pretty much have my number, but look what that knowledge did to their reputations. If I were you, after tonight, I wouldn't go crying in the streets to the townsfolk about how I'm some kind of monster." He grinned down at me, his eyes wide with excitement. "Because, sweetie, they ain't going to believe your story over mine."

I scooted to the side of the bed, calculating how much time it would take me to get to the door, wondering if I could get there faster than Sawyer could get to me. Since he was standing between me and the door, the odds were not in my favor. "Why now? Why after months of being a 'patient' boyfriend are you doing this now?"

"Because I can," he answered, his hands working over his belt. "And because I want to. That's all the justification I need."

I had to try. I had to make a run for it, because either way, Sawyer wasn't going to stop.

"So your brilliant plan is to rape the girl you just had a fight with in front of witnesses, with two hundred people around?" I was trying to appeal to his intelligence, what little he had in his drunken, crazed state.

"No, my brilliant plan is having consensual sex with my girlfriend, who's going away in the fall and wants to have one last romantic night before we part ways," he said, pulling his belt free and tossing it over with the shirt.

Shit. He'd thought this through. And I knew in a court of law, his story would be the one that would stick. Now was the time to run.

Scrambling across the bed, I dashed for the door and made it three strides before I took a clothesline to the neck. I fell to the floor, coughing, feeling like I was choking on my own throat.

"I wouldn't recommend trying that again," Sawyer said, standing over me, his hair leaking drops of lake water on my face.

Turning my head away, I tried to get my breath back. "One day, Sawyer Diamond," I said between clipped breaths, "someone is going to stand over you the way you are me and kick your ass. And I'm going to have a front-row seat."

He dropped down on me, pinning me with his weight. Shoving my legs apart with his knees, he ran his tongue up my neck to the tip of my ear. "Maybe tomorrow," he breathed into my ear, "but not tonight. No one's coming to your rescue tonight."

Wiggling my legs, trying to free them from his grasp, I lifted my head. "No, Sawyer," I said, just outside his ear, "no one's coming to *your* rescue." And then that self-defense class my parents forced me to take when I was thirteen paid out its weight in gold. Sinking my teeth into his ear, I wiggled one leg free and planted my foot once, twice, and a third time into his crotch.

He roared in agony, one hand grabbing his ear and the other grabbing his assaulted manhood. Scrambling to get the rest of me from beneath him, I slid along the carpet, knowing if I didn't make it to the door before he made it to the nightstand, no number of self-defense classes would matter.

Then the door I was crawling toward burst open, part of the jamb splintering off. Bursting through the door, Jude took one look at the scene playing out on the floor and went into a rage.

Jude threw himself on top of Sawyer, his fists going to work on him. Flipping Sawyer on his back, Jude straddled him and started pounding.

Each hit landed with a crack—each one released a little more blood. Deciphering whether Jude's grunts or Sawyer's groans were louder was impossible. When it became obvious Jude was not planning on just teaching him a lesson, but taking his life, I pushed myself off the floor and stumbled toward them.

"Stop, Jude." My voice wavered almost as badly as my legs. "Stop." Reaching out, I rested my hand on his shoulder.

He didn't stop, but his punches grew slower and less frequent.

"Yeah, you might want to listen to her," Sawyer said, spitting blood from his mouth onto the carpet. "Unless you want to find yourself locked up again. Who's going to be here to watch after Lucy when I corner her in some other room then, Ryder?" Sawyer winked up at Jude with a bloody smile, challenging him like he had a death wish.

Jude's muscles rolled beneath my hand, his breaths lifting and lowering his shoulders half a foot each time. "I told myself the next time I heard about you doing this to another girl, I was going to rip your dick off and stuff it down your throat. But since the girl I found you with was Luce"—he looked back at me, his whole face tense, before leaning down so his face was an inch from Sawyer's—"I'm going to kill you."

And the scariest thing that had happened so far tonight was that threat. Because it wasn't a threat; I could tell by the tone of his voice that he meant it.

Instead of crawling to them, I was crawling away from them, positioning my body in front of Sawyer's nightstand. It was the first place Jude would check for a weapon.

Jude stood over Sawyer, seething. "Luce," he said, keeping his eyes on Sawyer, "mind moving away from there so I can finish this son of a bitch?"

I swallowed—he already knew. "No," I said.

"Luce, this is between him and me right now," he said, his back quivering. "Move."

My fight had shifted from keeping Sawyer from assaulting me, to keeping Jude from murdering him. I should have hit my exhaustion point about one busted door ago, but I was a girl with a lot of fight in her.

"No," I repeated, my voice stronger.

"Damn it, Luce," Jude shouted, "he deserves this!"

I rose, taking a step toward him. "I know," I said, taking a few more steps until I could wrap my hands around one of his. I waited for him to face me, and when he finally did, I saw the conflict in his eyes. "But you don't."

"I'm going to get locked up for good one day, and I can't imagine a better reason for serving a life sentence than for taking out a bastard like him. I don't care, Luce."

Lifting one hand to his cheek, I traced his scar with my thumb. "But I do."

He stared at me, thunder still rolling through his eyes, and then down at Sawyer. His entire body stiffened again. "I want to kill him, Luce. I want to kill him more than I've ever wanted anything." A ripple ran down his back. "I don't know how to walk away."

"Let me help you," I said, waiting. I'd wait however long it took—I wasn't walking away until he walked away with me.

Below Jude, Sawyer chuckled, spitting another spray of blood. "The felon and the slut riding off into the sunset together," he laughed. "We won't have to hold our breath for that happily ever after."

Jude flinched, but I wouldn't let him go.

"Don't waste your life on this bastard," I said, refusing to look at Sawyer because I was good if I never had to look at that face again. I smiled at Jude. "Why don't you waste it with me instead?"

The lines smoothed from his face as he held my stare. And then finally he smiled. "I'll take that deal."

Nodding toward the door, I pulled on his hand.

Another laugh came from Sawyer. "At least someone's going to be getting a piece of that ass tonight."

I groaned—Sawyer had no sense of self-preservation.

Grabbing him by the shirt collar, Jude pulled him up. "You just don't know when to shut up," he said, drawing his fist tight. "Let me help you." He drove his fist square into Sawyer's mouth, sending him crashing back down on the floor.

"Luce," Jude said, his face composed. "Wait for me in the hallway. I'm not going to kill him," he added, answering me preemptively.

"Jude." I wasn't going to leave him alone with Sawyer.

"Look at me," he said, waiting for me. "I'm fine. I won't

kill him." And then he stared all meaningful at me. "Trust me."

This was my chance. My chance to show him the trust I'd denied him. The trust he'd deserved that I'd felt he didn't. How could I say no and expect us to ever have a fighting chance?

I didn't want to trust him. I didn't like leaving him alone with Sawyer. "Okay," I agreed.

That grin I hadn't seen on his face in so long I thought it had disappeared for good appeared. "I'll be right out," he said. "Could you send Holly in? She's waiting in the hallway, and I think she's going to want to see this."

Trust. Trust. Trust. "Okay. I'll wait outside," I said. "Don't keep me waiting too long." Heading for the door, I smoothed my dress back into place, trying to do the same with my hair.

Propped against the wall, Holly had obviously been placed there to make sure no one tried to interrupt Jude and the ass-beating he dealt Sawyer.

Her eyes ran down me, her face shadowing. "Are you all right?"

"Yeah," I answered, coming up to her. "Jude's asking for you in there."

She nodded, shoving off the wall. Turning to me, her hands found mine. "Are you all right?" she asked again as a silent exchange took place between us. On a very base level, I got it, I got her, and she got me too. We were like the sisterhood of girls Sawyer preyed on, and although it wasn't a common denominator to be proud of, it was a bond to be proud of.

"Yes," I answered.

Giving my hands a squeeze, she headed for the bedroom. "You are one tough cookie, Lucy Larson," she said. "I get what Jude sees in you."

Going against every urge to run back into that room, I didn't. I hadn't trusted Jude, I hadn't given him the benefit of the doubt before. I would now.

I earned a few sideways stares from a couple of girls sitting at the top of the stairs, but the second floor was mostly empty. Either the party was winding down or Holly knew how to redirect traffic.

Fiddling with the conundrum that was the dress I had on to pass time, I gave up. No amount of tugging and smoothing would magically create more fabric to cover the parts of my body I preferred to keep covered, and it looked like I owed Taylor a new dress, because thanks to Sawyer, it had a slit up the front to match the one on the back.

Another minute went by, and I assured myself everything was fine because no bloodcurdling screams or gunshots had gone off in the room down the hall, but I was still anxious as all hell. So I grounded some of that nervous energy by pacing the hallway like a caged lioness.

On my fifth lap past the stairs, Jude and Holly marched out of Sawyer's room. Jude's expression was unreadable, but Holly sported a shit-eating grin.

"Is everything all right?" I asked, rushing down the hall to meet them.

Jude glanced over at Holly. "It is now," he said, opening his arms for me. I curled into him, feeling like parts of me were melting into him. Six months of misery went up in smoke.

"What happened?" I asked against his chest.

"Vindication," Holly answered, patting her oversized tote. "I'm out of here. I've done what I came to do, and Mom's going to be pissed if I stay out all night."

"We are too," Jude said, tucking me under his arm and steering us toward the stairs. "I need to get Luce home."

"Wait." I stopped. "I drove with Taylor. I'm her DD tonight."

Jude groaned. "Hey, Hol, you mind hunting down Taylor Donovan and giving her a ride home?"

Her face twisted. "If you're referring to the woman who called me every name in the female book of cattiness, then yes, I do mind," Holly called back at us, winding down the stairs. "But since you're the one asking, I'll put on my big-girl, very not-bitter panties and drive the bitch home. I'm not walking her to the front door, though."

"You're a saint," Jude said, guiding me down the stairs, shoving a guy who almost spilled his beer on me to the side.

"Has anyone seen a raving bitch with nice hair?" Holly shouted at the bottom of the stairs.

Everyone who heard her pointed in a different direction.

"Looks like I've got my work cut out for me," she said, diving into the crowd. "See you guys later."

"Hey, Hol!" Jude shouted after her.

She peered back, almost out of view.

"My compliments on your handiwork up there."

She flashed us a rock-on sign and disappeared into the crowd.

"Come on," Jude said, keeping me close, "let's get you out of here."

Walking out the front door, I realized I'd never been to such a one-wrong-thing-after-another party, but as Jude led me down the stairs, I also knew I was glad I came. Slut-tastic dress, awkwardly enlightening conversation with Holly, and Sawyer trying to take advantage of me aside, I had Jude beside me, holding my hand like he was never going to let it go again.

I'd endure a lot worse to hold this hand.

"So what handiwork were you referring to back there?"

I asked, pulling Taylor's keys from my purse.

He didn't answer.

"Oh God. How bad is it?" I wouldn't even let my imagination go.

"Nothing less than he deserved," Jude said, opening the passenger door for me and taking the keys. "She just put a warning label on him." He shut the door and took his sweet time coming around the front of the car.

"What kind of a warning label?" I asked as soon as the driver's door opened.

Clicking his seat belt into place, Jude gave me a sheepish look. "The kind that's tattooed to his groin with a list of the STDs he may or may not have."

I choked on my saliva. "What? You're not serious."

Twisting the key over, he stared at me with an expression that bled serious. "As serious as a permanent marker can be."

"Oh my God," I breathed. "Crap, does he have an actual list?" I had even more to be thankful to Jude for.

He lifted a shoulder. "Well, let's put it this way. No girl will ever have to find out, because there's no way anyone will let his dick within a ten-foot radius of her again once she checks out that laundry list," he said, whipping the car around and heading down the driveway.

"Anything else?" I asked, fearing the answer.

The corners of Jude's eyes wrinkled. "We might have

Krazy Glued his hand to his dick and glued the index finger of his other hand up his nose."

My mouth fell open. It was as shocking as it was funny, so I laughed. I visualized the whole event, tattoo start to Krazy Glue finish, feeling totally . . . vindicated. Holly had said it best.

"Can't you guys get in trouble for that?" I asked when I calmed myself.

"Probably," he said, his own laughter dimming, "but there's no way in hell Sawyer will report it."

Sawyer had always struck me as the kind who was the class tattletale. "Why not?"

"Because Holly threatened to tell his parents that little Jude's his son, and then that would become a bona fide scandal," he said, gloating. "A family like the Diamonds can't afford to take a public hit like that if they hope to keep selling overpriced minivans and shit."

Holly hadn't had the chance to tell me, but I'd figured it out. The silent exchange in the hall told me everything I needed to know about who fathered little Jude. "You two had this all planned out."

He answered with a halfhearted shrug.

"How are you?" he asked, covering my hand with his.

"After almost being forced to have sex with my boyfriend? Or after finding out said former boyfriend is not only an ass, but a deadbeat dad? Or after finding out I'd been all wrong about you and you didn't speak up to tell me otherwise?" I wanted to blame someone else, or circumstances, but the only person to blame was myself.

"How are you feeling about all of it?" he asked, his voice gentle, such a contrast to what I knew he was capable of. "Give me a median score."

"I feel like shit," I answered, and then I looked over at him. I didn't know if it was just for tonight, or just as a friend who had my back, or as just a bit more than what he'd been to me these past six months, but he was here. "And I'm kind of great too. How about you?"

His eyes went light and warm. "I'm kind of great too."

Turning off Sunrise Drive, he pulled Taylor's car up to the cabin. We both stared at the house, waiting. It might be forward, it might be in bad taste, but this woman was grabbing what she wanted and not looking back.

"You want to come in?" I swallowed, expecting an acceptance as much as a rejection.

He paused, his eyes inspecting the place like it was heavily guarded. I knew that guy expression of concern.

"My parents aren't home," I said. "Mom had some work trip she dragged my dad on."

Jude opened his door. My heart lurched.

"Your mom got your dad to leave the house?" he asked,

when I stepped out of the car.

"After lacing his eggs with some hard-core narcotics," I answered, walking up to where he waited for me.

He was staring at the cabin again, chewing on his bottom lip. I also knew that man look: hesitancy.

"It's all right if you don't want to," I said, waiting beside him. "I understand."

"I want to, Luce," he said, studying my bedroom window. "I'm just not sure if I should."

The guy who could kick anyone's ass with his hands tied behind his back. The same guy who didn't care if all of Southpointe announced to the world he'd slept with every single—and some not so single—woman in the state. The same guy who was deliberating coming inside a parentless house with me.

He was a walking contradiction.

"Well, I am sure, so my certainty overrules your uncertainty." I grabbed his arm and pulled him up the stairs. "Right this way."

He sighed, but let me lead him up the porch and through the front door. The floorboards whined beneath our feet, echoing through the silent home.

"Do you want anything?" I asked, flipping on the kitchen light.

He shook his head, his eyes hesitant.

Wanting to get him to a floor above the most convenient exit, I pulled him toward the stairs, not about to let go of his hand.

"I need to get changed," I said, giving his hand another pull.

It worked.

I wasn't sure what I was doing as I led Jude into my bedroom, but it wasn't because my intentions were pure or impure. I didn't have any intentions right now; I was just going with what felt right.

"How did you know what was happening to me tonight?" I asked, pulling the chain of the lamp on my dresser.

"Holly saw Diamond and you have a fight and came and got me. And when it comes to predicting Diamond's next moves, all you have to ask yourself is what would a dickhead do and multiply it by ten and you have your answer." He leaned into the doorway, inspecting my room like it wasn't real.

I was looking at him the same way.

"Thank you, Jude." I paused on my way to the bathroom and studied him. I'd believed and assumed horrible things about him. I'd become another member of the mob letting the worst shit stick to him. It made my throat burn. "And I'm sorry," I said, hoping he could read in my eyes what my words could not convey. "Holly explained everything, and I'm so, so sorry, Jude."

Pushing off the doorway, he took a step inside. "I know, Luce." He gave me a sad smile.

I disappeared behind the bathroom door, pajamas in hand, tears in eyes.

"I didn't think your room would be so . . . girly." His nose was curled, from the tone of his voice.

Sliding out of the sausage-casing dress, I stuck my head out. "Don't we know better by now than to assume anything about each other?" I peaked a brow and smiled.

He chuckled. "I'd hope so," he said. "So you're saying this would be a bad time to mention the five children I've fathered with five different women? Or have you tailed me to all their trailers already?"

I flung the dress at his face.

Letting it slide off his face, he crumpled it up. If it was any indicator of how little fabric it consisted of, he was able to palm it in one fist before stuffing it in his jacket pocket. "I'm keeping this as a souvenir, Luce. You looked amazing."

"Like you were admiring the dress," I said, sliding into my nightgown.

"If you wear a dress like that, Luce, here's a pointer. Guys aren't going to be admiring the material."

Everything felt like it used to. Back to normal. Well, the only normal Jude and I could ever be, but it was ours, and enough. I ran a brush through my hair a few times, just so it didn't look like I was going for the ratty look, and stepped back into the bedroom.

Jude was propped up in my bed, flipping through my student handbook. "I heard you got in," he said, putting it back on the nightstand. "Marymount Manhattan, Luce. I may be a dumb hick, but even I know that getting into MM is something to be proud of."

I bent a knee beneath me and sat beside him. "And I heard you got into just about any university you want."

He bowed his head against the headboard. "Yeah, I guess."

"Have you made any decisions?"

"Not yet," he said, like it was no big deal. Like having a full-blown scholarship to whatever school you chose wasn't a big deal. If that wasn't, it was hard to imagine what Jude considered a big deal.

"Jude," I said, planting my hand on his stomach. "Why didn't you tell me about Sawyer? Why didn't you tell me you weren't the dad?" It was one of the many questions I couldn't even begin to answer.

"Would you have believed me?" he asked, his voice strained.

I knew the answer, but I didn't want to give it air.

"And I also knew that if you assumed I was little Jude's dad, and that I'd lied to you about that, it would be enough for you to be done with me for good. It was the only way I knew to keep you safe from me."

I lifted my hand from his stomach. "So you planned this? The whole time we were together, you were scheming some way to screw up royally so I'd leave you alone?"

"No, Luce," he said, grabbing my hand back. "So *I'd* leave *you* alone."

"That morning when I confronted you about Holly and the baby, you didn't deny it."

"But did I confirm it?"

I narrowed my eyes. "By not denying, you did."

Lowering his beanie, he closed his eyes. "That's because I knew that was the only way I could save you from me. I didn't plan it out that way, but when you confronted me about Holly that morning, I knew that if I was going to be a man and let you go, that was my only chance. And lucky for me, I had the balls to do it that day."

"What? Lie to me?" I asked with an edge.

Jude shook his head. "Walk away from you."

This whole thing between Jude and me had been one carefully managed miscommunication orchestrated by him. I was hurt, and I was pissed, and I even understood why, but most of all, I was done with it.

"You about done walking yet?" I asked, grabbing a pillow and tossing it at his face.

He tossed the pillow back. "Undecided on that one."

If I didn't know why he was undecided, that answer might have stung. "Why are you here now then?"

"Because I want to be," he said, confessing it like a sin.

"And you didn't want to be here before?" I scooted closer, wishing that for two damn minutes, we could be on the same page.

"I did," he said, staring at the ceiling. "I'm just tired of fighting it right now."

There it was, the breakthrough I was waiting for. The red light had changed. "Do me a favor and don't fight it again."

Sitting up, he looked at me. His stare was crippling. "I will, Luce. I'm going to keep fighting it, because you don't deserve some dead end guy with my past ruining your life."

Throwing my arms up, I exhaled. Humility was a good thing, but being a martyr was as bad as believing you were God's gift. I was done with the routine. "If you'd shut up about all the reasons I shouldn't want you, maybe you'd hear that I don't care," I said. Well, I shouted. "I know the worst parts of you and I know the best parts of you." I paused to get a breath. "And I want you."

Something flickered in his eyes before he looked away. His jaw tightened as he eyed the door, and just as I was contemplating barricading it closed with my body, he pulled me to him, his mouth finding mine.

He kissed me like he was trying to consume me, like he was making up for half a year's worth of missed moments, and like he was done fighting what I knew was a useless fight.

Cradling my face in his hands, he kissed me harder, so hard I couldn't breathe, but if kissing like this required breathlessness, I was giving up oxygen for good. The moment consumed me. The past, the lies, the pain—nothing could intrude on the world we were creating together.

Tugging his shirt free, I pulled it over his back and tossed it on the floor. It was the first time he'd ever let me take his shirt off, but my hands against his skin weren't enough. I wanted the rest of him against the rest of me.

Jude slipped his hands beneath my nightgown, sliding it up over my stomach, my breasts, and then my head. His eyes roamed over me, inspecting my body like he was committing every line and dip and curve to memory. I knew I should have been uncomfortable, sitting naked and exposed in front of a man who'd seen his share of women and could have his pick of any of them, but there was no way to feel insecure with the way he was inspecting me.

He smiled at me when his eyes made the final journey to mine. His eyes muted silver, his breaths short, his body ready. I knew I'd never want anyone else like I wanted him.

"Jude," I said, "I—"

The last two words got lost as his mouth crushed into mine, his hands digging into my hips right before flipping me back onto the bed. The warmth of his skin warmed mine, creating a sheen of sweat between us. His mouth moved to my neck, his hands to my breasts, and I felt close to falling over the edge. But I still wanted more, I needed more.

I was so ready for him I could feel it all the way down to my toes.

Sliding my hands between us, I grabbed his pants, tugging on the button of his jeans. It snapped free and I slid my hand inside. He moaned, his forehead leaning into mine as his body moved against mine. Sliding my hand out, I rocked my hips up toward him. Another sound escaped him. "Damn it," he moaned right before his mouth fell over mine again. His tongue parted my lips, touching the tip of mine, as his fingers slipped beneath my panties. He slid them off in one seamless move, his tongue never leaving my mouth.

I was in another world. A world that was foreign and a world I wanted to make my home. It was passionate and there was heat. The kind that went so deep it became a part of you.

I was so close to losing everything that was balling up inside me, I knew I couldn't hold on much longer with the way he was touching me. With the way he was consuming me.

Now, totally naked, I wrapped my legs around him, arching my hips against his, rocking up and down. His breathing stopped as every muscle in his body tensed.

"Not like this," he breathed, punching the pillow behind me.

Everything inside me screamed. "Not like what?" I said between ragged breaths, tightening my legs around him. I wasn't giving up when we were this close.

He closed his eyes. "Not right after you were almost raped by Sawyer Diamond," he said, leaning back.

His skin no longer pressed against mine, a cold crept up me almost immediately. "Jude, I'm fine," I said, leaning up on my elbows, not ready to let the moment go.

Shifting his legs off the bed, he hunched down. "But I'm not."

"Why?"

He washed his hands over his face. "Because this is all kinds of wrong right now."

That one hurt. "It didn't feel wrong to me," I said, trying not to think about the fact that I was probably the only woman the legendary Jude Ryder wouldn't go all the way with.

Retrieving my gown from the floor, he held it out for me, keeping his eyes down. "That's the thing. It didn't feel wrong to me either," he said as I snatched the gown from his hand. I wanted to chuck it across the room to prove a point, but pulled it on instead. "That's how I know it was."

"Could we save the mind benders for the morning?" I said, sticking my arms through the sleeves. "I'm running a little low on comprehension right now."

"I'm doing a shit job of explaining myself," he said, tugging on his hat, quiet for a minute. "My notion of right and wrong is so messed up, Luce, that my wrong is everyone else's right. And my right is everyone's wrong."

I wanted to wrap my arms around him and comfort whatever turmoil he was experiencing, but I felt too shunned for that. "So you're saying because what we were just doing felt right to you, it must be the wrong thing?" This was every definition of confusing.

He nodded. "I need a right and wrong recalibration, Luce, and until I'm able to get my shit figured out, I need to be careful with you."

I flopped back down on the bed, covering my head with a pillow. "Careful was not what I had in mind for tonight," I whined, my voice muffled.

"I know," he said, rubbing my leg. "But it's the right thing to do."

Lifting the pillow, I raised a brow. "Jude's right or everyone else's?" I asked with an innocent smile.

My snark had no effect on him. "I'm not sure," he said,

"and I need to be before we finish"—he glanced at the bed meaningfully—"doing what we were doing."

"Well," I said, sitting up and scooting close. "Hurry and figure your shit out, Ryder." I pressed my lips to his, pulling back as everything inside me started to boil.

"Yes, ma'am." He smiled, running his thumb down my cheek. "I just want it to feel right, okay? I want it to be perfect."

That would be nice if we lived in a perfect world. "If you're waiting for everything to feel right and perfect, I'll save you the suspense and tell you that's never going to happen," I said, weaving my fingers through his. "But if you can look at me and say you want to be with me and I can look at you and know I want to be with you, then carpe diem, baby. Because that's as perfect as it will ever get."

He nodded, giving my fingers a squeeze. "You're so damn smart, Luce," he said, kissing my forehead as he stood. "I'll see you in the morning."

Now this was just getting absurd.

"Yes," I said, grabbing his hand, "you will." I patted the space beside me, throwing the covers down.

Jude studied the bed as if it were an equation.

I guessed what equation he was trying to work out in his mind. "Right or wrong?"

One side of his face lifted. "I'm not sure," he confessed.

"Well, I am," I said, tugging his hand.

He stalled one more second, but whether he just gave in to me or decided on his own, he crawled into bed beside me and wound his arms around me so tight I couldn't breathe quite right.

I hadn't experienced such peaceful sleep since almost five years ago to the day.

TWENTY-TWO

*I*t was early. Like the-sun's-just-thinking-about-rising early. On a Sunday morning, I usually slept another three hours, but this one I didn't want to. I doubted I could have anyway.

I woke up with the same pit in my stomach I had each of the past four years on this day, that feeling that I wasn't sure whether I was going to throw up or pass out. The feeling of that day happening all over again, and then Jude's arm wound around me a bit tighter in his sleep, and today everything seemed easier to handle.

He'd stayed. All night. He hadn't let me go once.

He moaned something indecipherable in his sleep, tucking his face into my neck.

His beanie was still on. Topless and asleep, the man still kept that old hat in place. That couldn't be good for a head;

it needed to breathe every few years. Not sure why it felt like I was doing something I shouldn't, I slid the hat back from his forehead and pulled it off.

His hair was so short and so light it almost looked like he was bald. And then I noticed the puckering and scarring of skin, from the crown of his head to the neck I was so familiar with. Burn scars. I ran my fingers over them, wishing I could erase them from his skin and the event that made them from his mind.

Trailing my fingers down his neck, I looked down at the maze of scars that scattered all the way down his back. White scars protruded, some small, most large, like he'd been torn open in one hundred different ways and closed up by someone who didn't know how to use a needle and thread. I doubted cadavers came out with fewer scars.

I felt sick, sicker than I'd felt waking up to this day, as my fingers drew a line over each raised scar, not able or wanting to imagine what had happened to the man sleeping beside me.

Suddenly, he jolted awake. His eyes were peaceful for the shortest second before he noticed the expression on my face and what I held in my hand. Grabbing one of my wrists, he shoved it away before bolting out of bed, snatching his gray knit hat at the same time.

"What are you doing?" he cried, adjusting the hat back

over his head. He was angry and he was hurt.

"What happened?" I whispered, sitting up in bed.

He lunged across the room, grabbing his long-sleeved gray thermal and tugging it over his head, not answering.

"Those boys hurt you too," I guessed, wishing these conclusions weren't so easy to draw. "They burned you."

Jude wrapped his hands behind his head. "Not the same ones, but a few just like them," he said, his voice tight. "When I first moved to the boys' home. About five years ago."

"Why?" I leaned forward, trying to grab his hand.

He swung it away. "It was a welcome present."

"Oh my God," I breathed, wondering if the devastation in Jude's past ever ran out. "And the scars?"

Jude's eyes settled on me. They were black. "You don't want to know."

He was right, but also wrong. "Yes, I do," I whispered.

"I don't want to tell you," he replied, his chest rising and falling.

"Okay," I swallowed, accepting that Jude had just as many internal scars as he wore on his skin. "I'm sorry, Jude."

"I don't want your pity," he said, "and I don't want to rehash my whole childhood while you do that girl psychoanalysis bullshit. I'm a cancer, Luce. I told you that from the very beginning. You don't need to know the nasty details to accept that."

"Yes, you do," I said, going against every instinct screaming at me to embrace him. "You need the details so you know how to cure it. Let me help you," I said, reaching for him again.

"Dammit, Luce," he said, pacing around the room. "I'm not one of your pet projects. I'm not some dog you can rescue from being euthanized. I don't need to be saved, and I sure as hell don't want to be saved." Pausing, he finally looked at me. "So stop trying so damn hard."

I knew this was the point I should back off, but I couldn't.

"No," I said firmly.

He scowled at me. "I don't want to be saved."

I bit my tongue to keep any signs of tears away. "Yes, you do."

His eyes flamed. "No"—his voice shook—"I don't." Backing away from me, he hit the edge of my dresser, knocking over a storage box I'd pulled down from the attic yesterday.

It crashed to the floor, its contents spreading across the carpet. I was out of bed and collecting the items before he turned around.

Jude crouched down to help me. His eyes latched onto something in my hand, his face falling. Snatching the photo from my fingers, he rose, staring at the photo like he'd seen a ghost.

"How do you know this guy?"

A deep breath. "He was my brother."

"Your brother was John Larson?" he said, not blinking.

Now I was crying. This morning had just become too much for the woman of steel to keep the tears at bay. I looked up at the picture between Jude's fingers. My brother's senior year football photo. Only seven months before he'd been murdered. Five years ago today.

"Yes," I said, wiping my face.

The photo dropped from Jude's hand, his face blanching. "And your dad's first name is Wyatt?"

I nodded, grabbing the photo that had fallen to the floor.

Jude spun around, throwing his fist into the wall. It shattered through the drywall, as a cloud of white dust erupted. "How could you keep something like this from me?" he shouted, his whole body trembling.

I was so confused, so upset, I didn't know which one I felt more. "I told you my brother died," I said, settling John's picture in my lap. "Sorry if I didn't provide the gory details."

Pacing over to the window, Jude stared out it, his shoulders rising and falling with his breath. "Details would have been nice in this situation," he said, his voice about to break.

"What the hell are you talking about, Jude?" I whispered. Everything was falling apart, unraveling around me, and I didn't know what had pulled the thread.

"My full name is Jude Ryder Jamieson," he said, turning to face me.

That name hit me like a train.

"My dad," he said, gripping the windowsill, "went to jail for shooting and killing a young man."

I shook my head, whipping my hair back and forth. "Stop," I said, choking on the word. Everything was spinning out of control, and I wanted off this ride.

"My dad's name is Henry Jamieson." He paused, staring through the window like he was either going to escape out it or drive his fist through it. "My father murdered your brother."

The picture I held slid from my hands, flipping face-down on the carpet. I felt like sobbing, but I was too numb to move. I kept repeating to myself that this wasn't real, it wasn't possible. I had not fallen in love with the man whose father had killed my brother. God wasn't that cruel.

"Your dad," I began, not sure if I could get it out, "ruined my family."

Jude pounded the windowsill. "And your dad is the one to blame for setting in motion the whole damn string of events!" he shouted. "After working for one of your dad's companies for ten years, my dad got randomly selected for a drug test, failed it, and big Mr. Wyatt Larson got the final call. He fired him."

"Jude, he had coke and meth in him. He almost killed a man on the job site," I said, remembering every word that was spoken, every image portrayed during the trial. My parents were too gone in their loss to reason that letting their thirteen-year-old daughter sit in on the murder trial wasn't the best thing to do, but I wouldn't stay home. Hiding beneath a blanket when my brother's murderer was being tried felt wrong. I had been there for him, even in death.

"Because my mom had just bailed!" he shouted, the sinews of his neck popping to the surface. "He was going through a rough patch, but he would have come out of it, and as a reward for a decade of service, your dad fired him. The bank foreclosed on the house two months later, and we were homeless. He dropped me off at the boys' home the same day he shot your brother."

I wanted to run away, but I couldn't. I was still waiting to wake up from this nightmare. "He murdered my brother," I repeated, the words acrid.

"It was supposed to be your dad!" he exploded, everything draining from him. His shoulders rolled forward, his head falling. "It was supposed to be your dad," he said in a whisper.

"No"—my lip trembled—"it was supposed to be me."

Jude froze. "What the hell do you mean?"

I scooted against the wall, needing its support. "Mom had asked me to take Dad's lunch down to him that Sunday—he was working around the clock to get a project done on time—but I was being difficult and said I didn't want to. The job site was close to our home, and I could have biked." I closed my eyes as everything played back in my mind. "So John said he would, and that was the last time I saw him alive. Your dad put three bullets into him when he showed up at the work site. It should have been me, waiting inside Dad's mobile office, twirling the chair, when Henry Jamieson—who was so high on meth he wasn't able to make out who was in that chair—shot and killed my brother." Everything inside me deflated. "It was supposed to be me."

The silence was so loud I wanted to cover my ears.

Finally, Jude walked past me, stopping right before he walked out. "I really could have done without this shit."

He slammed the door behind him, and his footsteps thundered down the stairs, out the door, and out of my life for good this time.

Finally, I cried the tears I'd held on to for five years.

TWENTY-THREE

I stood in front of the mirror, studying the girl reflecting back. She looked like me, but she wasn't the same girl I remembered. Something had broken loose in the hours since Jude walked away, and it must have been vital to who I once was.

I felt flat, unable to muster any kind of emotion, and I felt lost, like everything I'd worked for and achieved had led me to a dead end. For the first time in my life, I wondered if the world around me I'd been trying to save wasn't worth saving.

"Lucy in the sky?" A gentle knocking sounded outside my door. "You ready?"

No, was my answer, but that's not what came out, because when it came to my brother, I never said no. I hadn't when I'd been asked to speak at his funeral, and I hadn't every year on the anniversary of his death, when Dad and I visited his grave. It was the only way I could still show him I loved him and I thought about him every day.

I took one last glance at the girl in the mirror before turning away. That girl was no longer me.

"Hey, Dad," I greeted, opening my door. Like the four prior years, Dad was in his black suit and had even managed to get his tie almost straight. "Just the two of us again?" I asked, glancing down the hall. My mom never accompanied us to John's grave, and for all I knew, she'd never revisited after the day he'd been lowered into the ground.

"Your mom deals with this in her own way," he said, wiping his palms on his jacket. "We deal with this in our way."

Most days I wished I could deal with it Mom's way.

"Come on, it's getting late." He headed for the stairs. I grabbed my purse and followed.

"You're driving," he said needlessly as he locked the front door. The last time he'd been behind the wheel of a vehicle was the day John died.

The cemetery was about an hour's drive from the cabin, but when you were sitting next to your father in total silence, it seemed more like an entire day, without pit stops. I came once a year because it was the right thing to do, but that was it. Besides, nothing of what I loved of John was buried beneath that gravestone.

Dad stayed silent, thinking the thoughts of a man who had ceased living, and I stared at the road ahead, trying not to think because my thoughts only led me down one road.

Like every other cemetery, it was empty. Rolling to a stop, I looked over at Dad.

"Dad." I set my hand on his shoulder. "You ready?"

He flinched, his eyes clearing as he came back to life. "Ready."

I slid out of the car and walked around the front. I waited.

And waited.

It was a practice in patience I'd learned five years ago. One I'd perfected.

Dad stood outside the passenger door, fidgeting and fighting with his demons. It took a lot out of me to come see John, but the torture Dad experienced was the kind entire mental illness books were dedicated to.

I'd never timed it, but I'd guess fifteen minutes was about average. This time, he rolled his shoulders back and smoothed his coat into place after only five. Walking up to me, he looked over. "Let's go say hi," he said, adjusting his tie for the fiftieth time.

John's headstone wasn't far, and about fifty paces later, we were kneeling beside it. Dad appeared close to fainting, but I knew he'd hold it together. He always did.

We never said anything, but I always sensed John heard what I wanted to say. The birds chirped, the sun shone down, I pulled my favorite memories of John to the surface, I tried to file the ones of Jude away for good. Life was slowly becoming one giant mess, and I wasn't sure if this was because I was somehow cursed or if life just blew by nature. I'd been buying into the whole one-person-can-make-a-difference thing this whole time, only to discover that, in the end, the world sucked.

"Would you like to tell me what's wrong?" Dad asked quietly, resting his hand on my lap.

I startled, whether more from his touch or the broken silence, I didn't know. "I'm fine." How was it so hard to make my voice sound normal?

"Lucy, I've never heard you once say you were fine. You're either wonderful or awful or exhausted or rip-roaring angry or anything else but fine," he said, gazing off into the horizon. "You're a passionate person. You take after me in that department." A smile shadowed his face. "Or at least the person I used to be." He stopped, taking in a couple of breaths, then shifted to face me. "What's wrong?"

"How did you know?" I asked, thinking of all the people on the planet, my dad would be the last person to detect that something was going gangrene below the surface.

"When you stop letting yourself feel your own emotions

like I have, there's more room to feel those of others," he said. "It's one of the many downsides to becoming a silent shut-in."

This was the first meaningful conversation my dad and I had had in five years, and the day and place it was happening made me feel that John had his hand in it. "It's about Jude," I said, fingering the grass around John's gravestone.

"I thought you weren't seeing each other anymore." Dad cleared his throat. He was really having a concerned-parent conversation with his teenage daughter.

"We weren't, but we kind of stumbled into each other last night." My dad might be exhibiting a margin of strength, but I feared that telling him about the event leading up to Jude's and my reunion would send him into another five years of absenteeism. "We worked things out and then, this morning, we found out there was something between us that we could never work out." I also knew this information might send my dad into a downward spiral, but he was sitting before me, looking so much like the beacon of strength I remembered as a little girl. Like a man who nothing could take down.

He nodded. "And what was that?"

I blew out a breath, the letters etched into John's gravestone going blurry. "Jude's last name is Jamieson." Even as I said it, I still couldn't quite believe it. I still didn't want to believe it.

Dad sighed. "I know."

My head snapped up. "What?"

"I know, baby," he repeated. "I've known for a while now."

Okay, Dad was having a moment. Another break with reality, but this one led him to lie through his teeth.

"Are you saying you knew Jude's dad was Henry Jamieson?" I felt I had to spell it out.

"I knew," he said. "Jude's name sounded so familiar, but since he didn't go by Jamieson any longer, it took me a while to piece it all together. I figured it out a few months ago, when I was going through a box of John's things and came across the newspaper article detailing his murder. It mentioned that Henry Jamieson had a young son named Jude. That's when I knew Henry's Jude and your Jude were one and the same."

I wasn't sure how much farther down the rabbit hole I could fall. "Why didn't you say anything?"

He hunched forward. "I should have told you, Lucy, but I didn't know how. I wanted to protect you, and I didn't want to see you hurt. I couldn't do both, so I chose to keep you from getting hurt. I'd seen you experience enough pain to last five lifetimes." He paused. "Maybe I didn't make the right decision keeping this from you. But there really wasn't a right decision in the first place, and you seemed to have moved on with Sawyer. I knew if one day the two of you ever got back together, you'd figure it out."

"We figured it out." I sank my teeth into my lip.

Dad patted my leg. "And you're wishing you hadn't?"

I bobbed my head.

"Because you cared about him and wanted to be with him?"

Another nod as I concentrated on keeping myself together. This day was bending my mind so far, I was bracing for it to snap at any time. "You should have told me."

"Maybe I should have, but I didn't. Jude shouldn't be judged by who his father is," he said, grabbing my hand. "What Henry Jamieson did is unforgivable, but that doesn't mean Jude is undeserving of happiness. We lost our John, but he lost his father." His voice wavered, but he caught it. "Everyone lost something that day, and I was glad to see one seed rise up from the ashes."

That was a seed that never had a chance to take root. "He blames you."

"And you blame his dad," he said, his eyes moving between me and John's headstone.

"That's because he killed John," I said. "I have every right to blame him." Blame was the least of it for murdering my brother.

"It doesn't matter who's to blame and who isn't when it

comes to you and Jude, sweetheart. What matters is what the two of you want. Both of you are searching for an easy way out of this because it scares you," he said, gazing into my eyes with real emotion and a presence I'd thought was long since gone. "Caring for someone is scary, because you both know how it feels to lose someone in the span of a heartbeat. But you can't let fear dictate your life or else you'll end up like me. Don't live life hiding behind your past. Live for the moment. When you find someone you want to spend forever with, you don't let them go, whether forever turns out to be a day or a year or fifty years." He rested his other hand over John's grave. "Don't let the fear of losing them keep you from loving them."

Wyatt Larson, who could talk to anyone about anything, the man who'd operated the largest commercial construction company in the state before his whole world came to an end, was lecturing me about living for the moment and not letting the past make you fear the future. I knew he wasn't a hypocrite. That's what he truly believed. He just was incapable of living like that now.

"I have lost him, Dad," I confessed, wondering if I'd ever had Jude.

Dad looked off into the distance, his expression flattening. "It always amazes me how when we're sure we've lost something for good, it winds up finding us."

I smiled. It was a sad one, but it still registered. My dad had said the same thing numerous times when I was younger and lost a favorite toy. He'd been right. Once I accepted Mr. Teddy was long gone, he somehow popped up in the most obvious of places.

"Even if we did get back together," I said, "how could we ever hope to move on from something like that? How can I get past his dad being Henry Jamieson? And how can he get past my family being the reason he lost his dad?"

"I'm fool-hearted enough to believe love can conquer all," Dad admitted.

I laughed a little, but it sounded all off since I was trying not to cry. "You *are* fool-hearted," I said. His words and voice sounded right, but his shoulders and head were still bent forward. He was a shadow of the father he'd been. But I'd take a fraction.

"What happened to you, Dad?"

He looked up, searching the clouds. Searching for shapes or answers or an escape, I wasn't sure, but seeking something. "When a child dies, a parent loses a part of themselves," he said. "Your whole world ceases to exist and you're nothing but a shell of the person you once were. Your mom has dealt with it in her way, me in mine, and you in yours." He lifted his hand off John's gravestone and rose. "Your mom hates the world, I avoid it, and you try to save it."

"Tried and failed," I muttered, not about to count the ways.

"I know why you try to save the world, baby," he said, extending his hand down to me. "Because you're trying to atone for John. To atone for the guilt you feel for it not being you that day."

I stared down at the dates of John's life. A life cut short because I was being a brat and made my older brother deliver Dad's lunch. "I've saved nothing."

"You saved yourself, Lucy," he said, his forehead lining. "You saved me. That first year, the only thing that kept me getting out of bed in the morning was you."

I stared at his outstretched hand, not able to accept it. "I didn't save John."

"Oh, sweetheart. John wasn't yours to save," he said. "I didn't save him. God didn't save him. How much longer are you going to let the guilt of the past hinder the present?"

I looked up at him, grayed, wrinkled, and sad. He'd aged thirty years in the span of five. "I could ask you the same."

"I know," he said, extending his hand again. "But you're stronger than me, my Lucy in the sky. You're stronger than you think you are."

I took his hand, letting him lift me up. "You are too, Dad," I replied, leaning in and kissing his temple. "You are too."

TWENTY-FOUR

The last couple of days leading up to graduation were packed with senior breakfasts, cap and gown distribution, cruises around the lake, and yearbook signings. I'd chosen not to participate in any of it. Despite Dad's "pep" talk at the cemetery, I couldn't seem to accept his words as truth. Fathers were meant to encourage their daughters and believe they were infallible creatures. I knew Dad believed in what he'd said to me, but it was because, as a father, he was incapable of seeing me in an impartial light.

I was his baby girl. His Lucy in the sky. That was all he saw when he looked at me; he couldn't see what I'd become. But he was right about one thing—I couldn't save the world. It wouldn't change what had happened, and it wouldn't bring John back. However, having accepted that, I no longer knew what to do with myself. My life felt kind of empty and upside down, and that was no recipe for celebrating with a bunch of people I'd known less than a year and wouldn't be in contact with in a week.

I'd been silent in my assigned metal folding chair, waiting to get this thing done with so I could put this year of my life up on a shelf and forget about it. The rest of the three-hundred-plus graduates were trickling in, everyone hugging and smiling and gushing about how they'd stay friends forever and would never, ever lose touch.

It was all way too much mush and bullshit for me.

A few more minutes passed, and the majority of the seats filled in. I bit at my tassel. Fifteen minutes down, two hours left to go of blah, blah, blah, our future is bright, blah, blah, blah, you can be anything you want, blah, blah, blah.

Blah.

One of the last remaining stragglers weaved through the row a few in front of mine. Sawyer was moving a bit awkwardly, like something wasn't working quite right, or something like his hand had been glued to his dick. I didn't even try to stop myself from laughing.

A few heads turned, including his, but as soon as he saw it was me, his head snapped away like I'd just clocked him in the jaw. I'd kissed that dirtbag. I'd done more than just kiss him. That was enough to make a girl swear off men forever. Especially a girl about to head to college, where I'd heard the guys who'd been dicks in high school changed into grade A assholes, and the few good ones were already taken by the time fall rolled around. Outlook in the man department was bleak, so I'd just pretend there was no department with that title. Better off alone and marginally happy than coupled and positively miserable.

Principal Rudolph appeared from behind the burgundy-colored curtains and headed for the podium. This was going to be painful. I actually felt bad for my parents, who were both in attendance, smiling and waving at me every time I glanced in their general area.

"Students, parents, faculty," he began, going for the fake-solemn thing, which just wasn't working for him, "this is truly a time to celebrate the past, the present, and the future."

What was it with these graduation speeches? Was there some law they all had to be the same, old, tired thing?

"I'd like to take this time to—" Principal Rudolph droned on as the rest of the student body and I tuned out.

Something coming toward me caught my attention from the corner of my eye. Someone big, dressed in a cap and gown, and someone who had a recognizable swagger even at a sideways glance. I blinked twice to confirm what

I was seeing. Jude was coming straight for me, right in the middle of a graduation ceremony, paying no attention to the murmurs directed his way. I hadn't seen Jude since Sunday morning, and everything about him was different. He looked like a man at peace. A man who'd uncovered all of life's mysteries. A man who still, despite all the revelations and words, made my heart throb.

"Hey, Luce," he said, stopping in the center of the aisle, right in front of me. "Sorry to drop this on you here and now—I know you hate these kinds of things—but I had to get this off my chest, so I wrote my own graduation speech."

Everyone was either whispering to their neighbor, or their jaws were dropping to the floor in surprise, or they were glaring at the center aisle. Most of all, everyone was hoping to catch a snippet of the exchange between two of Southpointe High's most talked-about students this year. However, Lucy Larson was smiling.

"This year wasn't like any before it," he told me. "I learned more about myself and life and even love than I have in my entire seventeen years."

Every head in the auditorium was turned my way. I wriggled down in my chair. I had no idea where Jude was going with this whole graduation, soul-baring speech, but I knew it would mean embarrassment, in the best-case scenario, for me.

"I learned I'm not the piece of shit everyone likes to believe I am. The piece of shit I believed I was," he said. He could have been up onstage, delivering a speech. "Someone told me that again and again and again, and it took me the better part of the year, but I think I finally believe her." His eyes flickered. "Because I don't need to believe where I've been is where I'm headed. And I don't need to believe that one tragedy can shape the future." He paused, clearing his throat. "Only I can shape my future. I see that now."

Another pause, and now the room was pin-drop quiet. "I also know that in the process of learning this, the person who taught it to me lost her belief in me, and maybe even herself, and the whole damn world." His fingers curled into fists at his sides. "I could go to jail a million times and nothing would be worse than what I did to her. She taught me how to love. She even gave me chance after chance to show her that I was capable of it. And I failed her every time." He winced, but he didn't look away from me. "I love you, Lucy Larson. And I'm sorry I had to ruin everything we had to recognize that. And I get why I lost you and I'll never get you back."

My eyes closed. It was too much. The confession, the emotion behind the words, everyone in the auditorium staring at me, everything I was feeling. It was too much.

"You saved me, Lucy, and I didn't return the favor. I'm

sorry," he said, his voice low. "I just wanted you to know."

Opening my eyes, I made myself watch him as he backed away from me. He was grinning my way, the grin he reserved for rare occasions. I smiled back.

In the midst of everything being so wrong, something right was pushing its way through. Something was rising up from the ashes.

Lifting his hand, he waved and walked out the auditorium doors, leaving his past behind and going after that bright future thing.

TWENTY-FIVE

y skin didn't have a chance to brown before I was packing up and moving across the country. I'd passed the short weeks of summer dancing, reconnecting with my parents, and dancing some more. It was the kind of summer that could be considered close to perfect. Except for one thing.

Or more like one person.

Jude checked out of the boys' home the morning after graduation, and no one heard from him again. Of course, more than a few rumors circulated, but after being a victim of the rumor circuit, I vowed I'd never give any credit to another. Some said he was at summer training camp for one of the best college football teams in the nation. Some said he'd skipped the country after holding up a bank down south and shooting one of the tellers. And some said Jude had an utter and irreversible break with reality and threw himself off Highman's Bridge.

I liked to believe that wherever he was, he was happy and, at last, at peace with himself and his past.

It was something I'd wished for myself after graduation and had made some progress toward. Happy was a stretch, but I leaned more toward the happy than the unhappy spectrum, and that was a victory. My past was still there, every morning and every night, ready to haunt me if I let it, but most days I didn't let it. I remembered John for how he was meant to be remembered, not for how he'd died.

And as for saving the world, I hadn't quite unloaded my altruistic ego. At orientation, I'd signed up to be a dance teacher at a studio where low income kiddos didn't have to pay to learn dance. An alum had even set aside a fund so they didn't have to buy their ballet shoes and tights. So I danced, and I taught, and I learned.

But something was still missing. I had to fight to get past my depression every day. Most days I won that battle, engaging in classroom discussions, smiling at my new friends at the right moments, but other days the ache went too deep.

It was a good life, and I felt guilty for thinking it, but I knew it could be better.

"Lucy, are you going to put that earring in or caress it all night long?" India, my roommate, said, giving herself one final once-over in the mirror.

"You're dragging me where again?" I asked, sliding the silver hoop into place.

Rolling her eyes, she tossed my purse at me. "To a party at Syracuse. There's guys and booze and music. It's meant to be fun." India was the queen of fun, for real. Her family had patented something like twenty board games, so fun was her middle name. As a perk, she had an innate sense of adventure, could turn an early morning pop quiz into a good time, and was invited to any and every party in the county.

"And you need me to go because?"

Another bonus to being a wealthy ambassador of fun? You never had to worry about rolling solo to anything unless you wanted to.

"Because you work too hard and play too little, and that kind of a Puritan work ethic is seriously messing with our room's Zen."

Grabbing my jacket, I followed her out the door. "Forgive me for mistaking college for something as taboo as hard work," I said, bumping my shoulder into her as we walked down the hall. "How can I set our room's sacred Zen right?"

She smirked over at me. "You can get tipsy. You can get

up on a table and shake your ass. And you can get laid by the finest, sweetest man God had the audacity to make."

"Oh," I said, waving my hand in the air, "if that's all."

"Sometimes I swear," she said as we left the dorm, "the creator forgot to install a fun button in you." India clicked her key chain, and the lights of her car flashed. Another benefit to growing up in a family of entrepreneur millionaires? You got to drive whatever the hell you wanted.

"And someone forgot to install a filter in you," I said, opening the passenger door and crawling in.

India groaned, pulling out of the garage. "My friend, you are in serious need of some tipsy, table-dancing, sweet lovemaking tonight."

"Well," I said, leaning my head against the headrest, "drive fast."

It was like stating the obvious, because India did everything fast, most of all driving, and on this trip, she didn't disappoint. "So," I said, looking over at her, "who's the guy?" I'd only known India for a few weeks, but it hadn't taken long for me to figure out that if we were going somewhere, a guy was always involved. India held a firm belief that men were the spice of life. Based on the men I'd seen her with, she liked her life spicy.

She shrugged a shoulder, staring out the window like she had something she was dying to say.

"You'll see," she replied.

Her mysterious act was all kinds of annoying. "Well, if you're driving to see him, he's gotta be hot. Possibly the hottest guy to ever be ogled by women."

She flattened her lips out, making a maybe face.

"But because you are who you are, you don't just roll out the India carpet for a pretty face. So he's got to be smart, witty, and wealthy as a sheik."

She lifted a finger. "Wealth isn't a requirement," she said, like it was offensive I'd even imply it. "Wealth can be created. Wit and intelligence can't."

"All right, Freud," I said as we finally cruised into Syracuse. "And here I thought you were majoring in music."

Braking to a stop, India killed the ignition outside what appeared to be a dorm hall. "Just get out of the car, will ya?" she said, opening her door. "Before you screw with my baby's Zen too."

I stepped out and waited for India to come around the car. "What is this?" I asked, watching students trickle inside the building, where neon lights blinked in the first-level windows.

"It's some sort of beginning-of-the-year student mixer," she explained, grabbing my arm and pulling me behind her.

"You brought me to some lame mixer?" I said, ready to turn and run for the hills. "I thought the reason we graduated from high school was so we didn't have to suffer through any more of these things."

"They're a little different in college," she said, walking up to the entrance.

"Really?" I said. "So there won't be any horn-dog guys trying to grind up on anything that moves?"

She shot me a sheepish smile.

"And there won't be any lamebrain music that doesn't carry even a hint of a beat to dance to?"

A more pronounced sheepish smile.

"Eh, India," I groaned. "If I wanted to go to hell, I'd just go up to the front door and ask Satan."

"Why is my roommate so damn difficult?" she said as we started weaving our way through the packed building. "You'll like this mixer," she yelled back at me over the, yep, lame music with no beat to dance to. "Trust me on this."

Breaking through the hallway where, yep, some horn-dog guy slid up to me and starting humping my leg before I could shove him aside, I yelled, "I can't give you trust until you earn it, Indie!"

"God, I need a drink," she said, pulling me along behind her as she beelined for what I guessed was the beverage table.

"Just pour me something!" India hollered over the music at the guy manning the drink table. He made a shotgun motion with his hand before mixing something that came out looking too pink and too strong.

"Pick your poison, beautiful," he said to me after handing off India's drink.

"Got anything back there that won't make me shit-faced in two sips?" From the looks of the crowd, it was doubtful.

Another shotgun motion, and he popped open a cooler and twisted the lid off a beer. The fist-pumping song came to an abrupt halt right in the middle of the obnoxious chorus, and then a slow, very familiar song wove its way through the room.

"Hey, my man!" he yelled at someone over my shoulder. "What can I get you?"

"I'm not sure if I can have what I want anymore," a familiar voice answered as Paul McCartney's voice echoed off the walls.

The breath caught in my lungs. Setting the beer down, I turned slowly.

"Hey, Luce."

It was him. Really him. Smiling at me with those liquid silver eyes.

"Jude?" I said. "What are you doing here?"

Not my best moment. With all the questions that had played out in my mind over the summer, this was not one of them.

Taking a step closer, his smile grew. "I kind of go to

school here." Over his shoulder, India snuck away, shooting me a thumbs-up and a knowing smile.

"Syracuse?" I said, stepping closer, wanting to reach out and touch him to confirm he was really here.

"Yep," he said, sticking his hands in his jeans. In his blue jeans. In fact, nothing was gray on him. He'd even lost the old beanie. He looked completely different, but completely the same too.

"So you didn't skip the border to keep from getting locked up for life?"

He chuckled, shifting his weight. "Nope. I've been crime free for a while now."

"So why are you here?" I asked. "Aren't there about a dozen schools with better football teams you could've gotten into?"

"Maybe," he answered.

"Then why here?" I knew I was asking idiot questions, but I couldn't stop them.

Rubbing the back of his neck, he glanced at the ceiling. "I was hoping that would be kind of obvious."

Nothing about now, or any of Jude and me, had been obvious.

"I'm here for you, Luce," he confessed. "Shit, if Marymount Manhattan had a football team and actually wanted me, I would be there."

I opened my mouth. Nope, words failed me.

"Hold that thought," he said. For once, he looked almost nervous. "I've been practicing this for a while, and I need to get it out before you slap me and walk out on me. Ready?" Squaring his shoulders, he inhaled. "Hi, I'm Jude Ryder Jamieson," he began, extending his hand. I took it, shaking it. He held on to it when I tried to pull it back. "My mom left when I was thirteen. My dad's serving a life sentence for killing a young kid. I spent the last five years in a boys' home being bullied, beat, and abused by the kids, the staff, and even the goddamn dog. I sold drugs. I did drugs. I got arrested. A lot. I screwed a lot of faceless women." He paused, sucking in a breath. "And then I met one whose face I couldn't forget. I fell in love with her. I hurt her because I fell in love with her and was afraid she was going to leave me the way everyone else had." He lifted his other hand, cradling mine between his. "I still love her."

"Jude," I whispered, not sure what to say next. We had so much history, history that made for the worst kind of foundation to build a relationship on.

"I love you, Luce," he continued. Clearly he wasn't going to stop until he said what he needed to. "And I'm sorry I ruined everything we had before I could admit it to you. Before I could admit it to myself. You didn't make me a better person, because no one can do that. You made me want to be a better person. You believed in me and stuck up for me. You cared for me when no one else would. You made me better, Luce. You're right—one person can make a difference. One person can change another person's whole world for the better," he said. "One person ruined my world, and that was my dad, and one person saved my world, and that was you." Raising his hands, he stroked my face. "The same tragedy ruined our families. The same tragedy brought us here today. Don't let it tear us apart."

"Jude," I began, determined to get more than one word out, "how can we even begin to move forward when the past will always be there to remind us of what we lost?"

His thumb ran down my cheek. "Because I know I will never love anyone like I love you. That's what will overcome the past every time it tries to rear its ugly head." He stepped closer. "So it's either you and me or me and me, Luce. And I don't really like myself, so I hope you'll pick the you and me option."

I took another step toward him, our bodies coming together. "I don't really like you either," I said, wrapping my arms around his neck. "I love you."

The long scar running down his cheek disappeared into his smile. "It's about time," he said, tilting his head down. "Because I'm not letting you go anymore. I want you forever, Luce."

He kissed me then, exhibiting the patience of a man who considered the future, and with the urgency of a man who lived for right now. It was, without doubt, the best kiss of my life.

"Dance with me," he said, winding his arms around my neck and pulling me close. Settling his mouth outside my ear, he starting humming along to the chorus.

"I thought you hated this song," I said, swaying against him.

"I did."

"And what made you change your mind?"

He grinned, dipping me low to the floor. "You," he answered.

Then, lifting me up, his head fell back and he opened his mouth wide. "Once I let Lucy Larson into my heart, I was able to take my sad, shitty song and make it better!" he sang, off-key and at full volume. Some of the students around us tipped their beers at him, some broke in during the "Nah, nah, nah," chorus, and a few stared at him like he was a crazy man.

But I just laughed—I already knew he was crazy. And I loved him for it. "I think that's called taking creative liberties with the lyrics."

"I don't really care what it is," he said, "because after everything that's happened in my life, I get to crawl into bed with you every night."

Leaning back, I studied that face I'd fallen for one hot summer day over a year ago, and now I'd fallen in love with the rest of the man behind that face. "How does a guy like you promise someone forever at eighteen?"

"Easy," he said, pressing a soft kiss into the corner of my mouth. "He finds a girl like you."

CHECK OUT
CLASH
THE SEQUEL TO CRASH

You know how they say it's always darkest before the dawn? Well, I'd lived five years of dark. I'd done my time—hard time—and I was officially done in on all things dark. I was ready for my dawn, and as I danced across the stage, I realized I was finally living my dawn.

I didn't let myself focus on the one thousand people who were watching me. Progressing into the difficult finale, I danced for only one. The lights that blinded me to the crowd, the pressure to perform that drove me forward, and the wardrobe malfunction that was one thread from snapping away—I pushed it all aside and danced for him.

As I took my final grand allegro into the air, my pointes

landed at the exact moment the music came to a close.

This was it. The moment I loved. The breath and a half of stillness and silence before I moved into a curtsy and the crowd applauded. A two-second window to reflect and revel in the blood, sweat, and tears I'd shed to get to this point. Job well done, Lucy Larson.

It was a moment I wanted to last forever, but I accepted it for what it was. A glimpse at perfection before it was swept away.

Sucking in a breath, I lifted my arms, and moving into curtsy position, I lifted my eyes. Right where Madame Fontaine had trained me to direct them at the conclusion of a performance. Front and center. A smile played at the corners of my mouth.

It was impossible not to smile when Jude Ryder sat front and center.

He leaped up from his seat, clapping like he was trying to fill the whole room with it, grinning at me in a way that made my stomach tighten. People were already peering over with curiosity, so when Jude jumped onto his seat and began hooting "Bravo" at top volume, those looks of curiosity got more judgmental.

Not that I cared. I'd learned a while back that being with Jude meant going up against the norm. It was a cost worth paying to be with him.

Taking one more curtsy, I met his gaze again and did the unthinkable. Thank the maker Madame Fontaine hadn't been here tonight, because her perpetually tight bun might have just busted something. I aimed a wink right at my man towering over the crowd, cheering for me like I'd just the saved the world.

The lights fell, and before I hurried offstage, I heard one more round of Jude hooting and whistling. He was breaking every unspoken rule of how to show appreciation for the arts. I loved it.

We did things totally outside the box, our relationship included.

"Think you could try, just for once, not to give a perfect performance? You know, so the rest of us don't look like such bush leaguers," Thomas, a fellow student and dancer, whispered at me as I scurried behind the curtains.

"I could," I whispered back as the last dancer took the stage. "But where's the fun in that?"

Smirking, he tossed me a bottle of water. Catching it with one hand, I waved it in thanks and headed to the dressing room to stretch and change. I had a ten-minute window before the performance would draw to a conclusion, and I knew from experience Jude would be barreling backstage to find me if I didn't find him first. He wasn't exactly a patient man, especially following a dance recital. My ultimate turn-on was watching him play football—his was watching me dance.

Sliding into the dressing room, I grabbed my foot, stretching my quad while I hopped over to my corner of the room, untying my pointe. The elastic band holding my corset in place so my performance didn't turn into a peep show snapped the moment I stretched my neck to the side. My wardrobe couldn't have picked a better time to "malfunction."

As I stretched the other leg back, my fingers worked to undo my other pointe. Tossing both shoes into my bag, I pulled out my jeans, sweater, and riding boots. It was Friday night, and since Jude had a home game tomorrow, that meant we got the whole night to ourselves. He had something planned, and he'd told me to dress warm. I would have rather been dressing for warm weather, but really, when it came to being with Jude, I didn't care what I was wearing. In fact, I would have preferred to wear nothing, but the latest patron saint of virtue, Jude Ryder, wasn't having any of that until he "figured his shit out."

I'd never wanted shit to get figured out faster.

I really needed to stretch a little longer, but I had two minutes max before Jude would come bursting through the dressing room door. Twisting my arms behind me, I worked away at my corset. Where was Eve, our costumer, when I needed her? That girl could fasten and unfasten a costume faster than a playa could lower his zipper in the backseat of his sports car.

I was searching for a pair of scissors to escape the satin straitjacket when a warm set of hands rested over my shoulders.

"May I be of assistance?" Thomas said, grinning at me as I looked over my shoulder.

"If your assistance comes with speed and precision, then yes, please," I replied.

His smile turned wicked. "When it comes to removing women's clothing, speed and precision are my top priorities."

I elbowed him as he laughed. "Anytime today, Mr. Hot Fingers."

"Yes, ma'am," he said, cracking his fingers dramatically before moving to the back of my dress.

Thomas was right—he had the undressing maneuver down pat. However, there was nothing even remotely intimate about one dancer helping another dancer dress or undress, male or not. You danced long enough, you got used to about every dancer in a three-state radius seeing you next to naked. There was no room for being a prude in the world of dance.

"Almost," Thomas murmured as his fingers worked toward the bottom rivet of my corset.

I was about to spit something witty back when the dressing room door flew open.

"What the hell?" he hollered, his face flaming red.

"Jude," I began.

"You're a dead man," he yelled, lunging toward Thomas.

Dodging in front of Jude, I pressed my hands into his brick wall of a chest.

"Jude!" This time I yelled. "Stop!" I put my arms around Jude to give Thomas a chance to retreat.

"Sure, I'll stop," Jude replied, his silver eyes flashing onyx. "Once this tool is dancing across the stage in a wheelchair."

I hadn't seen his rage monster in months. I was rendered speechless. Momentarily. This was the kind of anger people told stories about.

Jude gently removed my arms. Pivoting around me, he charged at Thomas, who was staring wide-eyed, half-confused, half-terrified, at the bull of a man trying to obliterate him. My strength was no match for Jude, not even a tenth of a match, but I had other powers that could render him into servitude. Sprinting in front of him, I jumped, wrapping my arms and legs around him as tight as they would go.

He stilled instantly, the murderous look dimming. Just barely.

"Jude," I said calmly, waiting for his eyes to shift to mine. They did. "Stop," I repeated.

I pointed to Thomas. "He was helping me get out of my costume. I asked him to. I wanted to hurry and get changed so I could be with you," I emphasized, "and unless you wanted to wait a year and a half for me, you should be thanking Thomas."

Jude now directed his glare at me. "Why didn't you have *me* help, Luce?" he asked, his jaw clenching.

"Because you weren't *here*" I said, feeling like I was stating the obvious, but if obvious was what it took to talk Jude down from the ledge, so be it.

"I'm here now."

I stroked his cheeks. "Yes, you are," I said, waiting for his eyes to lighten up completely. His chest was starting to lift and fall in a regular pattern again. "Thanks for the help, Thomas." I glanced back at Thomas, who was still staring at Jude like he was about to go all nuclear on him again. "Catch up with you later?"

Thomas sidestepped around us, never taking his eyes off Jude. "Sure, Lucy," he said. "Catch up with you later."

I smiled my appreciation. "Good night."

"Bye, Peter Pan," Jude called after him. "I'll 'catch up with you later' too."

Thomas was already out the dressing room door, but

there was no doubt he'd heard Jude's latest bout of name-calling threats.

Sighing, I ran both thumbs down his face. "Jude Ryder. What am I going to do with you?" I asked.

It was, perhaps, the question to end all questions. Nothing was easy about our relationship. Well, nothing but falling hard for each other. Everything else was like trying to fight an uphill battle. You never felt like you were making much headway, but the journey made up for the lack of ground you covered.

Latching onto my hips, Jude planted me back down on the ground. He spun me around, and his fingers worked the satin ribbon free of the last rivets. His hands just barely skimmed my skin, but "just barely" shot bursts of heat deep into my stomach.

"What am I going to do with you, Luce?" he threw back at me, his voice carefully controlled.

"Since you've almost got me topless, I'll let you fill in the blanks to that question," I teased, arching a brow at him.

His eyes weren't liquid like they usually were when we were sharing an intimate moment. The corners of his mouth weren't twitching in anticipation. Jude was all Mr. Stern on me.

"Don't do that again, Luce," he said, folding the ribbon in his hands before stuffing it into his pocket.

"What?" I said with a shrug. I feigned ignorance, but I was starting to boil. I didn't like being talked down to, especially by Jude.

"You know what."

I put my frown on. "Since I've obviously disappointed you, I wouldn't want to do it again, so why don't you spell it out for me?"

I cursed myself. The only thing that would result from fighting fire with fire would be some nasty first-degree burns. Jude and I didn't need our relationship to get any more complicated, so why was I pounding on complicated's door?

Sucking in a slow breath, I witnessed the effort it took for him to stay calm. He was making the effort to keep this from blowing up into a screaming match—why wasn't I?

"Don't let another man, tight-wearing fairy or not, help you out of your clothes again," he said, his eyes narrowing. "If you need help getting out of so much as a sock, you call me, you got it? That's *my* job."

Super. The possessive, overbearing police were back in town. He could deny it all he wanted, but overbearing implied he didn't trust me. Call me a fool, but trust wasn't only pivotal to a relationship, it was everything.

"Got it, Luce?" he said when I stayed quiet.

God, I loved him. Too much for my own good, but I

would not let him order me around.

"No, Jude. I don't 'got it,'" I said, about to blow a gasket. "So why don't you go wait outside and let that sink in while I finish getting undressed?"

"Alone," I added before he could open his mouth to object. Because if he did, I wouldn't be able to say no.

He paused, indecision written on his face. Finally, he nodded. "Okay," he said. "I'll be right outside."

"Is that so you can scare off any other guys who might help me with my costume, or just because you're waiting patiently and respectfully for your girlfriend?" I said, heading over to my bag.

Jude's sigh was as long as it was tortured. "Both," he said, his voice just above a whisper before he closed the door behind him.

As soon as he was gone, I felt it. Guilt. Remorse. Followed up by a potent dose of regret.

I knew what I was getting into when Jude and I got back together at the start of our first year of college. I went in willingly with both eyes open; I'd gladly gone in. Jude had been through more shit than any one person should, and along with that came certain characteristics that could be classified as extreme.

But you took the bad with the good. And when it came to Jude Ryder Jamieson, there was a surplus of good that always managed to not necessarily wipe the bad clean, but to make it a fair trade. If I was pointing fingers at damaged goods, I might as well turn that finger around. I was a far cry from flawless.

That was the beauty of us being together. And the problem.

I had as many triggers that ticked at my temper and as many ghosts from my past as Jude did. When his anger flamed, mine responded in kind, and vice versa. As in the last two minutes.

Then, as it always did, the anger I'd felt toward Jude shifted toward me. If I'd taken a time-out to take a step inside Jude's size twelve Cons, what would I have said or done if I'd walked in on some girl assisting *him* out of *his* clothes?

Shrugging into my sweater, I realized my reaction would not have been that far off from his. In fact, my claws would have been mid-swipe before he could open his mouth to explain. The old Jude, the one pre-Lucy, would have kicked ass first and asked questions later. The new Jude, although still not an anger management graduate, had allowed words to defuse the situation, not fists.

Progress. Significant progress he'd made for me. And how had I repaid it?

By yelling at him and throwing him out of the dressing room.

Tossing the rest of my clothes on, I stuffed my costume into my bag. I didn't bother letting my hair out of its headache-inducing bun. I didn't wash off the three-layer-deep pancake makeup covering my face.

I had to get to him. I couldn't get to Jude fast enough.

I threw the door open.

Leaning against the opposite wall, Jude was every shade of tormented. The emotion expressing itself on his face was the exact emotion I was sweltering in.

One side of his mouth curved up as he rubbed the back of his neck.

Dropping my bag, I rushed to him, wrapping both arms around him so tightly I could feel every one of his ribs hard against my chest. He embraced me with just as much urgency and maybe even more relief.

"I'm sorry," I said, inhaling the boy who, even in scent, exuded a hint of trouble just barely masked by a reluctant sweetness.

Tucking my head under his chin, he exhaled. "I'm sorry, too."

READ THE REST OF
CLASH
AS AN EBOOK OR PAPERBACK!

12